Wife Wanted

ALL FOR LOVE
BOOK 3

WREN ST. CLAIRE

ARE YOU SIGNED UP FOR DRAGONBLADE'S BLOG?

You'll get the latest news and information on exclusive giveaways, exclusive excerpts, coming releases, sales, free books, cover reveals and more.

Check out our complete list of authors, too!

No spam, no junk. That's a promise!

Sign Up Here

www.dragonbladepublishing.com

Dearest Reader;

Thank you for your support of a small press. At Dragonblade Publishing, we strive to bring you the highest quality Historical Romance from some of the best authors in the business. Without your support, there is no 'us', so we sincerely hope you adore these stories and find some new favorite authors along the way.

Happy Reading!

CEO, Dragonblade Publishing

A NOTE ON PRONUNCIATION

Comes is a Roman military title equated later with the Frankish Count and Anglo-Saxon Eorl (later "earl"). It is pronounced Co-mees.

Chapter One

WANTED: Secretary required for esteemed antiquities scholar. Respectable, unmarried, young (up to 30 years of age) lady, of good birth and character. Must have extensive knowledge of antiquities, excellent Latin and Greek, ability to sketch, and a neat and orderly mind. Experience with archaeological digs an advantage. This position is for a twelve-month project cataloguing dig sites and antiquities discovered in southern and central Britain and requires the lady to live in and be prepared for travel. All living expenses will be covered, and a generous salary will be payable to the right applicant. All proprieties will be adhered to.

DEODONATUS KININMOUNTH, 6TH Earl of Pendrell, Deo to his friends, reviewed for the dozenth time the advertisement he had placed last month in *British Antiquities*, his favorite journal. He had hoped to have received some applications for the post by now. *Perhaps I shouldn't have mentioned the living in bit? Was it putting them off?* But he had wanted to be very transparent about his requirements without baldly stating that he was looking for a wife who would also fulfil the role of secretary.

If she has half a brain—and I certainly hope she does, or what is the point?—she will understand what is implied. How can the proprieties be adhered to if we are not married?

He was a single man living alone, after all—except for the servants.

He put the journal away and returned to his desk to complete the next chapter on his book, *A Survey of Sussex Antiquities*. Kester, his lolloping red Irish Setter, rearranged his long furry limbs under the desk with a flop and a sigh.

He glanced under the desk at the dog. "Your walk is not scheduled until ten o'clock, Kes. Have some patience," he admonished gently. Kester raised his silky head with long floppy ears and rested it on Deo's knee. Deo stroked the head and scratched the ears absently, contemplating his next sentence.

The prospect out the window from his desk showed the rolling green of the south lawn of his Sussex country estate, with a glimpse of blue ocean in the distance. He always resided here for the summer months, when London became stiflingly hot. Last summer he'd spent the entire time unearthing and cataloguing a new find right on his doorstep before it disappeared into the ocean: a small hoard of Saxon coins and church reliquaries. He'd worked flat out for weeks to get it all done before the wind and weather destroyed the find. It had underlined for him his need for an assistant.

Now he was itching to get started on the new project he had been assigned by the Society for Antiquaries, but for that he really needed his secretary-wife. The prospect of having a companion who shared his passion for antiquities, who *understood*—a woman he could talk to—set up an ache in his chest.

At the age of thirty-two he had despaired of finding a lady of suitable birth who shared his interests, whom he could, in short, contemplate living with for the rest of his life. He was not an easy man to live with. He knew this. Finding a lady who could tolerate him was a tall order. Then his friend Emrys, Viscount Ashford, had suggested he advertise. Deo had thought the idea was brilliant, but perhaps he was wrong, and he was destined to be alone as he dwindled into old age. The prospect was depressing.

He shook his head to dispel the thoughts, pushing his spectacles back up his hawklike nose, and focused on the page before him, reaching for his notes, with one large, freckled hand.

Chapter Two

"EMILY! LIFT YOUR head up for goodness' sake. You will get stooped shoulders if you slouch like that. Now practice your curtsy again, as if I am the viscount. Hold out your hand for him to kiss, and for the love of all that is holy, smile! At least *try* to act like you are glad to see him!"

"Yes, Mama," said Miss Emily Grenfell softly, trying to obey all these instructions at once and almost losing her balance in the process. She was sure that she wasn't wearing a smile but a grimace. However, Mama seemed happy enough with the result, sniffing and going to the front parlor window.

"Gracious, he is here! Now remember everything I have told you. Sit there," she waved her daughter to the sofa, "fold your hands in your lap, keep your feet together, back straight, chin up, and smile!"

Two minutes later, the door opened, and their butler announced, "Viscount Bidenden, my lady."

The Countess of Efford rose and smiled broadly at their guest, a well-turned-out young man of medium height and build, with soft brown hair and green eyes.

"What a lovely surprise, my lord. Do come in. You know my little Emily, of course. But of course, you do," with a laugh so false it made Emily wince internally. "You danced with her twice last night at Lady Sefton's ball. Emily!" she prompted, and Emily rose and sank into the required curtsy, proffered her hand, and managed to raise her head, smile, and not wobble this time.

"My lord," she murmured, her eyes dropping in spite of herself.

The viscount took her hand and kissed it. "Miss Grenfell, I trust you are quite recovered from last night's frivolities?"

"I am," she responded, still looking at her slippered feet.

"Please take a seat, Viscount," said Mama, waving him to the couch beside Emily as she sat again, her heart beating uncomfortably fast. "I shall just see about the tea," said Mama mendaciously, leaving the room, much to Emily's anguish.

"Your mama is most accommodating," murmured Bidenden, managing to secure her hand in his and kiss it again. Emily tried to tug it away, but he kept a firm grip on it, "You must know the reason for my attentions, Miss Grenfell."

He spoke in a low, earnest tone that gave her goosebumps— and not the good sort. *Mama, come back!* Before she could respond, he went on quickly. "I am most smitten with your beauty!" He kissed her hand again, then turned it to most improperly press his lips to her exposed wrist.

Emily snorted inwardly. *Beauty indeed! I'm as plain as milk! Smitten with my fortune more like! Mama, for goodness' sake, come back!*

"I will speak with your father, Miss Grenfell. You must know what about. I hope to receive a positive response, hm?"

Fortunately for her, Mama reappeared at that juncture, sparing her the necessity of making a reply, and he let go of her hand hastily.

Tea was served, and stilted conversation, largely between the viscount and Mama, ensued. At the end of half an hour, Bidenden stood to take his leave. "When might I find Lord Efford at home, Countess?"

Mama flushed with pleasure and smiled so broadly, all her teeth showed. "Why, the earl is generally home until at least twelve o'clock most mornings, but if you are wishful to speak with him, I can let him know so that he will be at home to you when you call, my lord!"

"Please do so, ma'am," he said with a neat bow. He turned to take Emily's hand and kiss it again. "Until we meet again, Miss Grenfell." The throbbing accents in which this was uttered made Emily cringe and flush with embarrassment. Wholly unable to meet his no doubt ardent gaze, she mumbled something unintelligible, and to her relief, he let go of her hand and left.

She sank down onto the couch with shaking knees. *This couldn't be happening!* After two seasons with no offers (despite the temptation of her fortune), she was now facing the inevitability of being thrust into marriage with a man whose only interest in her was the settlements she would bring.

Her mother, unable to contain her transports, pulled her up into an embrace and polkaed her round the room. "My dearest, what a triumph! The heir to the Marquess of Malmsbury! Such a success for you! At last, my dreams are coming true!" Mama dabbed at the corners of her eyes.

"M-mama, I do not wish to m-marry Viscount Bidenden," said Emily shakily.

"What? Nonsense! Of course you do! He is a handsome young lord, and he clearly adores you. What is wrong with you?" Mama's voice escalated with each sentence. "This is an irritation of the nerves! A distempered freak! Go to your room. I've no patience with you, girl! You are all about in your head!"

Emily stared at her helplessly.

"Go!" said her mother, her face turning red. "And don't show your face until you are prepared to be sensible! Ridiculous! I never heard of such a thing! He will make you a marchioness, you stupid girl!" She waved at her in a shooing motion. "Go away! I cannot bear to look at you! After everything we have done for you, too! Such lack of gratitude. Go! Go!" Her mother screamed at her, and Emily bolted, shaking from head to toe and chased all the way to her room by the sounds of her mother's building sobs. Mama was going to have one of her fits of hysteria.

Shutting and locking her bedroom door, Emily sank down on her bed in despair. Her mother would rail at her and hector her until she accepted the viscount, she just knew it. She was trapped. She had thought if she could just hold out for one more year, she would turn twenty-one and be able to access her allowance. It wasn't her full fortune, for her father still controlled that, and if she married, it would pass straight into her husband's hands. But there was an annuity from her grandmother that was hers by right, and she would get that once she reached her majority. She wiped tears off her cheeks and sniffed. Perhaps marriage to the viscount wouldn't be so very bad. He was young at least, and not ill looking. She could have done worse, she supposed. Yet everything inside her rebelled at the notion.

Such a frivolous and fashionable young man would not tolerate her passion for antiquities any more than Mama did. He would force her to go to parties and be a hostess and expect her to be witty and pretty, and she wasn't any of those things. She was plain and shy and hated company. She was much happier with her books and musty artifacts.

She slumped back on the bed with a sigh and sat up quickly as something jabbed her in the back. It was a flat parcel lying on her bed. Distracted from her misery, she smiled, for she knew what it was. It was her copy of the latest volume of *British Antiquities*, her favorite journal. Gregory, the butler, who was her partner in crime, must have brought it up for her. He kept all her mail safe for her and made sure Mama couldn't steal it.

With a squeal of excitement, she tore the wrapping off and feasted her eyes on the precious volume. It took a substantial slice of her pin money every quarter to pay for the subscription, but she didn't mind. She would pore over the articles, reading them again and again, dreaming of the day when perhaps her name would appear below the title of an article that would be read and esteemed by other scholars—well, her pseudonym. She couldn't publish under her own name, of course. But *she* would know it was hers.

She opened the volume and read through the table of contents, savoring each title with delight. *There are hours of reading here. If Mama doesn't wish to see my face, she won't. I will stay in my room and read to my heart's content.* She banked up the pillows and settled back to devour each delight one by one.

It was three hours later when she found it. She almost skipped over it because she didn't generally read advertisements, but something about this one caught her attention. When she began to read it, her heart skipped and thudded so hard she thought it would choke her.

Her hand stole to her mouth to stifle the whimper of longing rising in her throat as she read. *Oh, if only . . .* She reached the end and reread it again and again, trying to decipher the meaning behind it. *I can't apply . . . can I?*

Even if she applied, she would never get the position. She didn't have enough experience. But oh! It was her dream come true! It must be a lady scholar who required an assistant, and that must be why she was asking for another lady. If that was the case, perhaps she wouldn't expect someone with lots of experience. Perhaps she would have a chance.

She squealed with excitement and drummed her heels on the bed. *I will apply. What do I have to lose after all?*

She spent an age over her reply, and it was quite late by the time she finished writing it out all fair, folded, and sealed it. No one had come to her room to see if she was all right or required food, and her grumbling stomach reminded her that she was famished. She hadn't eaten since breakfast and it was now after midnight. She went to her door and checked the hallway. Everything was quiet. Her parents had either retired early for the night or gone out, and as a consequence the servants had also retired by the looks of it. She crept down the stairs to the kitchens and the butler's room, where she knocked softly.

"Yes," said a voice.

She opened the door and poked her head round it. Gregory was sitting in his dressing gown, drinking a glass of some amber liquid with a book in his lap. He looked up startled and, rising, dropped the book. "Miss Grenfell, is there something amiss?"

"No, nothing, Gregory, I'm just hungry, and I need you to post this for me. Will you?"

"What's this, my lady? Mischief?"

"No, it's something very serious and important to me. Will you post it please and not tell anyone?"

"You'll be the death of me, you know," he said with a sigh, rumpling his grey hair. "Very well. Now, you want something to eat? Her ladyship said you were to be left alone." He put the envelope in the pocket of his coat hanging on the back of the door.

"Yes, she's punishing me because I told her I don't want to marry the viscount," said Emily, following him to the kitchen, where he fetched her cold meat, cheese, bread, and a cup of ale and sat with her while she ate. "Have they gone out?" she asked, referring to her parents.

"Yes." Gregory glanced at the clock on the mantle over the huge kitchen range. "They'll be back soon. You'd best get back upstairs. Do you need some water to wash?"

"Oh, yes. I'll take some back with me, thank you." She gave him a hug and took the jug of hot water from him and set off back to her room, which she reached without incident.

She washed, cleaned her teeth, put on a nightgown and crawled into bed, where she fell asleep over *British Antiquities* at a little after two o'clock, dreaming of scholarly fame.

To her immense surprise and joy, she received a response to her application a week later. It had been a hard week. She had stammeringly refused the viscount's offer and been confined to her room on bread and water by her irate mother. "Until you see sense," she said.

Papa had received word that his sister, Aunt Agnes, was gravely ill and used that as an excuse to go to Bath rather than stay and wrangle with the problem of Emily's intransigence, and she had no relatives or friends to turn to for help, she was trapped. The servants were under strict instructions to bring her nothing but bread and water for the entire week. She had been brought water to wash in daily, and her dirty clothes and chamber pot taken away and the bed made, but no other courtesies had been shown her. Her maid didn't even speak to her. Clearly the girl had been threatened with dismissal if she did.

She was close to changing her mind and accepting the viscount when the letter arrived. As she'd had no real hope of receiving a positive reply, she was beginning to think that she would have to give in after all. Her mother meant to starve her into submission, literally. She was lamentably lightheaded and weak by now. Gregory, bless him, had smuggled her a bit of cheese and the occasional apple, but it wasn't enough. He had also brought her the precious letter along with a bit of sausage and a handful of dates.

"I'm sorry about this, Miss Grenfell. It's not Christian, it isn't. But the countess has made it clear that if anyone helps you, they'll lose their position. I can't afford to be turned off without a reference, not at my age."

"I know, which is why you need to be careful. Thank you for this," she said, biting off a piece of the sausage and closing her eyes with a moan of delight as she chewed.

"I'll be careful, miss. She can't keep this up much longer, surely. If the earl were here, I'd speak to him. Except the countess has such a strong hold on him, I don't know if I'd be safe."

"No, no, you must not risk it. I think you're right and Papa would not intervene. He will never cross Mama, even for me."

"It's not my place to speak ill of his lordship . . ." He left the sentence unfinished and squeezed her hand in sympathy.

Emily smiled a tight smile and saw him out the door. She sat down to savor the sausage, bite by bite, and ate two of the dates before setting aside the rest for later. Then, with shaking hands, she turned to the letter and broke the seal, uttering a prayer beneath her breath for a favorable reply. *Surely it was a positive answer to come so quickly, or at all?*

With a fast beating heart and swimming head, she read.

Dear Miss Bromwich,

She had given a false name. What if she did get the position and her parents came looking for her . . .?

Your qualifications and experience are impressive for such a young lady.

She might have exaggerated slightly. And gosh, if her prospective employer thought twenty-four was young, what would they think if she confessed her real age was only twenty?

I would be pleased if you would present yourself for interview at Cheetham Court Sussex, on the 6th day of June, at ten in the morning.

Yours etc.
D. K.

The signature below the initials was an unintelligible scrawl.

"Yes!" Tears of happiness stung Emily's lids as she grabbed her pillow and hugged it.

All she had to do now was figure out how to escape from the house and get to Sussex by the 6th of June, which was four days away. Fortunately, she still had most of her last quarter's pin money in her purse. She wouldn't be able to carry a great deal, but perhaps when she had secured the position she could send for the rest of her things. Then again, perhaps not, as it would still be highly inadvisable to apprise her parents of her whereabouts. She had not yet reached her majority, which meant that legally her father could compel her to come home whether she liked it or not.

When . . .if . . . But what if I'm not successful? What will I do then?

She shook her head, refusing to think about that. She would cross that bridge when . . . if . . . she came to it. She just *had* to get the position.

Chapter Three

D EO KNEW AN unaccustomed excitement. Today was the day the applicant would arrive at ten o'clock. At least he hoped she was coming. He'd received no reply, but perhaps there hadn't been time. He'd been so anxious to move things forward he hadn't given her a lot of options. In fact, none at all. *Perhaps I should have?*

He got out her application and read it over again. Miss Bromwich. She'd signed it Miss E. F. Bromwich. He wondered what the E and the F stood for. *Esme, Elizabeth, Fanny, Fiona?*

She claimed to be fluent in Latin and Greek and had included some snippets of translations in the application in support of her claim. She had also included a couple of sketches. And she had said she had penned an article on Celtic burial customs which she had submitted to the *Quarterly Journal,* one of the most prestigious journals available. Admittedly she hadn't said it had been accepted or published, but at least she knew what the *Quarterly Journal* was. And clearly, she read *British Antiquities*, or she would never have found his advertisement. She was twenty-four years old. The perfect age. Old enough to be sensible—he hoped. Young enough to—well—his thoughts balked at that point and ran down another alley.

What will she look like? He had an image of a tall, slender lady with dark hair and striking grey eyes, with a calm demeanor and pleasant smile. She would be restful and competent. And best of all, she would put up with him. *I hope.*

Kester, picking up his mood, capered round his legs, anxious for a walk.

"It's not ten o'clock yet, Kes." Then it occurred to him, he had scheduled the interview for ten o'clock. *I can't take Kes for a walk and do the interview at the same time, can I?* He was reluctant to break his routine. He never broke his routine for anyone or anything. He didn't mean to start now. He hoped fervently Miss Bromwich would prove suitable, for he'd had no other applicants, which was disappointing. But *if* she proved suitable, she would need to fit into his routine and respect it.

IT WAS A warm day, despite the cooling breeze with the refreshing tang of salt to it, and Emily was hot inside her cloak and bonnet. She struggled with her bag, which seemed to have gotten progressively heavier throughout the journey. It was nearing ten o'clock as she battled up the driveway of Cheetham Court. But she was a day late.

It had taken far longer to get here than she had thought it would. Cheetham Court was on the coast, and when she had realized she wasn't going to make it on time, she had burst into tears. But she had continued on anyway. Because what else could she do? *I can't go home.*

So here she was. She trudged up the steps of the Corinthian-columned entry of the sprawling, two-storied, sandstone brick mansion and lifted the large brass knocker in the shape of a lion's head. After a few minutes, the door opened and let out a whoosh of cool air, revealing a dim entry hall with large black and white tiles and a wide, red carpeted stairway leading upward.

A middle-aged gentleman she assumed to be the butler

looked her over and said, "Yes, may I help you?" His disapproving look wasn't lost on her, and her tongue threatened to cleave to the roof of her mouth. But she hadn't come all this way to be stopped by a butler.

"I'm here for the interview," she said as forcefully as she could. "If—if you could tell your employer that I am here p-please?"

"You're late!" said a voice from the staircase, and her eyes widened as a giant of a man descended the stairs accompanied by a matching dog. Matching, because both man and dog had bright red hair—startlingly, shockingly red.

The man approached the doorway rather than allowing her to come into the entry hall, and she stammered, "I—know, b-but the stage took longer than I thought. I left as soon as I received the letter. Please, if you would tell the lady of the house I'm here? I've come a long way . . ." She trailed off, taking in the hawkish features of this giant before her. His eyes were a stunning deep blue, and he might have been handsome if his face were carved on less harsh lines. As it was, he was more brutish than hand-some, with a square jaw and hooked nose, frowning brows and grimly compressed mouth. His skin was covered in freckles. His frame was huge—well over six feet tall and broad through the shoulders and chest. He wore a jacket, breeches, and boots. The dog sat obediently by his leg, with floppy red ears and tongue lolling in a happy pant.

At her request, he looked confused. "I thought you said you were here in answer to the advertisement."

"I am," she said, equally confused. "Is this not Cheetham Court?"

"Aye." He frowned, his eyes roving over her. "Miss Brom-wich?"

"Y-yes." *Oh, no! He is not even going to let me see my employer— potential employer. He is going to throw me out. Who is he, her husband? He must be.* "Please, sir," she said, reaching out a hand to touch his sleeve. "I promise I can do the job, if you'll only let the lady of the house know I'm here. It truly isn't my fault I'm late. I'm very punctual as a rule, v-very orderly and—"

"There is no lady," he said, cutting her off.

"Oh!" She retracted her hand as if stung. "Then—then who placed the advertisement?"

"I did," he growled, looking, if it were possible, even more ferocious.

Emily's head swam. "I beg your pardon. I don't understand." She clutched the door jamb as the world threatened to tilt on its axis. She had managed a few meals during her journey, but she hadn't caught up from her week of privation, and the rigors of the journey had taken their toll. "*You* wrote to me? You're D.K.?"

He frowned at her. "Deodonatus Kininmounth, Earl of Pendrell," he said.

"Oh," said Emily again, and fainted.

DEO CAUGHT HER as she crumpled. "Damn and blast!" He lifted her easily into his arms; there was hardly anything of her. He turned back inside and headed for the front parlor.

"Send for Mrs. Blackthorn, she'll know what to do with a fainting female. And bring the lady's bag inside!" he said to Chiddick, his butler, as he shouldered his way into the parlor.

The room wasn't used much, and the furniture was swathed in Holland covers. "And remove these will you," he bellowed. Chiddick hastened to remove the cover from the settee, and Deo lowered his burden carefully onto the chintz-covered couch.

Chiddick disappeared. Deo gazed down at Miss Bromwich. She was as pale as a ghost and not at all what he had expected. She was a tiny thing for one, not only slender but short. Her hair wasn't dark. It was a sort of mellow, golden brown, and he was damned if he could remember what color her eyes were. He wished she'd open them so he could see. Her skin was creamy smooth, and she had a slight bump to her nose, which was long and a little aristocratic. Her mouth was a plump bow of curving lips.

Behind him, Mrs. Blackthorn bustled into the room. "Fainting lady, Chiddick said. Oh my, poor lamb. She's as white as a sheet. I've brought my smelling bottle; that will bring her around." She moved forward, and wafted the little bottle under Miss Bromwich's nose. The young lady stirred with a grimace and opened her eyes. Hazel-green, he noted with satisfaction. His previous image of Miss Bromwich shifted into the form before him. The dark goddess with grey eyes was forgotten.

"There, my poor love. Are you better?" crooned Mrs. Blackthorn.

Miss Bromwich blinked at her and nodded. "I think so. I—." She looked around and found him staring at her. She struggled to sit up, "I'm so sorry. I haven't had much to eat today."

"Well, that shall be remedied immediately!" said Mrs. Blackthorn, bustling away.

He bent forward to prevent her sitting up. "I think you should stay horizontal for a little longer. You're still alarmingly pale. Why the devil haven't you eaten?"

She subsided back onto the couch and said softly, "I'm so sorry! I didn't mean to be late." She closed her eyes, but the tears seeped out from under her lids and rolled out the corners.

Alarmed at this sign of feminine weakness, he said roughly, "Don't worry about it. It was my fault for not giving you enough time to get here." He searched his pockets and produced a handkerchief, which he handed to her. She took it gratefully and wiped her eyes.

"Thank you. If you will just allow me enough time to take some refreshment and recover a little, I will be on my way. I— there has clearly been some kind of misunderstanding."

"No!" He spoke rather more loudly than he should, judging from her startled expression. Moderating his tone with difficulty, he said, "There is no misunderstanding on my part."

She stared up at him bewildered. "But you could not have possibly advertised for a female assistant."

"I did," he said doggedly.

"But you're a man!"

"Well, yes."

"But you said all proprieties would be observed!"

He flushed. "They will be. If you'll just let me explain?"

At this moment, Mrs. Blackthorn bustled back in with a tray, which she set down on the low table by the settee. She then proceeded to pour tea and arrange a selection of cakes, biscuits, fruit, and cheeses on a plate.

Miss Bromwich sat up, and this time he let her, even propping a pillow behind her head and accepting a cup of tea from Mrs. Blackthorn. Kester, who had been observing all these proceedings from beside the doorway, inched forward and sat hopefully. Kes knew about tea. But he was too polite to help himself.

Mrs. Blackthorn stood back. "There then, you eat up, Miss Bromwich, and you'll soon have roses back in your cheeks."

"Thank you so much," said Miss Bromwich softly. She had a lovely voice, melodious and restful. She was clearly a lady of respectable birth.

"Thank you, Mrs. Blackthorn," he said, dismissing her. She left with a bobbed curtsy, and he watched in silence as Miss Bromwich devoured a whole plate of goodies. Sipping the tea, she sank back against the cushion with her eyes closed and sighed.

"That is so much better, thank you."

He sat in the Holland-covered chair to her left and sipped his tea. "Would you care to tell me why you are starving, Miss Bromwich?" he asked quietly.

"I haven't eaten for more than a week," she said wearily. "That isn't entirely true," she corrected conscientiously. "I've had some food, but not enough."

"Why?"

"My mother was trying to force me to accept a proposal of

marriage," she admitted reluctantly, looking at her fingers clasped in her lap.

"Good God, that's medieval!"

She gave a short smile. "Yes, it is rather. Fortunately, your reply to my application arrived in time before I was forced to capitulate. Of course I didn't realize it was from you. I thought it must be from a lady, because you specified that you wanted a young, single female." She swallowed, her cheeks flushing. "If I'd known—"

"You wouldn't have come," he said flatly.

"I can't imagine what you were thinking—"

"I was thinking, Miss Bromwich, that I wanted a wife."

"A w—" She stopped, her pretty rosebud mouth falling open. "But good heavens, why?"

His lips twitched and he said mildly, "Will you let me explain?"

She nodded.

"I am an antiquities scholar," he began.

"Yes, I know, quite a famous one—I recognized your name earlier. I've read several of your papers."

He flushed, inordinately pleased by her words.

"I have received a commission from the Antiquaries Society to undertake the cataloguing of artifacts and dig sites in the southern and middle counties."

"That was mentioned in the advertisement. It sounds most exciting!" she said with a smile and brightening of her eyes.

His heart gave a kind of leap at this sign of enthusiasm for the work. "Yes! It is very exciting; I'm heartened that you think so." He stopped. He hadn't thought the rest would be difficult to explain. It was a business arrangement after all, but with her sitting there looking flushed and pretty and excited, he was suddenly tongue-tied and awkward. A business arrangement was supposed to take the emotion out of it, but his heart was beating far too fast and his stomach churning. He hadn't bargained on her being pretty. But surely, he would grow accustomed to that—her prettiness. Once he got used to it, perhaps it wouldn't bother him so.

He swallowed. "I'm not a social man! I don't find it easy to talk to—talk to people."

"I don't either," she said.

"I don't like parties, and I can't dance—"

"I don't like dancing either!" She leaned forward, smiling. She was so pretty it almost stopped his tongue altogether.

"I despaired of ever finding a woman I could bear to be in the same room with, let alone"—he could feel himself going red as a beet, like he'd been out in the sun all day—"marry," he finished doggedly. "A friend of mine suggested I advertise for someone who might share my interests. So I did, and here you are." He swallowed again and waited for her to get up and walk out, to run in terror from the madman who thought he could get a wife via advertisement. *What was I thinking?*

"I see," she said slowly. "I don't quite know what to say." He peeked at her face. She didn't appear to be terrified, and she hadn't run—yet. "I was running away from a marriage proposal I didn't want. I wasn't expecting to run into one from a stranger."

Heartened a little, he said hesitantly, "I was going to suggest that it be in name only initially, until we got used to each other. Or decided that we didn't suit after all, in which case it could be annulled and no harm done."

She gasped, and he watched her, worried he'd gone too far. She must think he was insane. He probably was, he thought gloomily. If she wasn't prepared to run yet, she would once she got to know him a bit better. He was impossible. He knew it.

"That sounds like a perfect solution."

"Really?" He couldn't believe his ears. Raising his eyes to her face, he found she was smiling.

She nodded.

"Are you sure?" He bit his lower lip, best to make a clean breast of everything, so she knew what she was getting. "I'm not an easy man to live with. I'm very set in my ways. I like routine. I don't like it being disrupted. I have quite exacting standards, too, academically. I will expect a very high quality of output from my secretary." And he added, conscientiously, "I am hopelessly insensitive. I'm not emotional. In fact, I'm quite cold and lacking in affection. I don't do pretty speeches, and I don't tolerate stupidity. I'm quick tempered and frequently bellow at people if I'm not happy with them."

"Are you as bad as all that?"

"Worse," he said hollowly. He realized he'd been fiddling with Kester's ears while he talked and stopped. "Look," he said, leaning forward. "I'll give you tonight to think about it. We can spend the day going over the project, so you understand what's involved. And if you change your mind tomorrow morning, I'll send you home in my carriage. I won't have you riding on the stagecoach, it's not fitting. By your speech and the quality of your clothes, you are clearly a lady." He wondered who her parents were and whether he should make an effort to get her to tell him. Clearly, she didn't want to return home. If her mother was mistreating her like that, he didn't blame her.

She flushed. "Very well. You're most kind, but I won't change my mind."

"Don't speak too soon," he said, rising, his heart lighter than it had been in a while. "I will get Mrs. Blackthorn to make up a room for you. You would like to wash and change perhaps, before we begin?"

She nodded, rising. "Thank you." She added shyly, "Would you introduce me to your dog?"

"Of course. This is Kester. Sit and give a paw, Kes." Miss Bromwich bent toward him, and Kester bundled across to her, his plumy, red tail wagging, sat and offered a paw. She took the paw and petted an ear with her other hand.

"You are a gorgeous boy, aren't you?" she cooed. Kester stared up at her adoringly and Deo's heart did this odd little leap.

"How old is he?" she asked.

"Four. He's just starting to grow out of the puppy phase. Irish

Setters are slow to mature." He glanced at the clock; it was after eleven. "He's missed his walk. I normally take him at ten. In fact, I was heading out just as you arrived. I'd best take him now. I'll see you in my study at twelve?"

She nodded and headed toward the door. He held it open for her and bellowed, "Chiddick?"

The butler appeared. "Find Mrs. Blackthorn and tell her to make a room ready for Miss Bromwich. She will be staying for tonight. She'll need hot water to wash, that sort of thing."

"Mrs. Blackthorn's already prepared the green room, my lord. If you'll follow me, Miss Bromwich?"

LEFT ALONE IN the green room, Emily sank down on the bed, giddy with the events of the last hour.

She was being offered marriage to a man who shared her interests, her passion. She had never thought such a thing was possible. And she had the opportunity to work on an exciting project alongside him, to learn from him and hone her skills. And he was offering her a trial marriage, nothing irrevocable, so that they could both walk away if it didn't work. This was too perfect for words. By the time the project was done, she would be twenty-one and able to claim her inheritance, her independence, so if the marriage didn't work, she still didn't need to go home. She could forge her own destiny. *I will never need to be subject to Mama's bullying again.*

And he was an earl, not as lofty a title as a marquess per-haps—or heir to a marquess, as the case may be—but still highly sought after. Even her mother couldn't object to that. If only he had been the one proposing, she might not have refused. Not that she really cared about his title. She would rather be married to a plain mister who shared her passion than a duke who didn't.

She had listened with some amusement to his listing of his faults. If she believed him, he was a cold-hearted, unfeeling ogre with a foul temper and impossible standards. But his behavior gave the lie to that. He had clearly been anxious for her comfort, and he blushed deliciously when he was embarrassed. Neither of which argued for an unfeeling person. And she could not have failed to notice him petting his dog's ears or the look of blatant love he showered on the adorable canine. A man incapable of affection? She didn't think so.

And he was so big, and male! He made her feel—she groped for the description—petite, even feminine. And his intense attention, as if he really saw her, made her feel less invisible.

And even if he was a little gruff and bad tempered, she was used to that. She had lived with Mama's bad temper all her life. And she sensed his was not due to badness of disposition, but might perhaps be a method of defense? And his dog clearly adored him. If he were of a violent disposition, Kester would shy away from his touch, and he didn't do that.

She got up to wash and change her clothes. Refreshed, she ventured downstairs, wondering where his study was located. She made her way back to the front entrance to ask the butler, Chiddick. The man was most helpful and led her to a room at the back of the house overlooking a vast expanse of green lawn. *And look, I can see the ocean from here. The house is right on the coast!* She had never seen the sea before. Her heart gave a yearning leap. She longed to explore.

The room was large and clearly doubled as a library because its walls were lined floor to ceiling with books! In addition to the huge desk beneath the window, there was a bank of glass cabinets in the middle of the room containing a collection of artifacts. Emily was in heaven.

Chapter Four

W HEN DEO RETURNED from walking Kester, he found Emily on her knees in his study, staring at one of the glass cabinets, her round bottom outlined by her gown. He was so shocked, he barked, "What are you doing?"

She jumped and turned on her knees, her lovely little rosebud mouth falling open. "Oh, I'm sorry!" She scrambled to her feet. "I was just looking at that gold torc you have. It's beautiful. Where was it found?"

"Kilkenny, Ireland," he said, recovering from the shock of seeing her lovely bottom swathed in pale green muslin. Only to be confronted with the shape of her small, pert breasts served up in the same fabric. She was a slender little thing; he'd already established that fact when he carried her into the parlor. But at that time, her curves had been covered in a heavy cloak. Now they were on display and quite distracting. She was more than a foot shorter than him, which would make kissing difficult unless he lifted her up.

Kissing? Where did that idea come from? He didn't *do* kissing, not even with his mistress. He was *not* a kisser. He shook his head, becoming aware he had been staring at her for a full minute like an idiot.

When he had envisioned having a female companion to work

on the project with him, he hadn't expected her to be distracting. It must just be because he wasn't used to having anyone in his study. It was his solitary space—only he and Kester came in here. Kes had already settled himself under the desk.

"Your library is magnificent," she said, smiling shyly. "I hope you don't mind; I had a bit of a browse."

"No, of course not. You're welcome to read anything that takes your fancy. I've been collecting since I was fifteen. There are quite a few rare volumes. And I have complete runs of a number of journals dating back to 1801."

"How wonderful!" She clasped her hands together and her eyes danced. *Yes, danced.* He shook his head again. He was getting fanciful.

"Let me show you the brief from my sponsor, Lord Aberdeen," he said, going to his desk and opening the bottom drawer where he kept the papers he wanted most immediate access to. He had a meticulous filing system and knew where he could lay his hand on anything at a moment's notice. He would need to explain it to her so that she didn't mess it up. Nothing would more surely put him out of temper than that.

"Come and sit here," he said, moving a chair for her beside his own heavier desk chair. "I will need to rearrange things in here to fit in a desk for you."

"My own desk? That would be marvelous," she said with a smile, and he got a warm prickle in his chest.

"Of course, you're not going to be much use to me without a space to work." His tone was probably sharper than it should be, but then she was giving him prickles, and he wasn't sure what that meant. He retrieved his spectacles from his pocket and shoved them on his nose.

She took a seat and bent her head over the document he was holding out.

He then spent two hours explaining about the project and how his filing system worked, where everything was kept and the importance of putting something back where she found it. She nodded and took notes, which he was pleased about. It showed she was taking it seriously and had a methodical, well-ordered mind. *Really, this is working out well. I just need to be careful not to botch it, scare her off.*

Then somehow, she managed to get him talking about his book, *The Survey of Antiquities of Sussex*. He had been working on it for years in between other projects, and it was drawing to a close. He hoped to soon have a draft that could be read and edited prior to publication. If she stayed, editing it would be one of her major tasks.

He had been talking almost nonstop for four hours, and his throat was parched; to say nothing of his empty stomach. They had missed lunch.

"That, I think, is enough for now," he said. "I will get Mrs. Blackthorn to serve an early dinner. I'm famished, and you should eat—there isn't enough of you," he said, rising.

She rose, too, blushing adorably. "Thank you, this has been so fascinating; I cannot wait to get started."

"If you are of the same mind in the morning, we will discuss next steps." He cleared his throat. "I have already obtained a marriage license, so there need be no delay in—in making things respectable. I'm conscious of your reputation, Miss Bromwich."

"Oh, yes!" She flushed again. *Really, she must stop doing that. It is most distracting.* The blush travelled all the way up from the tops of her small, rounded breasts, revealed by the cut of her fashionable bodice, to her cheeks.

"That is, if you still want to, in the morning."

She nodded.

"What do the E and the F stand for, if you don't mind me asking?"

"The E?" she asked.

"Your name," he prompted.

"Oh, um, Emily Frances!" she blurted.

"Well, since you are of age, we won't need to ask your parents' permission."

"No! Ah, no . . . ."

"I gather," he said, with what he thought was considerable delicacy on his part—he didn't do delicate as a rule—"that you do not desire to return to your parents' house?"

"No, I don't," she said with a slight grimace.

"This proposal you were trying to evade—the gentleman was distasteful to you?"

"Oh, not exceedingly. He is quite young and handsome; and the heir to a marquessate. But I wished to ally myself with someone who shares my passion, you see, and he does not." She gave him a shy smile as she said this.

His heart jerked hard in his chest, and he felt himself flushing. "Then we are in accord on that score, Miss Bromwich," he said gruffly.

"Yes, I rather think we are," she said softly.

"If you would care to rest before dinner, I will see you in the drawing room at six," he said with a little formal bow and left the room before he embarrassed himself any further, Kester lolloping behind him.

⫸⫷

DINNER WAS AN unmitigated delight for Emily. Not only was the food good, but there was no awkward, silly conversation about trivial subjects such as the weather or gossip. Once the earl had satisfied himself that she had enough items on her plate, he said, "Tell me about your research into Celtic burial customs, Miss Bromwich. That is your specialty, is it not—Celtic artifacts?"

"Yes, it is," she said, flushing with pleasure. And she proceeded to wax lyrical about barrows, Celtic knots, and torcs for the next hour.

"You read Gaelic?"

"Yes, I'm self-taught, and I have been pursuing studies in Ogham also. You will be aware of the *Callan Stone in County Clare?*"

"Indeed, I've seen several different translations of it. Would you have another to offer?" he said, wiping mustard on a slice of beef.

She flushed and said shyly, "I would not yet. My studies are not far enough advanced. But the controversy surrounding it was irresistible as a lure. It is, I confess, the reason I began the study in Ogham."

"And would you venture an opinion on whether it is a forgery or not?"

"I would not be so bold, sir, no."

After dinner, it still being light outside, he invited her to accompany him on Kester's second walk for the day. "We can walk to the cliff overlooking the beach. Would you like that?" he asked, as she donned her cloak, for there was a breeze picking up.

"I would love that," she said with a huge smile. "I have never seen the sea," she confessed.

"You are in for a treat then," he said, holding the door open for her. Kester proceeded her down the steps, eager to be off.

They set out across the lawn, long shadows cast by the trees over the grass. Kester took off after a stick thrown by the earl, bringing it back with alacrity to have it thrown again. She couldn't help but be conscious of the man's musculature, even under his jacket, as he threw the stick. He had sizable shoulders and biceps, and shocking as it was to notice, very muscular thighs, shown to advantage by his well-cut breeches. She averted her gaze from this overt display of masculinity and concentrated on enjoying the fresh air and lingering warmth in the sun's fading rays. It would not be dark for another hour or so.

She could not believe how her life had transformed so quickly. Her every dream seemed set to come true. She had never enjoyed herself so much as she had these past hours in his company. To be able to speak freely of her passion for all things Celtic, and with someone so knowledgeable and genuinely interested—it took her breath away.

When he wasn't throwing a stick for Kester, he walked with

his hands behind his back and seemed content to let there be silence between them. They had, after all, talked for almost six hours today. Strangely enough, it didn't feel awkward, it felt . . . companionable?

It took them twenty minutes to reach the cliff edge. The breeze had picked up and the sun, which was setting to their right, cast a golden glow across the waves of the sea. Its beauty stopped her breath and made her throat seize up. A sandy beach stretched away to the right below them and waves rolled in, lapping at the sand with a hypnotic rhythm. The susurrant sound of it played in her head.

The wind made her cloak flutter, and she pulled it tighter round her. "It's so beautiful," she whispered. "You are so lucky to live here," she murmured.

"If you agree, you can live here, too," he said quietly.

"Y-yes, I was forgetting. This is like a dream. I can't quite believe it is happening." She glanced at his profile. He was staring, rather fiercely, she thought, out to sea.

"Likewise," he said abruptly. "Shall we turn back? We can explore the beach another day."

"Yes, of course."

"Kes!" he called, and Kester came racing back, tongue and ears flying, his plumy tail up and wagging. *He is the most adorable dog!*

AFTER THEIR WALK, Deo bade Miss Bromwich good night, intending to retire to his study to work. Instead, he spent an hour staring at nothing, while his mind chased itself in circles. *Will she agree to stay? Have I done enough to convince her? Am I entirely mad to propose tying myself to a woman I barely know, potentially for life, on the basis of one day's acquaintance?*

I have advertised for a wife, and heaven help me, I seem to have got one. He swallowed. The prospect was suddenly terrifying. *What do I know about women? Absolutely nothing.*

Yet the notion of letting her go was intolerable. He was almost too afraid to hope that his days of loneliness were at an end. His chest ached. He rubbed it absently.

"What do you think, Kes? Would you like to have her for your mistress?"

Kester put a paw on his knee and licked his face, which he took as a yes.

"I think I agree, old chap!" Deo scruffed the dog's ears. "Though I fear I may have wandered into foreign territory. I haven't the first notion how to deal with a female. I shall no doubt muck it up." He frowned. "She seems biddable enough. If I train her well in my habits and preferences, perhaps there will be little disruption to things. I don't like disruption." He sighed. "I wished for this, however, so I suppose I will just have to put up with a little discomfort until things get sorted out. The felicity of her company will no doubt outweigh any minor contretemps that occur. She doesn't appear to be a quarrelsome or naggish sort of female, nor is she hysterical or overly dramatic."

Kester pawed at him because he had stopped stroking his ears. "Perhaps we had best retire for the night. I may have to get married tomorrow. I should be well rested for such an event, don't you think?"

After passing an uncomfortable night plagued by wakefulness and vague dreams that faded with the light, Deo rose early, washed, dressed, and waited in the morning room somewhat impatiently for Miss Bromwich to appear for breakfast. He was conscious of his ill temper and aware enough to know its cause was nervousness. He was afraid that, all evidence to the contrary, she was going to say him nay. He had convinced himself in the middle of the night that the whole enterprise was mad, and he was on a disastrous trajectory. By four o'clock he was convinced she would refuse him anyway. By the time he sat down to breakfast, he was so confused, he took refuge in grumpiness. It was comfortingly familiar.

Thus, when she did appear just after eight o'clock, he snapped.

"You're late!"

She flinched slightly and changed color. "I'm sorry, I wasn't aware there was a set time for breakfast."

"I breakfast at seven," he said roughly, wincing internally at his own rudeness.

"I shall ensure I am here at seven in future," she said, quietly taking a seat. He sat down after her, and shook out his napkin. He had taken nothing but a cup of tea while waiting for her.

"You mean to stay then?" he asked, his heart thudding faster than it should.

"I do," she said and then colored further. "That is, if you still wish me to?"

A surge of relief filled his chest, and he said, his voice gruff to cover the emotion, "Yes." Then, "Of course I do!" He swallowed. "This damned project won't get done without you."

"Oh!" She smiled. "When will we begin?"

"Tomorrow." He reached for some toast and buttered it, placing it on his plate along with a generous serving of ham and eggs. "Today we will get married and set up your desk in my study." He corrected himself. "Our study. That will take some getting used to." He frowned across the table at her as she blinked at him in shock. "What's wrong?"

"N-nothing. I suppose I am a little shocked by how quickly things are proceeding. But I have no objection," she added hastily.

He nodded. "Very well."

She looked down at her gown and then up at him. "Where will we be married?"

"The local church. I have already warned the vicar. I obtained the license the other day from the archdeacon."

"Oh, but how could you, when you didn't know—"

"I had your name from your letter. You were my only applicant, Miss Bromwich."

"Oh," she said again. "And why was the chambermaid sleeping in my dressing room last night?"

"To observe the proprieties, Miss Bromwich. I told you all would be proper."

"Indeed, thank you."

"You needn't fear that I will be bothering you, either," he added, just to make sure there was no misunderstanding. "I said this marriage would be in name only initially. You have my word that I will respect that."

"Th-thank you." She flushed and looked down at her plate. After a moment or two she said. "My gown—"

He observed her gown of pale blue muslin, of similar cut and style to the previous day's green affair. Both gowns were plain, but to his eyes quite becoming to her figure. "What's wrong with it?"

"I—nothing." She twisted her fork around. "I suppose this isn't a romantic affair, is it?"

"No, it's not," he said, relieved that she was being so sensible. For a moment he had been afraid he was going to be subjected to female vapors. He was glad to observe that his initial impression that Miss Bromwich was a remarkably calm and collected young lady had not been wrong.

"We have an appointment with the vicar at eleven. Please be downstairs by ten thirty, ready to depart."

She nodded. He threw his napkin on his plate and left for his study.

EMILY STARED BLINDLY at her plate, wondering what to do. The man had obtained a marriage license using her name as he thought it to be—the name she'd put on her letter. If she married him under that name, would it make the marriage invalid? Would her age make the marriage invalid? She had no idea. But more importantly, if she confessed her real age, neither the earl nor the vicar would be able to allow the marriage without her father's consent. And it was possible that if she confessed her real name, he might just recognize it, too. For all she knew, he knew her father. Admittedly, her father was somewhat older, but they were both peers. It was not inconceivable that they knew each other. *Oh, dear.*

DEO NOTED THAT Emily was rather subdued throughout the morning, saying not a word in the carriage all the way to the village—which wasn't far. When they arrived, he wondered if he should ask her if she was having second thoughts, but having come this far, he was reluctant to entertain that possibility.

When they made their vows, she was pale but steady and did not falter, so he was glad he hadn't asked. He made his own with a faster-beating heart than he had anticipated. He couldn't help noticing the disparity in size of their hands when hers was put in his and when he slipped the ring on her finger. It had belonged to his mother; it was a little loose but not so loose she would lose it, he thought. He could have it made smaller if necessary.

As he stood holding her hand, he was reminded forcibly of how small she was. Her head barely reached his shoulder. With the vicar's eyes on him expectantly, he bent and kissed her cheek lightly. Her skin was soft, and she smelled faintly of rosewater. With a shock, he thought he might be smelling that scent for the rest of his life.

The vicar's wife was their witness, and after they had signed the registry book, Deo swept her back up the aisle and out to their waiting carriage.

Right, that was done.

He handed her up into the carriage and took his place beside her as the vehicle moved off, conscious of a wave of relief. Right up until the last, he had been convinced she wouldn't go through with it. At least now she couldn't leave him without a lot of botheration and paperwork. It gave him an unaccustomed sense of peace and comfort.

He had a wife, a companion, who shared his interests, was interesting in her own right, and didn't appear to need a great deal of care and maintenance. *Perhaps I can manage after all?*

EMILY TOOK HER seat in the carriage with a sense that she was in a dream and would wake up soon and find herself back in her room, faint with hunger and teetering on the brink of giving into her mother's bullying.

Her new husband smiled at her with a slightly anxious look. "Are you comfortable?"

"Yes, thank you." She fiddled with the ring he had given her. Concrete proof, if she needed it, that she was actually married to this quite magnificent man. Someone whose intellect she had admired from afar and never dreamed she would ever meet, let alone marry!

He had taken out the book he'd been reading on the way here, and she turned to look out the window, glad enough to be left to her own thoughts as the carriage lurched into motion.

She was married, but was it valid? If she were somehow found, could Mama still drag her home or make her marry Bidenden? And what would her rather fierce husband say to that? She rather fancied he would be a match for Mama in a confrontation. The idea that he might defend her, stand up for her in a way her father never had, made her heart leap and ache a little. *Would he?* She hoped that he would.

If she had told him the truth about her name and age, would he have still gone through with the marriage? She doubted it. In the twenty-four hours of their acquaintance, she had gained the impression that the earl was quite rigid in regard to rules and regulations. If he discovered her subterfuge, he would be understandably angry. Her heart quaked a bit at that.

She chewed her bottom lip and stole a look at his hawkish profile. She had noticed he favored a sandalwood cologne that seemed to meld well with his natural male scent. She liked it.

He was a mature man, not a boy like Bidenden. And most important of all, he shared her passion for antiquities. Was it possible—could this marriage become something more than a business contract with time?

What if it already was something more, and he is taking me home to make me his real wife? How do I feel about that? She gripped her hands tightly in her lap. He had said he wouldn't, of course. *But what if he changed his mind?* Her mind swirled.

When they arrived home, they discovered that Mrs. Blackthorn had prepared them a special meal in celebration, and after they ate, the earl took a footman to help him move a desk into the library for her and set it up. This necessitated moving a glass cabinet out and putting it in the drawing room—another room swathed in holland covers.

"I don't use most of these rooms," he admitted. "But if you want to use them, they can be made habitable again. I spend most of my time in the study."

"I'm sure I will too," said Emily with a smile.

After they had sorted out the furniture and reshelved some books that needed to be moved, he suggested a walk to the beach. "Would you like to explore the beach and the rock pools?"

"Oh, yes, very much!" she said.

"Wear some stout boots," he recommended. "The rocks can be sharp underfoot."

With Kester frisking about, they made their way to the cliff edge again in the late afternoon. He helped her down the steep sandy path, his hand clasping hers tightly, and when she seemed in danger of losing her footing, he grabbed her round the waist.

"Steady," he said gruffly. She leaned against him, breathless from more than the uneven terrain, his big body a shield against the buffeting wind.

They reached the beach itself, where the waves came in with a crash on the sand and the rocks, kicking up sea spray. She gasped in delight, running backward to avoid getting her skirts soaked. She turned to him, laughing with joy. "Oh, it's wonderful! I had no idea the sea was so magnificent!"

He grinned at her. "Come, if we go over here, we will be out of reach of the waves, and we can inspect the rock pools. I used to spend hours down here as a boy." He led her to a rocky platform at one end of the beach, helping her climb the rock and keep her balance with a hand on her arm, as they traversed the uneven surface, looking for pools with interesting inhabitants. The rock was slippery, and she was glad of his steadying grip. The surf pounded a few feet away, sending the odd bit of spray in their direction as he showed her fish, barnacles, brown crabs, and starfish.

He crouched down to look at something in the clear water of the pool, and she spied something to her left that drew her attention. She moved toward it, but still unused to this new terrain, she took an incautious step. She felt herself suddenly slipping, flinging out her arms with a cry, and found herself plastered firmly to a large warm body.

"Damn it, Emily, be careful!" he said sharply, lifting her clear off her feet.

"Oh!" she squeaked as he carried her carefully back to the sand and set her on her feet.

"I'm sorry!" she said, breathless from fright and the experience of being carried in his arms. He was not only big, he was also inordinately strong, her husband.

"I think that is enough for today," he said, gruffly, his face a little flushed. Perhaps it was the sun. "Kes!" he called the hound, and they made the trudge back up the sandy incline to the cliff edge.

Over dinner they discussed starting their project on the morrow and he bade her a formal good night at the bottom of the stairs when she retired for the night.

Undressing and climbing into bed, she reflected on a day that had changed her life forever. It was her wedding night, yet she was going to bed alone—that hadn't changed. If it were a real marriage, she would be preparing herself for him now. Instead of braiding her hair, she would leave it loose and wear her best night dress, instead of this serviceable cotton.

What would it be like? When he grabbed her round her waist today and clamped her hard against his body from behind, she had been shocked by the flush of heat that went through her. And when he lifted her and carried her—her heart had thudded so hard, she was sure he would hear it.

She pushed the thoughts away. This was a business contract, nothing more. He had made that abundantly clear.

AN HOUR LATER, Deo undressed in his own room, plagued by the memory of Emily's slender body pressed against his when he stopped her from falling on the rocks. He winced at his flare of temper at the time. But she had scared the living daylights out of him. The notion of her slipping and hitting her head, twisting an ankle, or even just getting a scrape or a bruise horrified him. She was such a little thing, and as of today, she was his responsibility. His wife.

He swallowed. In name only. That was the agreement. And it was what he wanted. Nothing complicated and—emotional. A simple straightforward business arrangement.

Three days later

WHERE THE BLOODY *hell was it?* He straightened from looking through the pile of papers on his desk. *I put it there, I know I did. Damn it!*

"Emily!" he bellowed.

"Yes, Deo?" She appeared from the stacks that took up the back half of the library, a pile of books in her arms.

"Where is the latest edition of *British Antiquities?*"

"Behind you, on the cabinet," she said calmly. "You put it there yesterday."

He turned and seized the volume, flushing. *Why did I do that instead of putting it back where it belongs?* "Thank you," he said gruffly.

She smiled. "You're welcome. I've just found a run of *Quarterly Journals* tucked between the *Gentleman's Gazette* and *Celtic Relics.* Would you like me to file them with the rest?"

"Good God, how did they get there? Yes, please."

She nodded and disappeared into the shelves again.

That was the third time he'd bellowed at her today and she had taken it without blinking. Really, she was a treasure.

Chapter Five

London

BRYSON PASSMORE, VISCOUNT Bidenden, stared morosely into his tankard of ale, tracing patterns in the moisture on the coarse-grained, wooden tabletop, and blanking out the surrounding hubbub of conversation in his favorite drinking establishment, the *Globe Tavern* in The Strand.

Things were not going well. Not only had the Grenfell chit turned him down, but now her parents were denying him entry into the house. *What did I say to them to cause them to do that?* Perhaps he had gone too far when he proposed. All he'd tried to do was give her a kiss to persuade her to consent to the engagement. For his trouble, he'd got his instep stomped on and an elbow in the ribs. It wasn't as if he'd have gone any further than a kiss. He wasn't a beast, just a little desperate.

His brown study was interrupted by a slap on the shoulder that spilled his ale just as he was raising it to his lips.

"Bryce!" Lord Kenrick Layne grinned as he straddled the bench Bryson was sitting on. The man was all long limbs, romantic blond locks, deep blue eyes, and cheeky smile. The ladies adored him. "Have you gone deaf, man?" said Kenrick, setting his own ale down on the table with a small thud. "I've been trying to get your attention for several minutes."

Bryson shook his head to clear it and grinned wryly at his

friend. "Sorry, old boy, I was miles away."

"Evidently!" Kenrick took a large swig of his ale and wiped the foam off his upper lip with his sleeve. "What's got you so down in the dumps?"

Bryson debated whether to confide in his friend, and while he was still thinking, Kenrick declaimed dramatically, "Don't tell me!" Putting a hand to his forehead in the manner of a seer, he said, "The pursuit of your lady love has gone awry!"

Bryson smiled ruefully at his nonsense. "Yes, something like that."

"Never mind, lots more fish in the sea, Bryce. It's not as if you're desperate."

"No," said Bryson hollowly.

Seeming to catch his tone, Kenrick asked, "Unless it's serious?"

Bryson lifted a shoulder, trying to adopt the air of a spurned lover. *Which I am, damn it!*

"Faint heart never won fair lady!" said Kenrick, raising his tankard.

"In this case the pitch has skewed, I fear," said Bryson in a hangdog sort of way. "Nothing for it but to rusticate for a while and try again in the autumn."

"Good idea! Where do you plan to go?"

"Not sure yet." He sipped his ale and waited.

"I'm heading to my brother's place in Leicestershire for a spell. Want to come? We could do a spot of fowling and fishing. He will have some house guests; he always does. You never know, there may even be some ladies to take your mind off your lady love."

"Are you sure the duke won't mind?"

"Of course not, Hereward and I have standing invitations to drop in whenever we like and bring a friend if we choose. I grew up there, you know. It's my home, too. Just because Robert got the lot, being the eldest, doesn't mean he's stingy about sharing his inheritance with me and Hereward."

"Don't mind if I do then, Rick. It will be good to get out of town for a bit. It's beastly hot in summer."

"Your father still being a curmudgeon?"

"A bit," he admitted reluctantly.

Kenrick nodded sympathetically. "I'll drop Rob a line to let him know we'll be there before the end of next week. That suit you?"

"Yes, thank you."

Chapter Six

Cheetham Hall, Sussex
Two days later

THEY HAD ONLY been married for a week, Emily thought as she sat down to breakfast, but she already felt a sense of companionable comfort in the daily routine they had established.

"It's from Aberdeen," Deo said, breaking open the letter beside his breakfast plate. "He says," his eyes scanned the page as he spoke, "that there is a find he wants us to investigate. Good lord, it's at The Castle!"

"Where?" Emily said, pausing with her buttered toast halfway to her mouth.

"The Duke of Troubridge's place. Well, well, that is a turn up for the books. You'll like this; it's a Celtic cross with a possible burial. How about that?" He lowered the letter and grinned at her.

"Oh!" *The Duke of Troubridge!* She swallowed a sip of tea, trying to compose her thoughts.

"Aren't you excited? This is right in your sphere."

"Yes, yes, very excited, I—I was just surprised, that's all."

"We will need to leave at once. It will take us several days to get there. The Castle is in Leicestershire."

Don't panic! Will the Duke of Troubridge even remember you? Yes, silly, he's not in his dotage! He danced with you several times. Mama was ecstatic, she thought he was a serious contender!

"Robert must have written to the *Antiquaries Society* to report the find. I remember him—or was it Emrys?—mentioning it last year. Aberdeen seems to think it might be significant and urges us to investigate immediately."

"You know the Duke of Troubridge?"

"Lord, yes. He's one of my closest friends. We went to Cambridge together."

"Oh. That—that's nice."

"He married Sarah Watson. Lovely woman, you'll like her—she's about your age," he said, oblivious to her internal turmoil.

What am I going to do? The duke will be sure to recognize me. There is no help for it. I will have to reveal my true name and age. But when will be the best time to do it? Not—not now. Her craven heart pleaded.

A week of marriage to Deo had already taught her to pick her moments. He had warned her his temperament was volatile. She should have listened to him. He could go from seemingly quite jovial and happy, like now, to a thundercloud in the twinkling of an eye and for a bewilderingly wide array of reasons that made little obvious sense. As his wife, however, she thought it behooved her to learn to understand those reasons and seek ways to ameliorate them. After all, he was a wonderful man with a brilliant archaeological mind, and—she trembled a little with giddiness at the reality—he was now her husband.

Her momentary euphoria dipped. Telling him she had lied to him about her name and age were going to be two reasons for him to be quite justifiably angry with her, and she needed to pick a moment when she could manage his response. Twenty years acquaintance with her mother had taught her a lot about handling people with an uncertain temper.

"Shall we take Kester?" she asked, postponing the inevitable.

"Of course. Go and have a look at the library, my dear, and select the texts you might need. I'll get out my dig equipment." He rose, rubbing his hands. "This will be fun!"

She nodded and rose as well, remembering to smile. *It is a wonderful opportunity. A literal dream come true, if I didn't have this cloud of deceit hanging over me.* Making her way to the library, she supposed it served her right for lying in the first place. She should have told him the truth before they were married. But she had been afraid he wouldn't go through with it and that he would contact her parents and send her home. *He might still do that!*

A little voice in her head said, *No, he won't! I won't let him!*

THEY LEFT FOR Leicestershire the next day. Deo had decreed they would stay in his townhouse in London on the way. What a difference there was between traveling in one's own, comfortable, well-sprung carriage with a team of fast horses and biding one's time in a lumbering stagecoach. The trip that had taken her over four days on her own, they accomplished in one. A long day it was, true—but a single day, nevertheless. But then they didn't have to trudge miles on foot, carrying a heavy bag, and wait for hours for a coach, all the while terrified her father would appear to drag her home. And they didn't have to change coaches twice with lengthy waits between each and then walk miles at the other end, again with a heavy bag.

This journey was quite pleasant, all things considered. Kester slept on the forward seat, and she and Deo shared the other. At one point Deo looked up from his book and said, "We should stay in London long enough for you to buy some clothes. You didn't bring many gowns with you, did you?"

Startled, she said, "No, I—" She had been going to say she had planned to have her things sent on, but of course she couldn't do that. *Oh, gosh, if I go shopping in Bond Street, I could run into Mama.* "I don't need gowns, Deo. Really, what I have is adequate for grubbing about in a dig!" she protested.

He shook his head. "We will be staying with the duke and duchess. They may well be entertaining; they often are. You will need evening dress suitable for dinner, apart from anything else."

"Oh dear, I didn't think of that."

He smiled. "Don't worry. Go and see a modiste; let her take your measurements, and she can send the dresses on. If you need something before they arrive, you can probably borrow something from Lady Ava's wardrobe."

"Lady Ava?"

"The duke's eldest sister. She is about your size, in height at least." He frowned. "I think she might have a bit more curvature. But that's all to the good. It is easier to take seams in than let them out, I should think."

Digesting this in silence and trying not to mind that the Lady Ava had more "curvature" and that he'd noticed, she returned to her book.

It was late when they arrived in London at his house in Grosvenor Square. At Cheetham Court they had made no changes to the sleeping arrangements—she had remained in the green room, and Deo remained in his. But the earl's sudden arrival at his townhouse with a wife threw the London servants into a flurry, and she was automatically shown to the suite belonging to her husband. This included two bedchambers, two dressing rooms, and a shared sitting room between them.

Mrs. Armiston, the housekeeper, was most apologetic. "I'm so sorry, your ladyship, but his lordship didn't tell us! I would have aired the room and dusted it. As it is, I'll have to change the sheets, and you're so tired after your long journey. But don't you worry. The mattress has been turned and beaten regular, and we've fresh pillows and coverlets in the storeroom."

The earl stood in the doorway, his hands on his hips. "Very good, Mrs. Armiston. And can you have Jenny wait on her ladyship? She doesn't have her maid with her." His gaze travelled to the portrait of a woman with a pair of Irish Setters above the mantle. "This room hasn't been used since my mother passed away."

Seeing Emily's expression, he said, "Don't worry, she didn't die here—it was at Cheetham. I'll leave you to freshen up and see you for supper downstairs. Send her to the library, will you, Mrs. Armiston? We will eat in there." He turned and walked off, leaving Emily feeling rather winded.

"If that's not just like him!" clucked Mrs. Armiston, who was a big-bosomed woman in her fifties. "I've known him since he was a lad," she said confidingly. "He never did have any sensibility, just like his father. Never mind. We will make you comfortable, your ladyship, and right welcome you are too. Thought he'd never marry, we did," she said, bustling about, stripping sheets off the bed. "I'll have Jenny bring up the hot water to you straight," she said and left before Emily could say anything.

She had visions of her mother telling her to depress the pretensions of servants being overly familiar, but she couldn't see herself doing so to the likes of Mrs. Armiston. When she had agreed to marry Deo, she hadn't thought about the position and responsibilities that would come with it. She was now forcibly reminded of both. She was reminded, too, that she needed to tell him sooner than later about her identity before he went introducing her to too many more people.

AN HOUR LATER Emily went downstairs, having washed and changed and with the knowledge that her bed would be ready and waiting for her when she returned. She found the library with directions and pushed open the heavy carved door to reveal a room made cozy by a large fire in the grate and the comfort of books lining the walls. She felt immediately at home, wondering what delights this second library held.

Deo was seated before the fire in a large comfortable armchair, his feet stretched out toward the blaze and by Kester's head. He had changed, too, and was looking quite casual and comfortable, sans neckcloth, and wearing a robe over his shirt and breeches. It was the most undressed she had ever seen him, and she felt herself blushing.

"My lord—"

He looked up from the book he was reading. "Ah, there you are." He rose and the robe, which was untied, fell open, giving her a glimpse of his shirt-covered chest. The swell of his pectorals was visible above his flat stomach, and she swallowed, dragging her eyes away hastily. Kester, seemingly worn out after sleeping all day in the carriage, raised his head, yawned, and put it back down with a sigh.

"Come, dinner's over here." He led her to a small, round dining table with two chairs drawn up to it and an array of dishes upon it.

Once she was seated, he began piling her plate with food. He still seemed to be convinced she needed feeding. "There," he said with a smile, passing the plate back to her. "Is everything in your room satisfactory?"

"Yes, thank you. Mrs. Armiston is very efficient."

"She's worked here all my life, I think. I don't remember a time when she wasn't a fixture anyway. She was one of the housemaids when I was a babe, I believe. She rose to become housekeeper and has been here ever since." He began eating with enthusiasm. She had noticed that he had a prodigious appetite, but then he was a big man.

She toyed with her fork. She really needed to tell him . . . but . . .

I can't tell him in London. What if he packs me back off home or— an odd idea occurred to her—*confronts my parents about their treatment of me? Would he do that? He wasn't impressed by it. All the same, I don't want to find out.*

He waved his knife at her plate, "Eat up. I don't want you fainting again!"

She swallowed the words hovering on the tip of her tongue and began to eat, rapidly finding she was famished.

"You should hire a maid while we're here, or you can take Jenny with us if she's satisfactory," he said. "Will you be all right to find a modiste and order some gowns? I'll be no use to you in that regard. I'm clueless as to feminine attire."

"What should I do about the bills?"

"Send them to me, of course. I trust you not to break the bank."

She swallowed a mouthful of wine to dislodge something that felt stuck in her throat. "I didn't expect gowns to be part of the salary package," she said, in an attempt at humor.

"I can't have my wife going about ill-dressed," he said. Then he added hastily, "Not that I meant to imply—"

"I know what you meant," she broke in with a smile. "Thank you, I'm grateful. It's very kind of you."

"Is it? It seems practical to me."

"I'll do my best not to embarrass you," she said quietly.

He put down his knife and fork. "You won't embarrass me. I'm the one who's grateful." He stretched out a hand to touch hers briefly.

She blinked, shocked and unexpectedly moved. His hand was warm, his touch comforting. She resisted the urge to clasp his fingers tightly. *This is a business arrangement, not one of affection.*

"I've bellowed at you at least a dozen times in the last few days and you haven't blinked an eyelid. I'm a grumpy curmudgeon. I'm sorry."

"I'm used to being yelled at. My mother does it a lot."

"Well, you shouldn't have to tolerate it. I'll try to manage my temper better," he said with a rueful smile.

"It's all right." She smiled back. "I think I understand why you do it."

"You do?" His blue eyes seemed to get more intensely blue as he looked at her. "I don't. Please tell me."

"Well, it generally occurs when you feel uncomfortable."

"Yes, when something isn't where it's supposed to be. Or my routine is disrupted."

"So, you yell to—to release the uncomfortable feelings and make things comfortable again."

"Yes, that's true. But I make you uncomfortable in the process, which is selfish of me. I'm not used to having someone else's feelings to consider. Only the servants, and I pay them to put up with me."

"Well, you're paying me too, aren't you?" she asked prosaically.

"Hm." He pushed his plate aside and picked up his wine.

She stole a look at him. He was frowning at the middle distance as if he was thinking about something he didn't like. She had thought his features too harsh to be handsome, and he was still fearsome when he frowned, but she must be getting used to his face because he seemed a great deal more attractive in general now, especially when he smiled. *It's a business arrangement,* she reminded herself sternly, again. *You shouldn't be thinking about him as a man. An attractive man . . . Oh dear!*

She pushed her plate aside. "I think I'll retire now, I'm tired."

He rose when she did. "Good night. I have a few things to attend to myself while we are in London. If I don't see you in the morning, we will no doubt catch each other later in the day. Sleep well." He hesitated and then leaned down and kissed her cheek. It was fleeting, like the kiss he gave her after they were married. But the warm pressure of his lips on her cheek sent a shiver through her body that made her jerk in surprise.

He jerked back, flushing, and turned away abruptly. "Good night!" he repeated brusquely. She touched her cheek and eyed his stiffened shoulders. Really, he would think she was a complete ninny if she jerked every time he touched her. Intuitively she sensed he was sensitive to rejection. Was that why he turned away when she reacted like that?

She left the room thoughtfully. *Perhaps I'm not the only one sensing some kind of attraction.*

WHATEVER POSSESSED ME to kiss her cheek like that?

He had promised her he wouldn't bother her, and it was clear from her reaction that she didn't welcome his touch. She had just got through reminding him that he was paying her to put up with him. She was his wife (temporarily, in name only) and a paid employee. He had no business touching her under their current contract. If he was going to do that, he would have to change the rules. And if he opened that particular Pandora's box, he would have to be prepared for what came out because it couldn't be shut again. He was not at all sure he wanted to find out . . .

If she weren't so damned pretty . . .

Chapter Seven

THERE WAS ONE thing Deo needed to sort out while he was in London which Emily definitely didn't need to know about, and that was to terminate his arrangement with his mistress. He had initially thought he would keep it, given that he wasn't intending to consummate the marriage, at least not yet. But considering that he wasn't going to be residing in London for several months anyway, it seemed sensible to terminate the arrangement now.

His arrangement with Damaris (he was sure that wasn't her real name, but he had never asked) had been in place for over ten years. When he was in town, he visited her once a week on Thursdays at three pm for an hour. There was no kissing, no conversation really beyond the commonplace, for what would he talk to her about? She had no understanding or interest, he was sure, in the things that interested him. She served a purely functional place in his life, nothing more, nothing less.

She stimulated herself to make herself ready for him, he popped his member in, and a little while later it was over. It served the purpose of enabling him to function sensibly. When he wasn't resident in London, he used his hand to relieve the tension, at three pm on Thursdays. The routine was so well established that his body knew when to get aroused and when to leave him alone.

He was aware this tightly regimented pattern was not the way others conducted their lives. His friend Ravenshaw, for example, was notorious for his affairs, mostly with willing widows. Before Troubridge was married, he had kept a mistress whom he visited regularly. And Ashford was married, and to Deo's knowledge, didn't have and had never kept a mistress.

Knocking on her door at a time that wasn't three pm on a Thursday—which was so wildly out of order it broke him out in a cold sweat—he was aware that it behooved him to provide her with some token of their time together. But he wasn't one for presents, so he'd simply brought her a check. Money would be of more use to her and allow her sufficient time to find another protector.

The butler answered the door and was startled to see him. "My lord, it's not Thursday."

"I am aware, Stoughton, is Miss Damaris at home?"

"She is, my lord, in the parlor. I venture she will be glad to see you," he said with a slight smile.

Deo didn't return the smile. He was feeling acutely uncomfortable.

Stoughton opened the parlor door, a room Deo had never been in, and announced him.

"The Earl of Pendrell, ma'am."

Damaris was sitting on a sofa and fully dressed. Since he never saw her except in a robe and half naked, he was taken aback.

She rose at his entrance, as startled to see him as Stoughton had been. "Pendrell! What brings you here today?"

The door had closed behind him. He swallowed and bowed to her.

"Forgive the intrusion. I have lately married, a week ago in fact. I came to inform you and," he thrust out the check, "give you this in token of our time together. I hope it is adequate to express my—ah—appreciation of your services. Henceforth, I will no longer be requiring them."

Damaris had stood opened mouthed through this recital. "I see." She took the check and looked at it. "This is most generous. Thank you." She appeared at a loss for a moment. "Would you care to sit down? A cup of tea perhaps?"

"No, thank you."

"Well, I wish you well in your marriage, my lord," she said a little stiffly.

He nodded. "Thank you. I wish you well also. I—" He stopped, flushing and flustered. "I apologize for the short notice in terminating our arrangement. It all happened very suddenly."

Her expression softened and she said, "Did it? I hope it makes you happy, Deo. All the best."

He nodded and bowed, turned, and left. He had a strange hollow ache in his chest that was very unpleasant. His throat felt tight, and there was a peculiar sting in his eyes. *It must be anxiety. I don't like change, and this is a big change to my routine.* He needed an outlet for the sudden flare of irritability that seized him.

He returned to the house, collected Kester and went for a very long walk. By the time he returned, the achy, anxious feeling had mostly dissipated, but he was strangely disinclined to eat anything and decided that more exercise was needed. Fortunately, there was no sign of Emily, so he didn't have to talk to her. He wasn't fit company in his current state. He might snap at her if she looked at him the wrong way. He took himself off to Gentleman Jackson's boxing saloon and spent a satisfactory hour sparring and sweating.

Thus, he was able to sit down to dinner that evening with his countess and ask politely about her day.

"I have ordered four new gowns and left instructions for them to be forwarded to the Duke of Troubridge's estate in Leicestershire," she said calmly.

"Have you had a chance to browse the library here yet?"

She flushed and smiled. "Yes, I spent a bit of time there this afternoon. You have a huge collection of gothic novels!"

"Ah!" It was his turn to blush. With embarrassment. "You have uncovered my secret vice. I'm addicted to them," he admitted sheepishly.

Her face glowed and she leaned forward. "So am I! Mama forbade me to read them but Gregory—that's our butler and my dearest friend—would smuggle them in for me. I had to leave them all behind, along with my other books and journals. I could only bring my research papers with me," she said sadly.

"Perhaps we can retrieve them when we return from Leicestershire."

She almost choked on her wine. "Y-yes, perhaps . . ."

"You're most reluctant to have anything to do with your parents, aren't you?"

"Yes," she admitted, flushing.

"The way they have treated you, I'm not surprised. I can deal with them for you if you like."

"Oh! That is most kind but—"

"It is not kind. I am your husband; it is my duty to protect you from—unpleasantness." He was conscious of his tone being peremptory and of a rising irritation at the way she had been treated. He would deal with the situation on their return.

It occurred to him that her parents may have set steps in motion to find her. *After all, if a daughter goes missing, surely her parents, no matter how self-serving, would want to recover her and know that she was well?* And they might be understandably annoyed with him for keeping her from them. Well, he was equal to that. As her husband, his rights outranked theirs. But he really should look into who her parents were, if she wouldn't tell him. He was strangely reluctant to force her to.

He pushed the problem aside; it would wait until their return. *If her parents are worried, they deserve to be. Starving your daughter to death in an attempt to coerce her into accepting a proposal that is repugnant to her is the act of monsters.* He had scant sympathy for them.

⇛⇚

THEY EMBARKED FOR Leicestershire two days later at first light. It would take them two long days of travel to get there, and Deo was anxious to get underway. Emily was a pleasant traveling companion, willing to converse, but also to sit quietly and read. *Really, she is an ideal wife. I must remember to write and thank Emrys for the suggestion.*

They spent eight hours on the road, stopping at Swinford for the night. He made an initial attempt to get them separate rooms, but the hostelry was close to fully booked, and the host was only able to offer him a single room. "It's a large one, my lord, one of my best," he said apologetically.

With a glance at Emily who was looking flushed and slightly embarrassed, he accepted the single room and had their luggage carried up with instructions that a bath was to be provided for the countess.

The room was indeed large and pleasant. Its predominant piece of furniture was a large bed, the sight of which made him uneasy. So far, he had managed to avoid any form of physical intimacy with his wife. Tonight, that was going to be impossible. The prospect was making him nervous. He was an intensely private person, and he had never shared a bed with anyone in his life. Only his valet had seen him naked as a grown man—and his former mistress, he added mentally.

Emily was staring at the bed, too, with flushed cheeks. He pulled himself together at the sight of her discomposure. He needed to reassure her that he wouldn't break the rules of their contract.

And to make matters worse, he had sent their servants, Jenny and Stevens, ahead to announce their arrival, so they would have to tend to their own dressing, too.

The two servants should have arrived at The Castle by now. Stevens was very familiar with the place and would ensure Jenny was looked after appropriately. Sending them ahead also ensured that the duke and duchess would have had ample time to prepare a suitable welcome for his countess. Emily wasn't shy with him, but he suspected she would be in company. Sarah's warmth would overcome that quickly, he was sure, but he wanted to assure her comfort as much as possible.

When the inn's servants left to fetch more hot water, he said, "Don't be concerned." He waved toward the bed. "I am a man of my word."

She jerked her head around to him and her cheeks deepened in color. His gaze followed the line of pink to her chest and jerked away in haste.

"Yes, of course!" she said quickly.

The bath had already been brought up and a procession of servants came with hot water to fill it. Making the excuse of checking on the horses, Deo took Kester and left Emily to enjoy her bath in peace and came back half an hour later to find her sitting in a robe by the fire, combing out her flowing hair. He stopped in the doorway, shocked, for it was the first time he had seen it out of its usual neat chignon, let down apparently after her bath was complete. It was an unusual color, brown with blonde streaks. It fell to the middle of her back in a cascade of inviting waves.

The room seemed smaller all of a sudden, and his earlier panic threatened to reemerge.

"I trust your bath was enjoyable?" he said, moving into the room and closing the door.

She began replaiting her hair. "Yes, very satisfactory, thank you."

"The food should be up shortly," he said and moved across to the dresser, where his valise had been left. The bulk of his luggage, equipment, and books had gone ahead with Stevens and Jenny. He removed his jacket, neckcloth and waistcoat and put on the robe he always wore to relax in. He removed his boots and put on his slippers. *That feels better.*

He turned to find she had finished plaiting her hair. It was now confined to a long, thick rope hanging over her shoulder. Her robe, which was of plain blue silk, was tied at the waist over a high-necked white nightgown. He could see nothing through the fabric, but even so, the intimacy of it made him flushed and hot.

A knock at the door heralded the arrival of dinner, much to his relief. He set out a bowl for Kester by the fire before sitting down himself. As they ate, he tried to distract her and himself by talking about The Castle.

"It's the ruins of the original Norman keep that give it the name of The Castle," he said. "The house itself is quite modern. It will be interesting to find out where this Celtic cross and burial are located on the grounds. The Latin inscription is only partially legible, but we may be able to take a rubbing and make out some of the lost letters."

"It would be terribly exciting if we could identify who is interred there," Emily replied. "From Lord Aberdeen's letter, I gather that the duke concluded the person had been subject to *damnatio memoriae*."

"Yes, which if true, would mean he had fallen out of political favor with someone powerful. Some long-forgotten king, perhaps." He smiled with excitement.

These were the moments he treasured most with her, when their shared love of history came to the fore, and she glowed at him like a portrait in candlelight. Her cheeks were flushed—with happiness, not embarrassment this time—and her eyes looked green in the soft glow of the room. Her rosebud mouth stretched wide in a smile. It was in these moments that she was most beautiful.

After the meal, Deo took Kes out quickly to relieve himself and upon his return suggested to Emily that if she was tired, she should retire, and he would join her shortly. He thought if she were already asleep, he could disrobe, wash, and slip into the bed without disturbing her.

Emily agreed and, getting out her book, she clambered into the big bed and nestled into the pillows with it. Deo settled himself by the fire with his book and tried to stop himself sneaking looks at her. He told himself he was checking to see if she was asleep yet, but it was more for the felicity of seeing her curled up in the bank of white pillows, the long plait of thick hair lying across the gentle rise of her bosom in its robe and gown that had him fascinated.

A strange possessive pride stole over him. *My wife.*

He dragged his gaze back to his book and tried to concentrate. She rustled around in the bed, and Kes, who had been lying at his feet, suddenly got up and leaped up onto the bed, shocking her into a yelp of surprise. "Kester!" she said, with a laugh and rumpled his ears, stroking his head.

"Kes—" he said peremptorily. "He's not supposed to do that unless he is invited. Kes, get down." Kes obeyed sheepishly, jumping down with a thud.

"Oh no! I don't mind; he will keep my feet warm," she said in protest.

"Very well, invite him up. Say 'Kes, up' and lift your hand."

"Kes, up!" she said, gesturing with her hand. Kester glanced at him for permission, jumped when he nodded, settling down on her feet with a deep sigh of contentment.

That was another thing in her favor: Kes was obviously very fond of her already.

The clock ticked on the mantle slowly, and eventually he looked up when a candle guttered to find she had fallen asleep over her book. Rising quietly, he moved the book to the bedside table and removed his shirt, but he left his breeches on. He always slept naked, but he thought it would be impolite to do so tonight. He might frighten her. She had probably never seen a naked man in her life. He performed a quick wash and, blowing out most of the candles, he crept to the bed and slid into his side of it. Lying back gingerly into the pillows, he looked across at her.

She is so damned lovely! He had never put much value on female beauty before. He had been so focused on wanting a woman he felt comfortable talking to. The pretty ones had just made him uncomfortable. Beautiful women disturbed his equilibrium and made him tongue-tied. Made him feel like he was fifteen again and making a fool of himself. Emily—Emily was different. He had thought her pretty enough when she first arrived, but not so beautiful as to reduce him to a puddle of incoherence. She was rapidly becoming much prettier every time he looked at her.

Just then her eyelids flickered, and she opened her eyes, staring straight at him. The impact made his heart stop, and his cock stirred to life, without his volition. He flushed and she smiled.

"Deo," her voice was soft and husky with sleep.

"Yes?" His voice came out croaky, and he cleared his throat.

She shifted in the bed, making the mattress dip and causing him to roll toward her. He was much heavier than her. He put out an arm to stop himself rolling on top of her and stared down at her, fascinated and terrified at once.

She blinked up at him. Then she bit her lovely, plump bottom lip, and he swallowed a groan with difficulty. *I need to get out of this bed, now!*

But he didn't. He continued to stare down at her.

"Deo, there's something I need to tell you," she said hesitantly.

"Yes?" he said again.

"I—I lied to you."

Her words penetrated his brain slowly, and he pulled back a fraction, the thudding of his heart interrupted by a skip and an uneasy roll of his stomach. "What do you mean?" His voice came out harsher than he meant it to.

She flinched back into the pillows, and he cursed his sharp tongue.

She dropped her eyes and worried at the sheet with her fingers. "I lied about my family name. It's not Bromwich, it's Grenfell. My father is Viscount Efford."

"I see." He breathed out slowly. "Why are you telling me this now?"

"Because the Duke of Troubridge will likely recognize me. He—he courted me briefly last year. I'm an heiress, you see." Her tone became wretched. "I'm really sorry. I should have told you sooner."

"Yes, you should!" He sat up, pushing a hand through his hair.

"Does it make our marriage invalid? Because my name isn't correct?"

"Very possibly. I don't know." He stared at the canopy above his head. "Damn and blast, I should have made you tell me who your parents are. I thought—." He stopped, his throat working. "It doesn't matter what I thought, I should have—bloody hell, Emily! Is that even your name?"

"Yes, yes. Emily and Frances are my given names. I only lied about my family name. I was afraid you would force me to go back to them if you knew who they were."

"Was it true about them starving you, or did you make that up too?"

"No, it's true. I swear!" She sat up and swiveled toward him. "I'm so sorry. There—there's one other thing—"

"What?" he asked ominously, his heart thudding hard in his chest.

She dropped her head. "I lied about my age, too. I thought you would think I was too young for the position, that I wouldn't have enough experience. And then when you proposed marrying me, I—I was afraid—"

"How old are you?" he asked, looming over her.

"Twenty," she said faintly, flinching.

"You're not of age." His voice was flat. He sank back against the pillows. Somewhere he was conscious of a smoldering rage, but the uppermost emotion was disappointment. A deep, heartrending disappointment.

She nodded. "I was afraid you'd pack me off back to my parents if you knew, or if they found out and came after me, they'd drag me back home." She stopped, her voice cracking. "I don't want to go home. I've been so happy with you. Please don't send me home!" She flung herself on his chest, openly weeping.

Stunned, Deo froze. He didn't know what to do with a weeping female. Especially one half dressed and draped across his naked chest.

"Please, Deo, don't send me home!" she begged, her little hands clutching at him. The gentle swell of her small breasts was pressed against his chest, her scent of roses and something else filled his nostrils, and her body was warm and shaking against him.

Kes, woken by the disturbance, came and rested a comforting jaw on her leg, and Deo found himself patting her soothingly and saying, "Don't cry, I won't send you home." He swallowed; his throat was tight. "Damn it, Emily," he said softly, "don't cry. I can't stand it!"

Her sobs tumbled down into a hiccoughing mess, her hot tears dripping down his bare skin. He put his arms around her and discovered anew just how small she was. The rage and the disappointment were still there somewhere, but right now they were buried under a layer of need to get her to stop crying. Her sobs were tearing him to pieces.

"Hush!" he said a bit more loudly. "Stop it, Em, please!"

This seemed to reach her, and she made an effort to stifle the sobs.

"I'm s-sorry!" she said woefully.

He pulled her away a bit with his hands on her arms, so that he could see her face. It was blotched and her eyes were red and swimming in tears. He knew he was frowning fiercely. "I won't send you home, Em, but this is serious. I've married you without your father's permission."

She nodded, a hand to her mouth to stifle the sob. "I know. I'm sorry."

"Stop saying you're sorry. It doesn't help!" he said irritably.

"What a damned coil!"

She swallowed and wiped her face on the sheet and sniffed.

He got up and fetched her a handkerchief and climbed back into bed. She sat up and blew her nose. Wiping her face, she said thickly, "What will you do?"

"Seek the advice of my solicitor. I need to understand the legal ramifications. Damn and blast!" He stared angrily at the bed post. "Is there anything else you haven't told me?"

"No, no, I swear. Everything else was true. I should have told you; it was stupid not to."

"Yes, it was," he said harshly.

She nodded dolefully and wiped fresh tears off her cheeks.

"Bloody hell, Em!" he said helplessly and pulled her into his embrace. "I'm no good at this!" he said, his voice anguished.

She buried her face in his chest, wetness on his skin. "I'm so—"

"Don't!" he admonished and kissed her hair. *Fuck! I don't do kisses, I don't do hugs, and I cannot cope with her crying.*

"Thank you," she whispered, and the anger leeched away, leaving him feeling drained and slightly heartsick.

"We'll sort it out when we get to The Castle. I'll write to my solicitor and find out where we stand. Once I know that, I'll write to your parents. We may need to be married again; I don't know."

"You'll still marry me?" she asked, raising her head.

"My reasons for marrying you haven't changed," he said roughly, flushing. "You make me comfortable—when you're not crying all over me."

She smiled tentatively, and she leaned forward and kissed his chin. "You make me so happy," she said softly.

His whole body flushed with pleasure, and his traitorous cock stiffened in his breeches. *Good thing I left them on.*

"We need to sleep," he said abruptly, pushing her away.

She nodded, dropping her head and moving away to her side of the bed. He heaved a sigh of relief to have the temptation of her body separated from his treacherous cock. Yet his body now felt cold without her warmth. He pushed the thought away and suppressed the ache in his chest. He had a contract to uphold. And in any case, she might not be legally married to him, in which case there was even more reason to keep his distance.

Chapter Eight

THEY ARRIVED AT The Castle late in the afternoon. The consequences of her confession or rather her deceit, were felt keenly by Emily. While Deo was polite, there was a constraint between them. Their companionable peace was destroyed, replaced by an awkward silence, broken only by necessary conversation. It was making Emily feel miserable, and Deo didn't look happy either. In fact, he exuded thundercloud more strongly than an incipient storm. Surprisingly though, he didn't snap or raise his voice. She almost wished he would. It might clear the air and break the tension.

As a consequence of this, by the time they arrived at The Castle, her confidence was very low. She found herself wishing the ground would open and swallow her up, rather than having to face the Duke and Duchess of Troubridge.

In desperation, as the carriage entered the grounds of the estate, Emily reached out to touch his arm. "Deo?"

He looked up from his book and raised an eyebrow.

"Please," she said. "I cannot bear to face them with you so angry with me. They will sense it, and I'll die of embarrassment."

"I'm not angry—" he protested.

"Yes, you are, I can feel it!" she interrupted him.

He took a breath and huffed it out. "Very well. But I cannot just wave a magic wand and *not* be angry."

"No, but you could yell at me, and you might feel better?" she said, peeking at him.

He glared at her for a moment and then surprisingly, he laughed.

"Is that what I do? You said something like that the other night."

"Yes, you do," she said with a tentative smile.

He took her hand and squeezed it. "I'm sorry. I'm like a bear with a sore head." He shook it as if to shake off his mood. "But you don't have to worry about the duke and duchess. They are very nice people."

She shuddered. "The duke is terrifying. I've met him!"

"Oh, that's just his starchy public face. He's not like that at home, I assure you. And Sarah is a vicar's daughter, the eldest of eight. She is very warm and friendly."

"Oh, well, if you will not glare at me too much, I should be able to manage, I suppose. I'm not good at social situations."

"Neither am I, but this is different. You'll be among friends. My friends. They will welcome you simply because you're my wife."

She nodded, and he surprised her by raising her hand to his lips and kissing it, then he gave it a reassuring squeeze. It was comforting, as she was sure it was meant to be.

"We're here," he said as the carriage rolled to a stop before the very imposing front entrance of a sprawling three-story mansion. Opening the door, he let Kes jump out and then followed, turning to help her down, which he did by lifting her. He did this so effortlessly, he made her feel like thistledown. The whole sensation made her heart flutter and gave her gooseflesh— the good kind. He was so big and handsome, her husband. Her eyes ran up his length, and she breathed in his scent. His masculinity was overwhelming sometimes—that chest, those arms.

Last night, she'd flung herself against him and cried all over him. And he'd hugged her, held her, and begged her not to cry. No one had ever done that before. She swallowed a swell of emotion as he set her on her feet, and he turned her toward the entrance, which was suddenly full of people.

She recognized the duke, and she thought the other rather carelessly dressed gentleman looked vaguely familiar, too, but she couldn't be sure. The rest was a blur of ladies and three children who, with loud squeals, descended the steps at a run, heading straight for Kester, who wagged his tail at this greeting and capered about barking madly. Pandemonium reigned for a few moments until Deo got Kes to settle down and the rumpled man who wasn't the duke managed to subdue the children somewhat.

Deo greeted the man with a hug. "Emrys!" He smiled. "I took your advice," he murmured obscurely. Then he said, "Meet my wife, Emily. Em, this is Emrys, Viscount Ashford. He was at Cambridge with the rest of us."

Emily curtsied and murmured something that she hoped was appropriate, while the man, who had very kind eyes, twinkled at her. "My pleasure, Lady Pendrell."

"Hey, precedence!" protested the duke, stepping forward. "Why does he get the first introduction?"

Deo laughed, clapping the duke on the back. "Your Grace, I would like to introduce my wife, Emily Frances, Countess of Pendrell. But Em tells me you've met?" There was a faint challenge in that tone, and Emily's heart turned over.

The duke, ever the polished gentleman, took her hand. "Indeed, we have. When we last met, you were Miss Grenfell, so this is a happy change in your circumstances. Welcome to The Castle, my dear. Let me introduce my wife, Sarah," he said, sweeping a tall, brown-haired young woman forward.

"I'm delighted to meet you!" The duchess enveloped Emily in a hug. "Come and meet everyone else." She swept Emily up the steps, making introductions as she went. "This is Annis, Lady Ashford. And the children are Elizabeth, Charlotte, and Ewen. As you might have guessed from his peace-keeping duties, they belong to Emrys. Now do come in and put off your cloak. You must be thirsty and hungry, yes?"

They entered the house with Kester and the children, rounded up by Deo and the viscount, and the duke bringing up the rear with instructions to the butler to take care of their luggage. Tea was served in the drawing room on the first floor, and a very elegant apartment it was, too. Emily found herself seated next to Deo on one of the couches as the duchess served and handed round cups of tea, biscuits, cakes, and sandwiches.

"We're expecting Kenrick any moment too, with a friend, so we will have quite a house party."

"Hereward has a standing invitation, but I think he has gone to a friend's for a spot of hunting," said the duke.

"Well, it's quite like old times having everyone here, isn't it?" said Sarah. "And some new, very welcome faces, too," she said kindly with a smile at Emily.

"So, you've come to investigate the cross, eh?" said the duke to Deo. "Stevens gave me your note, of course. I had no idea when I wrote to Aberdeen about it that he was going to send you."

"What can you tell me about it?"

"Emrys found it," he said.

Emrys leaned forward to take another piece of cake. "Actually, the Watson boys found it, last summer. It's about fifty yards from the ruins. We did a bit of digging, and it seems likely there is something buried underneath it. So, we left it to the expert. Which is you."

Deo took Emily's hand and said, "*We* are. In fact, Em is more of an expert than I am in this one. Celtic burials and artifacts are her specialty."

Emily blushed with pleasure at his praise. "It's so very exciting. Thank you for the opportunity."

AT THE END of tea, the duchess said to Emily, "You'll want to wash up and rest before dinner, which is at seven. I've put you and Deo in the yellow suite. Deo will show you where it is."

With a slightly sinking heart, Deo left his friends to escort Emily upstairs to their room. He had specifically asked Stevens to secure them a double suite. Either he hadn't asked, the message had gotten lost in translation, or the duchess had chosen to ignore the request. The yellow suite had only one bedchamber, dressing room, and sitting room. They were likely to be here for weeks, and the prospect of sharing a bed with Emily for all that time . . .

He opened the door of the sitting room, off of which the bedroom ran. It was a light and airy chamber done out in yellow brocade furnishings and gold-and-white striped wallpaper. The sitting room had a generous-sized desk, and perhaps that was the reason the duchess had assigned the suite to them. This room would become their headquarters while they worked on the burial. Stevens had laid out their books and papers on the desk and made a neat pile of Deo's archaeological equipment in the corner.

He led her through into the bedroom which boasted the same style furnishings as the sitting room and poked his head into the dressing room to check that their clothing had been put away.

"Dinner," said Emily in a panicked tone. "What shall I wear?"

"Oh, don't worry. I had a word with Sarah, she said they wouldn't be dressing for dinner tonight as it's just family. She'll sort you out with something tomorrow."

"That is very kind of her."

"I told you she was kind."

She nodded. "Thank you," she blushed, "for what you said downstairs, about my expertise."

He smiled. "It's true. You'll be taking the lead on this one."

"B-but I can't! You know far more about archaeology than I do."

"True, I'll be applying the methodology, but *you* will provide the contextual and interpretive knowledge."

"Oh, Deo." She wrapped her arms round his middle and hugged him. It was so unexpected, he just froze. Looking down at her head pressed against his chest, he slowly put his arms up to hug her back and irresistibly, he lowered his head and kissed her hair. Her rose scent was intoxicating, and the feel of her slender form pressed against him was having a disastrous effect on his equilibrium. It was Wednesday, not Thursday, and way past three in the afternoon.

He wanted to push her away and flee and at the same time pull her closer and—kiss her. *No, no, no! That way lay disaster.*

Unfortunately, his body wasn't listening to his brain. She raised her head, and those rosebud lips were so close. She stared up at him with such a softened expression in her bright hazel-green eyes, her lips slightly parted, plump and inviting. And he couldn't resist.

He lowered his head and set his lips to hers, gently, softly, tentatively, as if he were afraid he would startle her. He hadn't much of a clue about kissing. He'd never done it, not properly. When he was a raw young lad, there had been a few sloppy attempts along with some heated groping in the barn with the dairy maid that had ended abruptly when he came all over himself. Her disgust and the humiliation had made him retreat, and he'd not tried that again.

Now here he was, a thirty-two-year-old man with a beautiful woman in his arms and not a clue what to do with her. Well, not much of a clue anyway. Instinct made him move his lips a little and the effect was searing. A kind of heady, tingling pleasure exploded outwards from the caress of her soft lips, and he pressed a little closer, chasing the delicious feeling, moving his mouth around to try different angles and get more of the delectable sensations.

He was drowning in sensation. Nothing had ever felt this good in his life. Her lips were pure heaven, and his cock was rigid in his breeches. It was that realization that made him pull back. His boyhood terror of disgracing himself cut through the bliss and made him let her go with a groan of longing.

He stepped back, turning away to hide the effect she had on him. "I'm sorry. I shouldn't have done that. We may not even be legally married at this point. I—" He swallowed, his throat clogged. "I'm going to take Kes for a walk." He moved to the door, calling Kes. But Kester was looking at Emily as if reluctant to leave her.

"Kes!" he said peremptorily, snapping his fingers for emphasis. Kes came, his ears and tail down. Deo held the door for him and left the room rapidly.

EMILY, LEFT ALONE in the bedchamber, put her fingers to her lips and closed her eyes. The sensation of his mouth on hers had sent a thousand delicious tingles through her body and a warm, nagging heat between her legs. She sank down on the big bed to contemplate what it meant. She had felt the hard heat of his body pressed to hers through their clothing. She knew just enough to hazard a guess at what that signified. And a smile curved her lips. The agonized groan he'd uttered as he pulled away from her told her that he hadn't wanted to let her go but felt compelled to—by his scruples, she supposed.

She sighed. Perhaps she could persuade him to kiss her again. *After all, what could a few kisses hurt? And they felt so good . . .*

DEO, TROMPING OVER the lawns while Kester romped round him, tried to sort his brain out. *What is wrong with me? I barely touched her, and I'm stiff as a poker. And it's not even Thursday!* Mind you, he wasn't in the habit of kissing pretty young women, so how was he to know what was normal and what wasn't? *If I did it more often,* his logical brain pointed out, *I might find out.* He groaned.

I've opened that damned Pandora's box. Just a crack, and it's already ruining everything.

He didn't even know if they were truly married. He had to stop hurtling down this slippery slope immediately. At least until he knew what their legal status was. Then if he needed to marry her again, he would, and that would solve *that* problem. And by then perhaps he would have figured out how to approach the *other* problem. *How to kiss my wife without making a mess of myself.* Because he had to admit, he wanted to. Very much. So much, it scared the living daylights out of him.

The fact was he hadn't a clue how to make love to a woman. He knew the mechanics of intercourse, but that was the problem. It had all been mechanical with Damaris. That was how he liked it. Because it put him in control of the situation. He could very clearly see, just on the basis of that kiss, he could very rapidly lose control of the situation with Emily if he wasn't very, very careful.

What am I going to do?

Chapter Nine

A FTER DINNER, EMILY was yawning, so Deo sent her up to bed first in the hope that by the time he joined her she would be asleep. Eventually bidding the other fellows good night, he returned to their suite, nervous and reluctant. Entering the sitting room, he contemplated sleeping on the couch, but it was far too small for his big frame, and he resigned himself to the prospect of sharing the big bed with Emily.

To his relief, she appeared to be fast asleep, worn out with traveling, no doubt. He was tired himself. They would inspect the burial site tomorrow and begin the work after a good night's rest. It was an exciting prospect.

He stripped in the dressing room, had a thorough wash, re-doned his breeches, and approached the bed quietly, slipping between the sheets. The bed was big and comfortable. Kes rearranged himself at their feet, and Deo lay back against the pillows, trying to relax and ignore the fact that Emily was lying about a foot away from him, sleeping.

With any luck, they would both sleep through and there would be no awkwardness. The best thing would be if he rose extremely early. With this laudable ambition in mind, he rolled onto his side and tried to sleep.

The next thing he was aware of was a wave of pleasure pulsing through his body. He was lying on something soft. A woman's body, but he couldn't see her face, yet somehow, he knew it was Emily. He was dreaming, of course. Another wave of agonizing pleasure rolled through him. He was rubbing his cock on her, and it wasn't enough! Horror seized him at what he was doing, and he woke abruptly, his eyes popping open, and he rolled panting onto his back, his cock stiff and quivering inside his breeches.

He glanced over at Emily, but she was curled away from him, oblivious of his tumescent state. He stared down at this inconvenient state of arousal, visible as a bulge through the cloth, and his balls twitched, his stomach muscles pulling tight with need. There was no way around it, he had to do something about it. Sliding from the bed, he went swiftly to the dressing room and found the little bottle of oil he kept for his needs in a side pocket of his valise. Exiting the dressing room as quietly as possible, he groped his way to the door into the sitting room, opened it and with a glance back at the bed, slid through and closed it softly behind him.

The sitting room was lit only by the glow of the banked fireplace. He crossed swiftly to the fire, leaning on the mantle, his breathing erratic and his cock quivering and hard, demanding his attention.

He undid the buttons on his breeches, allowing his aching cock to spring free, and applied the oil with shaking fingers to the silky, warm shaft. He took himself firmly in hand and stroked. He could deal with it quickly and return to bed as if nothing had happened. *This is just an aberration; it has nothing to do with kissing Emily or sharing a bed with her . . .*

A hushed groan escaped him as he recalled the feel of her mouth under his, her delicious lips, and her soft, lovely body pressed against him. He closed his eyes tight. *God, I want to kiss her again, properly, deeply. Oh, fuck!*

He came rapidly and hard, his seed splashing onto his hand and splattering his belly, breeches, and even into the fire, as a faint hiss from the hot ashes attested. He gasped for breath, hanging onto the mantelpiece as his knees trembled from the force of his release, tingles spreading all through his body.

Oh, God! He caught his breath and shook his head as the tingles gradually faded, and he got the use of his legs back. *Fuck! That was . . .* Words failed him for the intensity of the sensations. He looked down at the mess on his hand, clothing, and belly. And nothing to clean it up with. *You did not plan this well, Deo! Of course I didn't. I didn't mean it to happen! And it mustn't happen again. No more kisses or lascivious thoughts about my wife—if she even is my wife . . .*

He must write to his solicitor first thing and get that sorted out. Once it was settled—he could think about perhaps approaching the issue of consummating his marriage, changing the rules. With Emily's agreement, of course. But only in such a way as he maintained control of the situation. He couldn't be putting himself in a position of losing control, of—*of humiliating myself again.*

He turned back toward the bedchamber. Reentering very quietly, he crept across the room to the dressing room and slipped inside to clean himself up. Then he climbed back into bed, seemingly without disturbing Emily. *Thank goodness she seems to be a heavy sleeper.*

Relaxing back into the pillows, he slipped into sleep.

The next thing he knew it was morning. Emily was still asleep, and he rose quietly from the bed, washed, shaved, dressed, and took Kes out. On his return, the first thing he did was pen a letter to his solicitor at the desk in their sitting room, before sorting through his equipment for the dig and writing up a quick methodology to discuss with Emily.

The door to the bedroom opened, and he turned to the sight of Emily dressed in a plain gown and sturdy boots, her hair confined in its usual chignon. She smiled at him and his heart lifted. *She is so dashed pretty . . .*

"I was just getting everything ready," he said. "Shall we go down to breakfast? We can leave straight after that for the site."

"Yes, please. I am so excited; I can't wait!"

He smiled and held out his hand without thinking. Emily's enthusiasm and warmth were infectious. She took it, and he was conscious of a little rush of pleasure. *This is what I dreamed of. If I can just keep my physical responses under control . . .*

They descended the stairs to the breakfast parlor and found Ashford and his wife there before them.

"Ah, our intrepid archaeologists!" said Emrys. "Annis and I will be happy to show you where the site is after breakfast if you like?"

"That would be delightful. Do tell us about it!" said Emily, taking a seat, while Deo fetched her a plate of food. It was becoming a habit for him to fill her plate up. *She is still slender as a reed. I don't want her fainting on me again. That is an experience I can do without repeating.*

"We were there when the boys found the cross," said Annis, as Deo came back to the table with two plates piled high with eggs, ham, sausages, mushrooms, and crispy potatoes.

Emily looked at her plate and said, "Gosh, Deo, I can't eat all that!"

"Try," he said, taking his seat. "We will be working all day; you'll need something substantial to keep you going."

Emily made a manful attempt at her plate full of food. After everyone had their fill, they collected flasks of water and tea to take with them; Deo shouldered his rucksack of equipment, and Emily put on a huge floppy brimmed hat to keep the sun off her face, and they set out to find the site, with the Ashfords showing the way.

It was a fine day, not too hot, some cloud cover and a light breeze, but no immediate threat of rain. *A perfect day for a dig.* As they walked across the lawns toward their goal, Deo reflected that while they were here, he should write up the ruins, too. There was only a paragraph on them in John Nichols's great work. Surely there was more to be said about them than that.

When he voiced this, Annis said, "Oh yes, I found some material in the library on them; I must show you. There was probably a moat originally. The dip in the ground is still there." Annis had been the Layne sisters' governess before she married Ashford and was well acquainted with The Castle.

Emrys turned to Emily. "So, what date would you put on this cross, do you think?"

"If it's what I think it is, most of them date to the immediate post-Roman period in Britain. But I won't know for certain until I look at it," she said cautiously.

Deo smiled with pride. *Emily understands the importance of checking the evidence first before making an interpretation. She will make an excellent archaeologist.*

"Are those the ruins?" asked Emily excitedly, pointing to the remnants of the stone tower ahead.

EMILY WAS SO excited she had to stop herself racing ahead like a child. As they approached, she could see the dip in the ground encircling the tower that must be the moat that Lady Ashford spoke of. There were lots of large stone blocks scattered about, half overgrown with creepers and covered in moss, as well as a fragment of wall around the broken tower, with its exposed side open to the weather and showing the staircase within.

"According to the floor plan I found, there were four towers originally, but this is the only one left," said Lady Ashford.

They poked about a bit, but Emily was anxious to see the cross, and she suspected Deo was, as well, so they headed toward a stand of trees and a rising bit of ground, behind and to the right of the ruins—about, as the viscount said, fifty yards away.

"The bit we uncovered may have got covered up again. It's been a few months since we did the exploratory dig and a year since we found it originally. That was last summer when we were here with all the children," said the viscount.

They stopped at the base of the rising ground, which was covered in grass and leaf mulch and was roughly circular and about fifty feet in diameter. Emily clasped her hands, trying to contain her anticipation. "Deo, do you think this could be a burial mound?"

"A burial mound? How thrilling!" said Lady Ashford. "Emrys, here we were tromping all over it like hobgoblins, showing no respect!"

"What would you expect to find if it is?" asked the viscount.

"There could be multiple graves or just one. Or it could be nothing, just a bit of a hump in the ground. But it does look auspicious, I must say. What do you think, Deo?" she prompted him again, worried she was getting ahead of herself.

The viscount continued before Deo could. "When we dug into it, there seemed to be something there. We hit stone with what looked like markings carved into it. That is why Robert wrote to Aberdeen. It seemed like something that should be investigated by people who knew what they were doing instead of us amateurs."

"I think the first thing we need to do is uncover the cross fully and see what we can learn from that, then we will investigate the mound and any possible contents. Where is the cross?" said Deo.

"At the top of the mound, just under the shadow of that tree." The viscount pointed to a huge gnarled oak tree looming over the higher ground. The tree seemed to have taken root on the sloping base of the farthest side of the mound toward the east. Its trunk seemed to lean toward the mound, its lower branches brushing the sides of the mound, almost as if it were embracing it.

They walked up the slope and the viscount crouched down to scrabble through the leaf mulch that had accumulated until his fingers scraped against stone and part of the cross re-emerged from the covering of leaves. "There," he said, rising and standing back to let Emily and Deo have a closer look.

Deo crouched and Emily knelt, while Deo brought out a trowel and a brush from his rucksack. He then scraped away the rest of the mulch and ran over the revealed surface of the cross with the brush to remove the finer fragments of dirt. It took several minutes of careful work to reveal it all.

Emily ran her fingers over the revealed inscription. "I think if we take a rubbing of this, we might be able to make out some of the missing letters. What do you think?" she asked.

Deo nodded. "It should certainly reveal more than we can see with the naked eye." He withdrew some paper and charcoal from his rucksack, and Emily went to work on the rubbing.

"Before we can excavate the mound, we will need to move the cross," said Deo, rising to his feet. "I expect it is exceedingly heavy. It will need a few of us to lift it."

"That shouldn't be a problem, Deo," said Emrys. "There are the two of us and Robert, and I believe Kenrick is due today. That should be enough. If Hereward were here, I daresay the two of you could do it between you—he's a big as you are."

"Surely the duke wouldn't want to lift a dirty stone?" queried Emily.

"He wouldn't miss this for anything," predicted Emrys with a grin.

Emily went back to her rubbing and soon held it up. "I believe we have something. Deo, look at this."

Deo got out his spectacles and jammed them on his slightly beaky nose.

"*Hic iacet* something GYN," he read. "This next bit is hard to make out. Something starting with a C? And another word starting with a C? *Filius* WIG something?"

Emily peered over his arm and pointed to the C words. "These must be some kind of title or epithet, wouldn't you think?"

He nodded. "Yes, I agree. What is a Latin title starting with C?"

"*Comes*," they both said at once. Emily grinned and he smiled back. *Comes* was a Roman military title, which became equated later with the Frankish Count or the Saxons' Eorl.

"We will check if it fits when we get back to the house and see if we can figure out what the other word is and the conjunction between them," said Deo, rolling up the rubbing carefully and sliding it into a tube he had brought for the purpose.

Straightening, he turned his attention back to the cross.

"We will need some ropes to lift the stone and turn it. We will want to check the verso for any other inscriptions. I have some rope here, but I don't think it will be enough. I think we should come out this afternoon and raise the stone. In the meantime, we should sketch it in situ and measure it. And if we have time, we can begin on the identification of the damaged names back at the house."

The program laid out for the morning, the Ashfords left them to it, and Deo and Emily worked together until lunchtime when they headed back to the house with the rubbings, sketches, and measurements, leaving the rucksack on the mound for the afternoon's work. Emily was bubbling over with ideas about the cross. It was so out of place. No crosses of this design had been found in England. To her knowledge, all of the ones so far identified were found in Scotland or Ireland. They were a symbol of British Christianity dating to the post-Roman period up to early medieval times. Scholars were divided on their exact dating.

"I must ask Robert if he has a copy of John Nichols's *History and Antiquities of Leicestershire*. I have one at home, but it's in six volumes, so I didn't bring it. I seem to recall he mentions some burial mounds or barrows around here somewhere," said Deo.

"Oh, how splendid," said Emily, skipping to keep up with his long strides. He was frowning at the rubbing he held in his hands.

Emily reflected that the morning had been one of unalloyed pleasure. Working alongside him had been the best experience of her life, and his deference to her knowledge and expertise had her bursting with pride. She couldn't wait to start investigating the inscription. *Would it be a name they recognized?*

He had rolled the rubbing into a scroll and put it back in its tube. She caught his other hand and squeezed it for sheer joy.

"Thank you," she said, unable to keep her feelings in.

"For what?" he asked, startled. He looked down at her, his eyebrows cocked and his shocking red hair all mussed from rubbing it with his fingers. He had such a dear face, she decided, all those hard angles softened when he was relaxed and made him positively handsome.

"For treating me like a colleague," she said shyly.

His face did soften then, and he said gruffly, "Of course. That was the whole point."

She chewed her lip. "Everyone has been so kind and welcoming; I've never felt so comfortable."

"I told you they would be."

"Yes, you did. I like your friends, Deo."

"And they like you."

They continued onto the house and discovered that Lord Kenrick had indeed arrived with a friend. Lord Kenrick was exceedingly tall, possibly taller than her husband, but not as broad or solid in the chest. He had a mobile face that was more cheeky than handsome. But it was his companion that took all of Emily's attention.

"Lord Bidenden," she said through numb lips and thought that she was going to faint for the second time in her life.

Chapter Ten

D EO, SEEING EMILY turn white as a sheet, clasped her arm in alarm.

"Miss Grenfell," the dandified fellow Kendrick had brought to The Castle with him said with a bow. "What a surprise to see you here."

"This is my wife, the Countess of Pendrell," growled Deo.

The other man changed color. "Really? I had no notion. This must have happened very quickly." His lips compressed into a thin line. "Now I understand why your parents said you were indisposed when I came to call!"

Emily didn't seem to have a reply to that, but Deo didn't give her a chance in any case, saying peremptorily, "I believe my wife has a touch of the sun. If you will excuse us." And he swept her off upstairs. When they reached the top of the first flight, he picked her up and carried her the rest of the way. She looked so pale he was afraid she was going to faint again, and he didn't want her tumbling down the stairs and hurting herself.

"Deo, I can walk," she protested.

He ignored that and, pushing open the door to the sitting room, he strode in, taking her through to the bedroom, where he laid her down on the bed. Seizing her hat, he tossed it aside, and felt her forehead.

"Do you have a headache?"

"No."

"You must be dehydrated," he said. Fetching a glass and pouring her some water from the jug, he offered it to her, helping her to sit up, so she could drink it.

She drank and lay back against the banked pillows.

"Better?" he asked, frowning at her.

"Yes, thank you. I don't have sunstroke."

"Then what made you go so white?"

"You recall that there was a gentleman my parents were trying to force me to marry?"

He nodded.

"It was Lord Bidenden."

"That dandified prig?" he said, revolted.

"Is he? A dandy, I mean? I just thought he cared more for his clothes than anything else."

"That is the definition of a dandy," he said shortly. "Why was your mother so set on you marrying him?"

"Apart from the fact that I hadn't had any other offers? He is the eldest son of the Marquess of Malmsbury," she said with a sigh.

"Well, I'm glad you had the sense to reject him." Deo paced away from the bed, unaccountably agitated. Turning back, he barked, "Did he force his attentions on you, behave inappropriately?"

She flinched a little, and he cursed his bad temper.

"No, not really. Mama left us alone and he kissed my hand and my wrist here." She held her hand out palm up and indicated the soft skin of her inner wrist, and Deo was outraged at the notion of this man touching her with such intimacy.

She went on. "When he proposed, he tried to kiss me. I elbowed him in the ribs and trod on his instep."

A powerful desire to hit Bidenden in the face for daring to touch her possessed him; and a flare of pride made him smile at her spirit.

"But Mama came back before he could do anything else."

"Hmph," he grunted. "Why did you refuse him?"

"Because I knew he was only interested in my fortune, for all his protestations to the contrary. He kept telling me that I was very pretty and he"—she paused, blushing an adorable pink—"that he desired me," she finished on a low note. "I knew he must be dissembling. I'm not pretty or desirable."

Deo gaped at her, caught between an overwhelming urge to take her in his arms and kiss her and an almost more powerful urge to march downstairs, drag Bidenden out into the garden, and punch the living daylights out of him.

With a supreme effort of will he did neither, growling instead, "You are both pretty *and* desirable." He cleared his throat. "And your fortune has nothing to do with it."

She stared at him, her color rising again, and her eyes taking on a glow that made him mortally afraid she was going to cry again.

"Oh, Deo," she said softly, and her tone touched something inside him. That she should look at him so, with . . . admiration and desire? He must be mistaken. The old panic threatened momentarily, and he fought to find some control in the midst of a flood of reactions he didn't understand.

He turned away, discovering he was shaking. *This will never do. I am going to lose control again. What is it about her that brings me undone like this?* He muttered something incoherent and left the room.

EMILY STARED AFTER his rapidly retreating back and slumped back onto the pillows. She was so confused. One minute he was telling her she was pretty and desirable and the next he was fleeing from her as if she were a banshee or a succubus. She had thought there for a moment he was jealous of Lord Bidenden, which was ridiculous of course. There was nothing to be jealous about. Lord

Bidenden held no attraction for her, especially not compared to Deo, who was not only a God in face and form, but the embodiment of her ideal husband and partner. She swallowed, feeling her heart swell and burst with emotion. *Oh, gosh, I am in love with him . . .*

She lay against the pillows, letting the feelings wash over her. *Of course I'm in love with him. How could I not be? He is perfect! He treats me as a colleague and a friend, a companion. He is intelligent and learned and as obsessed with antiquities as I am. We even share a secret passion for Gothic novels! And his kiss, brief as it was, was wonderful. If only I could get him to do it again . . .*

But if he kept running away from her, how could she? Was she repellent in some way? Physically? But he had said she was pretty and desirable. Was he just saying that so that her feelings wouldn't be hurt?

No, he had reacted to her physically—she knew that. She knew enough to know that heat meant something. But she also knew that gentlemen could feel that kind of desire without more tender emotions. Her governess had warned her of that, warned her against being taken in by protestations of false love by gentlemen.

She sighed. *Is it just his scruples that keep him away from me? Or is it the fact that I lied to him and broke his trust? Does he despise me for that?*

Tears stung her lids at the thought, and regret seared her heart. How she wished she could meet him again for the first time and tell him the truth from the start. But if she had, would he have married her or packed her off home immediately? She wiped her eyes. *How can I regain his trust?* Her heart ached. *Is my perfect love affair over before it even begins?*

Deo reappeared in the doorway and said stiffly, "Luncheon is being served downstairs. We should join them, if you're fully recovered."

She rose hastily. "Yes, I am fine." She splashed some water on her face and tidied her hair before joining him. Silence reigned between them as they descended the stairs. She desperately wanted to say something to break it, but her tongue had cleaved to the roof of her mouth and her head was empty of anything sensible to say.

DEO SAT THROUGH luncheon barely aware of what was going on around him. The knowledge that it was Bidenden she had fled from had rattled him to the core. She had made it clear she wasn't interested in Bidenden, which ought to reassure him, yet . . . He glanced surreptitiously across the table at the other man. He had denounced him as a dandified fribble, but the man was attractive in a dark and brooding sort of way. Deo understood females often had a weakness for such a style of male. But Emily had run away to escape his attentions, so she surely wasn't one of them.

But the man was clearly experienced with women, in a way that Deo wasn't. While his boldness might not have been welcomed by Emily, it spoke of a confidence that Deo lacked and made him feel at a disadvantage. His only comfort was that Emily was his wife. She had agreed to marry *him*. *She couldn't be having second thoughts about that, could she?*

He glanced sideways at her, but her head was turned away from him. They hadn't spoken since they sat down to eat. All their previous camaraderie was broken. How could they go from this morning's blissful accord to this state of discord in such a short time? He was inclined to blame the man on the other side of the table for casting a shadow between them, even if he didn't fully understand how he had done it. He glowered at Bidenden, and the man's eyes clashed with his. Bidenden raised a dark eyebrow, and his lips curved in a sneer. He took a sip of his wine and looked away, but not before Deo caught the flash of contempt in his gaze. It lashed him, rubbing him raw.

SOMEHOW EMILY GOT through luncheon, but she was unequal to eating anything but a mouthful; and Deo for once didn't attempt to fill her plate or tell her to eat up. In fact, he said nothing to her at all. And to make it worse, she felt Lord Bidenden's eyes on her for most of the meal.

It was agreed over luncheon that the gentlemen would all assist with the raising of the cross. But the silence between herself and Deo was making her wretched, and at the end of the meal, she vowed she had to do something to fix it or all her peace and happiness would be destroyed. Thus, when they left the dining room, she dragged him into an adjoining antechamber and blurted, "Are you still angry with me about the deception over my age and identity?"

"Not precisely, no," he said. "I am simply concerned that it may have invalidated our marriage. I sent a letter to my solicitor this morning, seeking his advice on the matter. Fortunately, we have not consummated the marriage, so no irrevocable harm has been done. We must await his advice before I can take any steps to rectify the matter."

"Rectify—? What do you mean?"

Deo flushed. "I mean that in the event the marriage is invalid, we would either need to repeat our vows or, under the terms of our agreement, we could part ways, no harm done."

"Why would I do that? I've no wish to return to my parents' house. You know that!"

"I am simply giving you the option," he said doggedly.

"Oh! You wish to be rid of me?" Anguish gripped her heart along with a lick of anger.

"No!" he barked. "No, nothing of the sort. I simply wish to be fair to you. You have another suitor—" He swallowed visibly, and she thought for a moment he was going to be ill. "If he is more to your taste—"

"You know he isn't! Deo, why are you being like this?" she almost wailed.

DEO STARED INTO her face, his heart thudding hard in his chest. He was being irrational, he knew it, but his brain was scrambled. He was assailed by so many different damnable sensations and emotions at once—jealousy, anxiety, fear—he didn't know if he was on his head or his heels, and he didn't like it. Not one bit. Everything in his life to date had taught him that if he followed the rigid set of rules he had laid out for himself, if he was true to his principles, then his life would proceed in an orderly fashion. He would remain in control, and he would not be humiliated or hurt by the actions of others. Right now, he felt perilously close to both.

He swallowed again and said quietly, "I told you that I am not an emotional man, that I do not feel as others do! I think you chose not to believe me at the time, but it is true." *It has to be.* "I'm sorry." He gave her a bow and left the room, almost running into Lord Bidenden in the hallway. Deo glared at him, shucked his cuffs, and strode off.

Chapter Eleven

EMILY, STUNNED BY Deo's behavior, clutched at the back of a chair to keep her feet and tried to swallow the tears that threatened to fall down her cheeks.

"Emily!"

She jumped and looked around to find Lord Bidenden standing in the doorway.

"I could not help overhearing!" he said, advancing on her. "You poor girl! You have been deceived, lured into a false trap!"

"What? No—"

"Hush." He put his hands on her arms. "Your innocence does you credit, my dearest Emily. You would not know—how could you—that there are men in this world who do not like women, whose intimate tastes veer toward men. The fact that he did not consummate your marriage immediately tells me all I need to know. This matter of the legality of your contract is just an excuse.

"He clearly regrets his decision and wishes to be free of you. He has given you a way out, my dear, and do not fear that I will spurn you after. We could be married quite swiftly, if your current alliance is proved invalid. I do not fear gossip from this household for I feel sure the duke wouldn't allow ill rumor about his friend, Pendrell."

She gaped at him. "What are you talking about?"

"Emily." He contrived to get his arms round her. "You cannot have failed to understand how much I adore you." He made an attempt to kiss her, but she evaded him, pushing her hands against his chest. "My dearest little Emily," he said thickly, crushing her to him. "I was heartbroken when you rejected my suit!"

Since Emily could feel the heated bulge in his trousers, she was seriously frightened now. She gave him a shove and, breaking his hold on her, stepped away. "You are mistaken, Lord Bidenden. I ran away rather than marry you. I cannot understand why you are persisting in this fiction that you love me!"

His face took on a despairing expression. "Emily, I must prove my devotion to you."

"To my fortune more like!" she snapped. "You must be desperate indeed for your own money. Does your father keep you on a tight leash?"

For a moment his expression flickered, but in the next he said, "You must be confusing me with someone else, Lannister perhaps. Everybody knows he hasn't a feather to fly with. I have no need of your money, my darling, and I shall prove it to you. Just know that you have me to turn to when Pendrell cruelly spurns your sweet overtures of love. A man such as he will not know what to do with a lovely, innocent girl like you."

He gave her a deep bow and left the room.

Emily sank into the chair, her legs giving out.

THE MEN WERE getting ready to set out to lift the cross, all except Bidenden, which was a good thing or Deo might be tempted to punch him after all. Emily joined them, putting on her hat. She must have gone upstairs to retrieve it. Kester followed her, and Deo's heart did an odd sort of thump to watch him come to a stop by her side and her hand go automatically to the dog's head and stroke it.

She didn't meet Deo's eyes, and he couldn't blame her after that conversation following luncheon. He didn't know what had possessed him to offer her the option to take Bidenden. If she did—no, he would not contemplate such a possibility. He dragged his eyes away from her as they set off across the lawns again. The men were loaded with several lengths of rope looped around shoulders and a couple of spades and a pick borrowed from the duke's gardener, Smiggens.

They arrived at the site, and Deo discussed with Robert his plan to flip the cross so that he and Emily could inspect the verso for markings, before dragging it off the mound altogether to make way for the dig, which they wouldn't commence until tomorrow. Emily listened to this plan but made no comment. Nevertheless, he was highly aware of her presence. Even if he wasn't looking at her, he knew where she was as the men organized themselves to lift one arm of the cross sufficiently so that they could slip a loop of rope around it and lift and flip it.

With two of them on the rope and two to steady it via the head and base, they accomplished the flip easily enough. Settling it back on the mulchy, worm-filled ground, the other men stepped back to allow him and Emily to look at the reverse side of the cross. Brushing away the dirt and debris, they found only knot-work patterns on this side, no inscription. Emily took a rubbing of the knotwork and sketched the flipped cross. Then she stepped back to allow the men to carry the heavy object off the mound and deposit it on the ground at the base.

BRYSON HAD SPENT the afternoon penning a letter to Emily's mother to apprise her of her daughter's whereabouts.

My dear Lady Efford,

I felt compelled to write to you and advise you that I am staying at the Duke of Troubridge's Leicestershire estate and was surprised to find your daughter among the guests. I was even more surprised to discover that she is here masquerading as the wife of the Earl of Pendrell. How Pendrell has persuaded her to undertake this enterprise, I know not. But I have it on excellent authority that their ostensible marriage is invalid, as it was contracted without Lord Efford's permission. It is also a sham. The earl himself claims the marriage has not been consummated. If he is to be believed, Emily is not ruined entirely.

This is an extraordinary circumstance. I can only conclude that the earl is a man of certain appetites and has hoped to hide his proclivities from the ton by contracting a sham marriage. If I am correct in my assumptions, Emily is in no danger from the earl, but neither will she ever give you grandchildren, should this sham marriage continue.

I hasten to assure you that you can rely on both my discretion and my assistance in bringing this lamentable affair to a satisfactory conclusion. I propose that for a reasonable initial settlement, plus a generous allowance until such time as Emily should come into her full fortune, I will take Emily to wife and assist you to hush up the scandal.

I remain ever your humble servant to command,
Bryson Passmore, Viscount Bidenden

Satisfied, he took it into the nearest village to post.

Over dinner it was easy to see that the strife between Emily and Pendrell had not been resolved, and Bryson was emboldened in his plan, despite Emily's rebuff. Once her parents arrived, as they would no doubt set out for The Castle upon receipt of his letter, it would be a simple matter to have the marriage declared invalid. Emily would then have no choice but to accept him. Indeed, the poor girl would be grateful to him for his rescue, after the humiliation of Pendrell's rejection.

Bryson knew Pendrell to be an antiquities scholar of some

standing, as Bryson's father had more than a passing interest in antiquities himself, and he had grown up in a house stuffed full of ancient artifacts from all over England and the world. His father's secret passion for such musty objects had been of no interest to Bryson until this moment. But listening to the conversation over dinner, another means of obtaining money began to percolate through his brain. A highly satisfactory one, too, if he could pull it off. Assuming there was anything of value to be had in this burial mound they were discussing.

He smiled as he cut into his beef and listened attentively to the conversation. The idea of getting money from his sire for valuable objects of this nature pleased him very much. He would of course use a third party to do the deal. He knew his father would pay well for something rare and would never know the money was going to his son, whom he had cut off without a penny. If there was anything to be had, of course. There may be nothing in the ground but old bones.

Chapter Twelve

EMILY RETIRED EARLY, unable to bear the tension of the situation any longer. Neither of them had any heart for investigating the inscription, which was a painful end to what had been such a promising day. Her thoughts were in such a whirl between Deo's words and Bidenden's interpretation of them. *Could Deo truly be a man who preferred men to women?* Everything in her rebelled at this notion, but the sliver of doubt ate at her. As she washed, slipped on her nightgown, and climbed into bed with her book and Kester, she determined to talk to him and perhaps put things to the test. *If I can get him to kiss me again, perhaps things will become clearer.*

DEO CAME UP to bed late in the cowardly hope that Emily would be asleep. They had barely conversed all afternoon beyond the necessary, which was heartbreaking when he—and she, he was sure—had been so looking forward to beginning the investigation of the inscription. But with everything so strained between them, that was out of the question.

At dinner she had ignored him completely and conversed

with surprising animation with Lord Kenrick, which had him clutching his knife and fork so hard he was surprised he hadn't bent them. Kenrick was known for his charm and winning ways with females, and he contrived to keep Emily so well entertained she even laughed at several points in the conversation.

Bidenden, who was seated on the opposite side of the table and down two from Emily, watched her with covetous eyes, which provoked Deo to glower at him. He wanted to gnash his teeth and growl at the man. *Back off—she's mine!* He didn't, of course; he wasn't a dog. But he felt like one. The worst cur imaginable.

He was so discomforted, he drank more wine at dinner than he probably should have, and was conscious, as he made his way upstairs, that he was mildly tipsy, a state he didn't often find himself in. For one thing, because of his size, it took a fair bit of alcohol to affect him. And for another, he was of a generally abstemious habit, not given to excessive drinking. He didn't like the loss of control it brought with it.

He checked his progress at the bedroom door, for Emily was not asleep as he'd hoped. She was sitting up in bed with a book, and her hair was loose round her shoulders. The collar of her nightgown was open, showing an expanse of neck and bosom. Not that it was more than showed when she wore a gown; it was more the context that made it alluring.

"I thought you'd be asleep," he said.

"I wanted to talk to you," she said, putting the book aside.

"Oh," he said, and then cravenly, "I'll just go and wash." He dove into the dressing room and stripped and washed. Stevens had laid out his dressing gown for him, and he slipped that on. Should he redon his breeches? He wasn't going to walk out there naked for Emily to gawk at him. He debated, reaching for his breeches, but they were uncomfortably hot to sleep in. He reached for a shirt instead and, removing the robe, put the shirt on and then the robe over top. Girding his loins mentally, he returned to the bedroom. Emily had picked up her book again, and even he, who was remarkably insensitive to emotions from others, could feel her latent anger.

Emily had never demonstrated anger toward him before. He found the idea oddly thrilling. He approached the bed and got into his side of it, but he didn't remove the robe. That would be tantamount to removing his armor. He didn't feel strong enough for that. Even the shirt which reached to mid-thigh wasn't sufficient on its own to stop him feeling more than half naked in front of her.

She put her book aside. Kester, who had come up with her and settled on the bed, lifted his head to acknowledge him and settled back down across Emily's feet. It occurred to him that if it came to a choice, Kester would side with her, and he wasn't sure that he blamed him. Before she could say anything, he blurted, "I'm sorry. I behaved abominably earlier. I know I upset you, and I apologize."

Emily, who had opened her mouth, closed it and swallowed. Clearly, she hadn't expected him to say that. Visibly regrouping, she said, "Thank you." She seemed at a loss for a moment, and then she reached out and touched his hand resting on the coverlet. "Deo, can you explain, please?"

"Explain what?" he said helplessly. He was so wretchedly bad at this.

"Why you're acting this way."

"I need more context. Which way, exactly?" he asked, taking refuge in pedanticism.

"You said that you don't feel as others do. What did you mean?"

He slumped back against the pillows and let out a sigh. He never talked about this sort of thing. *Dash it, I don't even think about it. Or I try not to anyway.* He was so used to being different to everyone else, he took it for granted. He had tried to warn her, but clearly his warning had fallen on deaf ears. But he had wanted a wife, and this was the price he had to pay for it.

How to explain?

"My parents, my father in particular, was a—very cold man. My mother was much the same. My father believed emotions denoted weakness." He swallowed. Just talking about it made him feel sick. *But Em deserves to know. She said it is her duty as my wife to understand me, as I should strive to understand her. She is so sweet and . . . perfect. How could I know the advertisement was going to bring me the perfect woman? I don't know how to manage—*

"Deo?" she prompted, squeezing his hand and recalling his wandering thoughts. Jerked back to the present, he cleared his suddenly clogged throat and sought for the right words.

"I don't think either of them knew what to do with me. I have no siblings." He paused, breathing deeply. *Who knew this would be so damned difficult?*

"Neither of them showed the slightest desire to show me any affection." His voice sounded hollow as he spoke this self-evident truth out loud. He'd never said that to anyone. Never confessed that his parents didn't love him. He was slightly surprised by how much it hurt to admit such a humiliating fact.

Her hand squeezed his again, and he squeezed back involuntarily. *It helps a bit, having her hold my hand.* A little curl of comfort stirred in his breast.

"I was raised by the servants as a small child. I have the vaguest recollection of my infant nurse. I believe my father dismissed her from her post for showing me too much affection." He frowned, trying to bring her face into focus and failing. He shook his head. His heart was beating too fast, and his chest felt tight. He tried to breathe through it.

"He chose tutors for me who were strong disciplinarians, and I was rewarded only for academic excellence." The lump in his throat refused to be pushed down, and he stopped speaking because his throat had seized up entirely.

"Oh, Deo!" Emily's soft cry of anguish made him look at her, surprised, as she launched herself at his chest, her head coming to rest on it, her small, warm body nestled into him. He could feel the gentle swell of her breasts pressed against him.

"I'm so sorry," she whispered. "That is awful!"

Hesitantly, he moved an arm up to wrap it around her. "Thank you," he said thickly. "So, you see why I—" He stopped and cleared his throat. "I have difficulty with emotions, both expressing them and responding to them."

"Yes, yes, I understand." She raised her head, and he could see the tears in her eyes. As she blinked, drops rolled down her cheeks.

"Sweet Emily," he said, husky voiced. "Don't cry over me. I'm not worth it."

"Yes, you are," she said fiercely and kissed him.

He froze at the touch of her lips against his. But the explosion of pleasure her touch provoked made him raise his hands to her face and move his lips over hers, testing, nibbling, experimenting. Her lips parted on a gasp as she responded to his touch, to his tentative kisses. He closed his eyes and concentrated on the feel of her mouth moving against his. Without conscious thought, his tongue licked her lower lip and then ventured more boldly beyond her lips, and the feeling that provoked in his body made him groan involuntarily.

The effect on her was equally electric. Her whole body moved closer, molding itself to his, one leg straddling his thigh as her lips widened, and she used her tongue in imitation of his to explore his mouth, too. And the sounds in her throat as she did this made his already inflamed body harden further.

This was nothing like the sloppy kisses he recalled with such horror from his teenage years. This was exquisite. *Why, oh why, have I never tried this before? Because I have been waiting for her. I've been waiting to kiss Emily, my wife.* The pleasure of it took his breath away.

He deepened the kiss, giving more, taking more. His heart thudded so hard the pulse beat in his ears threatened to deafen him.

She moved her body over his in an effort to get closer and nudged at his cock that was straining against his belly with her hip. The touch sent a shudder of hard desire through him. His cock twitched and leaked on his belly beneath the cloth of his shirt and robe, triggering memories of his humiliation. Of the hot rush of his seed exploding all over Marah's rucked up petticoats and bared lower belly, and her subsequent disgust and contempt.

He broke the kiss and a cold shiver of self-loathing passed through him as he caught his breath, his cock withering a bit as if he'd doused himself in cold water.

"What's wrong?" asked Emily, staring up at him.

"I can't," he said brokenly.

"Can't what?" She sat up and the removal of her warmth made him shiver. "Deo?" Her expression of bewildered hurt cut through the fog of his past terror.

This dear, sweet, innocent woman wanted him. And here he was behaving like the humiliated adolescent boy he had always felt like on the inside. But he was no longer fifteen. He was a thirty-two-year-old man who was incapable of pleasuring his own wife! For a moment his self-contempt threatened everything. *What would my friends think of me if they knew?*

He shuddered and then some stubborn pride rose to the surface. He was tired of being kept a prisoner by ghosts from the past. He had an opportunity here and if he passed it up, he would, he suspected, lose the greatest treasure of his life. But he was miserably aware of his own inadequacy.

"Deo?" she prompted him again, her hand coming up tentatively to stroke his cheek. He caught her hand and kissed the palm. He prided himself on his self-control, yet he realized with a sudden flash of insight, that he had shown little real control at all, only able to keep his baser impulses in check by a rigid set of external controls. *It is time to do better.*

"Emily," he whispered. Pulling her gently back into his arms, he cupped her face and kissed her, a dozen small kisses, gradually deepening into full open-mouthed ones, that had them lost in each other for minutes at a time.

His lips strayed to her neck and her ear and along her jaw and back to her mouth, for more deep, drugging kisses. *It feels so good. Nothing has ever felt so good before.* Her neck was delicious, her skin so soft, the little noises she made so sweet. He found her mouth again, unable to stay away from it. More kisses, more deep, slow kisses. Minutes passed in just kissing. Kissing. Kissing. Kissing. His senses were completely swamped in the shared delight. He had never known it was possible to feel this close to another human being.

She moved her body against his restlessly and he let her, his hands sliding over her, feeling her warmth through the thin fabric of her gown. Over her back, glancingly along the side of her breasts, up to her shoulders, down to her slender waist. *Divine, adorable Emily.* Venturing down from her waist to hold, squeeze, and press her buttock with his palm, pressing her against his thigh where she squirmed with increasing urgency, her breath coming in little pants, those little noises becoming more imperative.

More kisses, lips, tongues, tasting, biting, rubbing.

Her hands on his chest, shoulders, face, in his hair. Touching, stroking, grabbing.

He had not anticipated this when he placed that advertisement. Emily was the perfect wife he never knew he needed. So deliciously perfect she made him dizzy with wanting her. All so new and enticing and terrifying. *My perfect little wife . . .*

But is she? My wife? His conscience poked him. They shouldn't be indulging in this kind of intimacy, no matter how delightful it was, when their status was unknown. A cold shiver sluiced down his skin. *This is wrong if we aren't married. Unfair to her.*

Breaking the kiss, breathing hard, he cupped her face gently, "Em, we shouldn't, not while we don't know if you're legally my wife."

"Oh!" She flushed. "I—I suppose you're right." Her hand moved on his chest, the fingers gently teasing the bare skin revealed at the shirt's opening. He swallowed a groan at the tingle this provoked in his groin. His cock was hard and hot beneath his robe and shirt, and he was mortally afraid she would discover it at any moment and get the fright of her life.

He picked up her hand and kissed the fingers. "We should stop."

Her lips were swollen, her chin reddened from the scrape of his whiskers, her eyes wide and dark. For the first time, he felt a visceral rush of desire just from the way a woman looked at him. He had never let himself feel that before, not so strongly, at any rate. Whenever he had looked at a beautiful woman, he had perceived her through a veil of the unattainable and put a barrier up mentally. Beautiful women weren't for him. But this one was, she was here in his bed. *She is my wife . . . I hope . . .*

Everything in him rebelled at the notion of stopping something that felt so damned good, but he must for her sake. She was such an innocent, so sweet and affectionate. She overwhelmed him with emotions he didn't know how to deal with. He needed to put some space between them, even as part of him clamored to pull her back into his arms and never let her go. He had never felt so conflicted and confused in his life.

Which told him more clearly than anything else that this needed to stop.

He pushed her very gently away. "You need to sleep," he said firmly.

She blinked at him, and he caught the flash of hurt in her eyes, the bewildered look she had given him earlier.

"Just until we know our status, Em. It's the right thing to do."

She nodded slowly and withdrew to her side of the bed. He watched her turn her back on him and curl into a huddle beneath the sheets.

He got out of bed and padded into the dressing room, where he shut the door and leaned against it, his legs shaking, and his heart thudding hard in his chest. He felt slightly sick. And his groin ached abominably.

He found the oil and took himself in hand and stroked firmly and rapidly. It didn't take long as he was so overwrought. Stifling his groan of release, he leaned against the door, his knees trembling and fought to get his breath back. Then he cleaned up rapidly and returned to the bedroom. Em had her eyes closed and didn't move or speak as he climbed back into bed and rolled onto his side away from her.

Chapter Thirteen

EMILY LAY STILL, curled up in a ball, listening to Deo's steady breathing. She rather thought he was asleep at last, but she couldn't be sure. She was a mass of quivering tension and longing. *He is right, but how I wish he hadn't stopped! My body wants more. I am wicked to think like that—he is trying to protect me.*

One thing she was fairly sure of after their marathon kissing session was that Deo did not have a preference for men over women. His restraint ought to be admirable, but a nagging doubt chewed at her. Was he not as affected as she was? Was he not as eager to go to the next step? But why wouldn't he be? As far as she understood it, men were always eager for that. It was women who had to stop *them*, not the other way around. *Unless . . .*

The idea was so fantastic she almost gasped aloud. Covering her mouth with her hand, she bit her bottom lip. *Is he a virgin? Like me? Does he not know what to do? Is that why he is avoiding . . .*

But why would a man as old as Deo still be a virgin . . . unless there was something wrong with him, physically? Was he incapable? Was that why he offered her a marriage in name only in the first place? Why he'd said he wouldn't be bothering her . . .

Or was it all to do with his childhood? The terrible way his parents treated him? That tale had wrung her heart. She could just imagine him as an earnest little boy desperately wanting his parents' attention and affection and receiving only rebuffs. Eventually that would make him retreat into himself, build a wall round his heart. *Oh, Deo!*

She wiped tears from her eyes. She knew what it was like to long for affection and not receive it, or only in small conditional doses, as a reward for good behavior. If she did what her mother wanted, she might receive a hug or even a kiss, an occasional word of praise. But it never lasted. Her mother's temperament was so volatile that it wouldn't be long before Emily did something to displease her.

And her father . . . well, he really wasn't there very much. He would pat her vaguely, maybe give her an absent kiss on the cheek. He was no effective shield from her mother's wrath. He knew better than to provoke his wife and would never take Emily's part against her. Emily secretly believed he had never got over the disappointment of her not being a son. He needed an heir and didn't have one. *If I had been born a boy . . .*

Will Papa approve of Deo? Is he the kind of husband Papa wants for me? Or does he care? She suspected he wouldn't care as long as Mama was happy. *Will Mama approve? He is an earl after all. That is almost as good as a marquess and definitely better than a viscount.* She shuddered, thinking of Bidenden and his poisonous words that had made her doubt Deo. *No, Deo does not prefer men. I am sure of that.* But she was sure of nothing else. Least of all how he felt about her.

She sighed. So many questions and no answers. She had sworn she would talk to him, but then they'd started kissing and talking had stopped entirely. *And oh, those kisses . . .*

She moved her body restlessly. She was damp, sticky, and swollen between her legs. She had felt such a fiery heat there when he kissed her. Now it was a dull, itchy ache. She felt as if she needed to get up and go for a long walk to get rid of the feeling of tension in her body.

But really, she just wanted him to wake up and kiss her again. She wanted his arms around her. She felt so safe wrapped up in his big embrace, clasped against his great chest. She glanced over her shoulder at him, but he was rolled away from her, his back toward her, just a big shape under the covers. There wasn't even enough light for her to see his fiery red hair. That hair had shocked her at first, but she was used to it now, and she loved it, along with his freckles and his somewhat hawkish features that she thought were quite majestic.

She stifled a sigh of longing, her heart aching. She wished she were brave enough to roll over and wake him up and make him kiss her again.

BRYSON LEANED ON the spade, breathing hard, sweat congealed under his jacket, despite the cool night air. He'd been digging solidly for half an hour. It was harder going than he had anticipated, and he suspected he was more out of condition than he knew. He'd brought a lamp with him to supplement the moon's silvery light, but it mostly just emphasized the shadowy shapes of the trees and the tower that brooded in the dark around him as he worked.

He couldn't rid himself of the sensation that hidden eyes watched him, nor the creeping sensation that something was going to leap out at him at any moment.

Perhaps this idea, conceived in the safety of daylight, wasn't so good a one as it had seemed. After all, he had no way of knowing if there was anything in this mound. And even if there was, his chances of finding anything on his first go were probably slim. He had chosen to enlarge the hole already dug six months earlier by the viscount when he and the duke had concluded that the mound probably housed at least one burial. The viscount, according to his account, had hit stone with his spade and dug out sufficient dirt to reveal what appeared to be a series of stones piled up like a barrow. Some of what the viscount had dug out had been filled in again with dirt, and Bryson had spent the last half an hour removing it.

He had a sizable pile of dirt accumulated beside the hole, and his spade had hit rock. But he needed more light to see by. Raising the lamp, he peered into the hole. If he could remove one of the stones, might he reveal what was underneath? Picking up the mattock, he used it to try to pry one of the stones up. They were irregularly shaped and each about the size of a small storage box for papers. If he could pry one loose, he might be able to lift it up.

He picked at it for a while, and eventually he thought he had the stone loose enough to lift. Ideally it would be better to lever it out with a rope, but he didn't have the equipment for that. Brute strength would be needed. He wasn't sure if he had sufficient of that. The giant earl would be able to do it, he reflected. Not wishing to be beaten by the man, Bryson spread his weight, got the mattock wedged under one side of the rock, and heaved it sideways. After two tries, it toppled away to the side and a rush of cold dank air blew upward, bringing with it stale dank air.

Wiping his brow, he picked up the lamp and held it to the space revealed, but could see nothing that made any sense. Just dark shapes and the smell of damp earth. The hole he had made wasn't big enough to fit through, and the prospect of digging out more rocks held little appeal.

He straightened, weighing the potential rewards with the effort involved. Perhaps he would leave the digging to the experts. If they found anything, he could always steal it and send it to his agent to sell to his father. On the whole, that seemed like a better plan. *Why didn't I think of that in the first place?*

He pushed the stone roughly back into place over the hole. He knew enough not to leave it open for creatures to get in and wreak havoc.

He staggered down the mound with the lamp and headed back toward the house. Entering quietly via the servants' entrance, he used the servants' stairs to make his way to his room, disgruntled that all that work had given him nothing.

Fortunately, he and Kenrick had arranged to go shooting first thing and would be well away from the house by the time his attempt at grave robbing was discovered. Since it was well known he had zero interest in antiquities or grubbing about in the dirt, hopefully he would be the last person they would suspect of digging up the mound in the middle of the night.

DEO WAS DISCOVERING that his wife was not habitually an early riser, which was fortunate as it allowed him to slip out of bed and take Kes out without disturbing her. Or having to deal with the potentially embarrassing state of aching need she seemed to be able to reduce him to by just being herself. He spent several minutes just watching her sleep, terrified that she would wake and catch him at it, and by the same token, unable to tear himself away. She looked so peaceful and sweet, clutching the pillow, her hair, which she had left loose last night, a tousled mess around her head.

He finally dragged himself away from the temptation that was his wife, washed, dressed, and took Kes out, his thoughts still a jumbled mess over last night's kisses. *How to avoid a repeat? At least until I can determine our legal status . . .* He groaned and picked up a stick to throw for Kes. The truth was he didn't *want* to avoid a repeat. *Who wouldn't want to experience that kind of delight again? And more . . .*

He wanted to bed his wife . . . desperately. And, more to the point, properly. And he hadn't much of a clue how to go about it.

Well, he had time to think about it. It would be a few days before he heard back from his solicitor, and found out if he had to organize another marriage license . . .

In the meantime, he needed to prevent Bidenden sniffing around Emily. The cheek of the man to persist in showing his interest when she was a married woman. *What, does he think I will give her up? Not bloody likely!*

Chapter Fourteen

EMILY WOKE TO an empty bed. Both Kester and Deo were absent, gone out for Kester's morning anointing of the flower beds, no doubt. She stretched and rubbed her thighs together, sticky with the residue of last night's activities.

She sighed and sat up, flinging back the bedclothes just as the door opened and Kester burst through to jump up and greet her, followed by Deo. His face was flushed from exertion which made his freckles stand out, and his eyes blazed a deep blue this morning. His hair was tousled as if he had forgotten to comb it.

"Kes, down!" he said as Kester tried to lick her face.

She ruffled his ears and said, "I don't mind! Was your walk invigorating? You look quite refreshed."

"It was." He gave her an odd look. *Speculative? Shy?* "I am in a buoyant mood this morning," he admitted. He approached the bed and sat beside her, putting an arm round her waist. He kissed the top of her head as she leaned into him, and he said softly, "I think that might have something to do with my wife."

"Oh, Deo," she said on a sigh and slid a hand inside his jacket and rubbed it over his great chest. The man would be magnificent without his clothes on. She couldn't wait to see him naked. *Does that make me a wanton wife?* She stifled a giggle at the notion.

"Would you like to come back to bed?" she said shyly, peeking up at him.

He made a gruff noise in his throat. "That would be inadvisable. We have a lot to do today."

"Oh," she said, trying to stifle her disappointment.

"Don't look so woebegone, wife. I will make it up to you tonight," he said with equal gruffness.

She smiled and flung her arms round his neck. "You will?"

He flushed and nodded as she kissed his cheek. His hand clenched hard on her thigh, and he gave her a quick kiss on the lips before rising abruptly. The kiss was disappointingly brief. He reached the door and said, "I asked Jenny to bring you water for bathing. She will be up shortly."

"Thank you," she said. With mixed feelings, she watched him disappear into the sitting room and close the door. On the one hand he was acknowledging that she had made him feel good. On the other he didn't share her desire to climb back beneath the sheets and continue her education into all things lewd. *Am I a bad wife to want more this morning?*

FAR FROM NOT sharing her desire to climb back into the sheets, Deo was fighting his own desire tooth and nail. He wanted it too damned much, which meant he had to fight it. Giving into a sudden debauched desire for marital congress was a recipe for disaster. Last night was a revelation to him, and he needed time to accustom himself, to contemplate his next move, how far he should go with Emily. There was no question of consummating the marriage yet—he needed to know their status. Once he knew that . . . He swallowed, a flush of heat washing through his body.

His groin felt hot and heavy, and he couldn't wait until tonight.

Over breakfast, they discussed the plans for the day with the Ashfords. Surprisingly, Kenrick and Bidenden were present, although neither participated in the conversation. They were planning a fishing trip by all accounts and thus were up earlier than usual. Of the duke and duchess there was no sign. Apparently, their child had been colicky and, unlike other wealthy parents, neither was prepared to surrender the heir to the dukedom to the care of the nursemaids. The two of them had been up with him most of the night.

"Oh, poor little fellow. I hope he is better this morning," said Emily.

Annis nodded. "I believe so. Babies often suffer with colic; it can make them fretful."

They arrived at the dig site after breakfast, and Emily and Deo surveyed the mess in consternation. *What has happened here overnight?* It was just herself and Deo this morning, everyone else having other things to occupy them.

"Deo, who could have done this?" asked Emily, peering into the hole. "Oh, they have uncovered the stones of the barrow, look!" She pointed into the hole, and Deo came to her side to see.

The morning sunlight showed a chink between the stones, as if one had been moved and pushed back into place but not properly aligned.

"Whoever they are, it looks like they gave up before they dug any further. Perhaps they were disturbed in the act?" Deo knelt and, grasping the stone that had been moved, lifted it out of the hole entirely and set it aside, revealing a black hole from which wafted the smell of dank air.

"My God, Em!" he said, staring at the dark hole. "It's a hollow chamber!"

She dropped to her knees beside him to peer into the hole. "It must be a burial chamber, don't you think? Oh Deo, this is so rare! Most barrows are earth filled, but this one looks as if it was once a stone-built cairn that has been covered over!" Emily clutched his arm in excitement.

"It definitely seems like we have a burial then." He smiled at her excitement. "A rare find indeed." He paused, staring down into the hole thoughtfully. "Bring me the lamp, Em, let's see if we can make out anything inside it from here."

She brought him the shuttered lamp, and he raised the glass shutters so that it could shed maximum light and lowered it into the hole. It threw shadows on the stone walls of a chamber.

"Em, you're smaller than me, lean in and tell me what you can see," he said, wrapping one arm around her waist to hold her while he extended his other arm holding the lamp into the hole as far as he could.

She leaned forward and poked her head fully into the hole. Gazing around, she could see the sides of what she guessed must be a rectangular chamber because the lamp light failed to illuminate the ends. "It's a chamber that runs east-west," she said, "with stone walls and roof and an earthen floor. I can't see either end of it so it must be several feel longer than it is wide. I'd estimate the width at roughly six feet?" she added, settling back on her haunches as she withdrew her head from the hole. "Deo, this is magnificent. What a discovery!"

"Could you see anything inside it?" he asked.

She shook her head, "No, but the light didn't reach very far."

He set the lamp down and shuttered it once more, frowning down at the stones he could see on either side of the hole. The one they had removed had been sitting on top of two others, plugging a gap.

"Em, I think we need to find the entrance. If we try to come in through the top as we would with an earth-filled barrow, we will likely make the whole thing collapse."

"I agree. How will we find it?" she said, trying to contain her excitement.

"Digging around the perimeter until we find it." He stood. "Em, can you sift through the pile of disturbed dirt to check for anything of interest and move it off the mound as you go? I'll start digging for the entrance to the barrow."

She nodded and set to work with buckets, trowel, and sieve. "Who do you think could have dug into the mound?"

Deo stuck his spade into the soft topsoil on the western side and shoveled a load aside, adding to the pile she was working on. "I don't know. Someone who thought there might be something to find, obviously." He shoveled another load. "I wonder if there are any local legends kicking about that would send someone on a treasure hunt? But why last night? Unless they have just got wind of what we are doing here."

Em glanced up at him and tried not to stare. He was only wearing breeches and a shirt today, anticipating that he would be digging, and the sight of his shirt open at the neck and the play of his muscles beneath as he worked was creating havoc within her body. His brief kiss this morning had done nothing to relieve her condition, and she was an aching ball of longing. She dragged her eyes away from him and tried to concentrate on her sieving. But she was conscious of every move, every heave of muscle, grunt, and expelled breath.

Biting her lip, she kept sieving, her fingers running through the dirt, looking for sherds of pottery, coins, anything really that indicated human occupation. She had done four bucket loads and was on the fifth when she came across her first find.

"Oh, Deo. It's a coin!" she said, rubbing the dirt off, trying to figure out what denomination it was. She dunked it in the bowl of water she had and washed it clean, holding it out in her palm for him to see.

He stuck his shovel in the dirt upright and wiped his face with his handkerchief, then picked up the coin in his large, blunt fingers. He squinted at it. "A Queen Anne shilling, not of much value, but proof that it is worth continuing to screen through the debris. You never know what we will find." He smiled down at her, and she grinned back, her heart swelling with warmth. This is what she had dreamed of, working on a dig with someone who shared her passion for it. The fact that he was gorgeous and her husband to boot meant that all her dreams were coming true at once. *If only I can get him to kiss me again . . .*

He paused to take a drink from a flask of water and passed it to her. They were fortunately standing in shade for the moment, but even so he was sweating with the effort of moving all that earth. She went back to sieving.

He removed several square feet of topsoil down to the barrow rock and stopped to review. "This doesn't look like the entrance," he said, propping a hand on his upright shovel and squinting up at the sun, which had come out from behind a cloud. "But it isn't necessarily built on a perfect east-west axis, so we will need to dig in an arc on this side to determine where the entrance is."

She got up and came over to him, looking down into the area he had uncovered.

"I think you're right," she said, pointing to the overlapping layers of rock. "That looks like the base of a domed wall."

"We definitely seem to have some kind of structure here. What do you think?"

She nodded, "I agree, it looks like a stone-built cairn, and there should be an entrance to the chamber. There are several examples that I have read about that were uncovered in East Anglia with what are believed to be Anglo-Saxon burials inside ancient stone tombs. What if it is one of those? From the period *after* their conversion to Christianity? The cross certainly indicates a Christian influence."

"Celtic Christian rather than Roman Catholic. Bede references the struggle for power between the two factions." He frowned in an effort of memory. "I think that all came to a head in the reign of King Oswy of Northumbria. If that is the case, given its location, shouldn't this burial predate Oswy? Eighth century?"

"Seventh century, early to mid-600s was his *floruit*." She grinned. "This is so exciting!"

"It is." He caught her hand. "All the more so for sharing it."

She reached up on tip toe to kiss his chin which was all she could reach. "Thank you."

He leaned down and kissed her forehead. "Thank *you*." His voice had dropped to a husky note that made her heart race. In the next instant his arms came around her, almost lifting her off her feet, and he kissed her full on the lips.

Her heart thudded and heat flooded her body as she wrapped her arms round his neck and kissed him back. Held securely in his arms, his great chest pressed close and the scent of his maleness made her dizzy and glad of the support of his strong frame to cling to. His mouth explored hers with increasing boldness, and she responded, parting her lips and pressing closer against him, quite forgetting they were standing in the middle of a field in broad daylight where anyone might see them.

He broke the kiss all too soon for her, setting her gently away from him. She was reminded of him pushing her away last night. She gazed up at him, dazed. He cleared his throat, his color high, and said gruffly, "I'll help you with the sieving and start clearing the rest of the base of the mound after lunch. And tonight, we can take a look at the inscription."

She looked away and nodded, swallowing the irrational lump in her throat. Her body was a battleground of desire and need. She wanted to fling herself back into his arms and seek the comfort only his kisses and caresses could offer. But she could see that he was trying to do the right thing. If they continued kissing like that out here—well, it wouldn't be appropriate.

He caught her hand and kissed her dusty fingers, seeming oblivious to the dirt on them. "Later, Em, hm?"

She nodded and forced a smile. "Yes, please, Deo."

"Emily Frances, you are killing me," he said, agonized.

"It's mutual," she whispered, placing a hand on his chest. His shirt was slightly damp with sweat and his skin felt hot through the fabric.

"Em!" It was halfway between a groan and a warning. "Work, please!" he begged.

She nodded again and returned to her sieve.

In a few minutes they had set up a rhythm, working through the soil he had dug up. The tension dissipated somewhat as they worked, replaced by the joy of companionship, of a shared task that both of them loved. They found several pieces of pottery, a couple of coins, and a copper pin. None of which were ancient.

Heading back to the house for luncheon, they discussed possibilities of what they might find next. She couldn't suppress a skip of excitement.

OVER LUNCHEON, IT was agreed the viscount would help Deo clear the base of the mound and Annis offered to help Emily sieve. The children went, too, and played chasey around the stones with Kester. It was a pleasant afternoon of camaraderie, and Emily felt for the first time like she was truly where she belonged.

She and Deo shared some intimate glances, and when he came over to check on how she was going, his hand squeezed her shoulder and he murmured, "Well done," quietly in her ear. His warm breath made her shiver and sent a tingling heat to settle between her thighs. She was still overwrought from last night's kisses; this morning's kiss hadn't helped.

By four o'clock the men had cleared three quarters of the exploratory arc at the base of the mound on the western side. The eastern side was dominated by the old tree, as if it stood sentinel beside the mound, protecting it.

Surveying what they had accomplished, Deo said, "No sign of the entrance yet. I thought we would have uncovered it on this side."

"Perhaps it is on the side sheltered by the tree?" offered the viscount.

"That's what I'm afraid of. If it is, the tree roots are likely to have spread into the structure and we will have a much bigger problem to deal with."

Emily listened to the men discussing the engineering problem of the tree. Deo had put the dislodged stone back in situ to prevent any creatures getting into the barrow and also hopefully to prevent water getting in. They needed to find the entrance urgently and remove any finds before the weather damaged them. England, even in summer, was not known for its dry weather. They had been lucky to have several dry days in a row, but it wouldn't last.

Deo and the viscount concluded that they would need to examine the extent of the tree's root system and figure out how to complete the search for the entrance tomorrow under its spreading branches.

"The trouble is that we have no way of knowing how far and deep the roots go into the mound," said Deo. Wiping his face with his handkerchief. "We know they are spread quite wide, on the side sloping away from the mound because there are a lot of them exposed on that side already. But if they have penetrated the stones of the barrow, it will be impossible to get them out without wrecking the barrow itself. I fear we may have to cut the tree down."

DEO WAS PAINFULLY conscious all afternoon that he had promised Emily more kisses that night, and he was in a lather trying to decide how to proceed. He was adamant with himself that the marriage could not be consummated until he was sure that they were indeed legally married. Therefore, nothing they did could progress past kisses. But kisses were so tempting. *Surely it would be more sensible not to risk temptation?*

They only needed to wait a few days, a week at most. He would explain it to Em—it was for her protection after all . . .

After dinner, he and Em repaired to their sitting room with the inscription and the books they had brought with them. With the rubbing spread out on the desk and as much light as they could manage with the candles and lamps, they sat and stared at it for a while in silence.

HIC IACET ___GYN C______ __ C_____ FILIUS WIG____

"*HIC IACET*—here lies—someone with a name that ends in *GYN* . . ." mused Deo aloud.

"If the first C word is *comes*," said Emily, "and this preposition looks like it has two letters. What are our choices? *AD*, *DE*, or *IN*."

He nodded. "So, *at*, *of*, or *in* or *on*. *At* or *of* would make most sense and would mean the second word is a place name."

"Yes." She leaned closer to the rubbing and pointed. "I think it's *DE*—of—see here, that looks like a D to me."

He pushed his glasses up his nose and peered closer. "Yes, I agree. So, we have someone with the second part of his name ending in *GYN* who is a *comes* or earl—"

"Like you!" she quipped with a grin.

"Well, earl is an Anglo-Saxon title, so perhaps this fellow is English rather than British?"

"Most likely, given the location, Leicestershire was Middle Anglian territory prior to being absorbed into Mercia."

"So something *GYN COMES DE. GYN*, Earl of something starting with C . . ."

They stared at each other blankly. Then Deo pointed to the last name. "This should be his father's name, 'Wig' sounds Saxon to me, but 'Gyn' sounds British. Do you agree?"

"Yes, but this period was a melting pot for Saxons and Britons, particularly in this part of the country. If you're right, and this burial is say sixth or seventh century, this might be the last remnant of British occupation on this area."

"If the son has a British name, but the father was Saxon, it's likely his mother was British."

"Yes, that makes sense! I do love this!" She bounced a bit in her seat, and he put an arm around her, unable to resist her enthusiasm.

"Em, you make everything a pleasure," he said. "I love it, too—I just thought I was strange. Even my friends think I'm odd."

"You're not odd," she said, placing a hand on his thigh and making his semi hard cock jerk to attention. "At least no more odd than I am."

"Emily," he murmured and kissed her, because he just couldn't resist any longer. She snaked a hand around his neck and kissed him back. Her lips were warm and soft, and tingling pleasure exploded through his veins like it always did every time he kissed her. Reluctantly he broke the kiss and pulled back.

He cleared his throat. "So, any ideas about this place name?"

She let out a breath slowly and bent over the rubbing. Her other hand was still on his thigh. "It should be something local if he was buried here, you would think." She chewed her lip, and he swallowed a groan.

"Do you think this is perhaps Caer something?" she said.

"Yes. Yes, most likely, but there are dozens if not hundreds of Caer place names."

She got up and rummaged through the pile of books they had brought with them. Pulling out a slim volume, she came back to the desk brandishing it. "I haven't had a chance to read this, but I was glancing through it and grabbed it to bring because it's newly published and it relates to the post-Roman period."

He glanced at the cover: *Nennius' Historia Brittonum*, translated by Gunn. "Oh God, I'd forgotten I ordered that! An excellent idea. I haven't had a chance to read it yet either."

She sat down and opened the volume. "I'm sure I saw a list of Caer place names—yes, here on page 3, and there are notes in the back." She turned to the back of the book and scanned until she found the list of place names with their modern locations. "Oh, gosh. Look, Deo, Leicester! 'Caer Lierion' is listed as being Leicester. Could it be . . .?"

"I'm not sure if there is enough space for that . . ." He leaned over the rubbing. "I think this is a y. Yes, it could be 'lyr,' Caerlyr perhaps? A variation in the spelling. Medieval spelling is notoriously unreliable."

"Yes, yes! It must be, surely! Oh gosh, Deo, we did it!" She bounced up and danced round the room, and he swung around in his seat to watch her, a smile curving his lips. He got up and captured her, pulling her close.

"You did it," he said, lifting her off her feet and kissing her. She flung her arms round his neck and clung to him as they shared a warm, tingling kiss.

"We did it," she said, breathless and flushed.

"We still have to figure out the full names, but we know his title and location, and that is a lot," he said, setting her on her feet gently but not letting go. He couldn't. Holding her was so addictive.

Kes, who had been watching their antics from the fireplace, got up and ambled over to paw at his leg.

"Need to go out, do you?" he said, reluctantly letting Emily go. "All right, I'll take you." He glanced at Em, suddenly feeling awkward. He had promised her kisses and more tonight. He was both eager and nervous at the prospect.

"I'll just take him out," he said.

"Yes, of course." She flushed faintly and began tidying up books and papers. "We can write it up tomorrow and maybe continue the search for the names?"

He nodded and held the door for Kes.

Chapter Fifteen

R ETURNING TO THEIR suite half an hour later, he found the sitting room tidy and empty with most of the lights doused. *Em will be waiting for me . . .*

He opened the bedroom door and found Emily dozing over her book in bed. It had been a big day. He signaled to Kes to go to the fire, he didn't want Kes to wake her. Then he crossed quietly to the dressing room to disrobe, wash, and clean his teeth and decided to wear a night shirt. It might afford him some protection.

He blew out the candles and slid into bed, congratulating himself on not having woken her. He was just settling into the pillows when she said, "Deo?"

"I didn't mean to wake you," he said apologetically.

"I didn't mean to fall asleep," she said. The room was dim, but not completely black, and she moved toward him, nestling into his chest. His pulse raced, and his cock, which had been quiescent, stirred to attention from her proximity. A waft of rosewater assailed his nostrils, and he wrapped an arm around her warm body before he could stop himself.

Her fingers traced patterns over his chest. "Are you pleased with the progress we made today?"

"I am. Are you?"

"Yes. I am so excited about what we might find tomorrow."

"It may take several days before we are able to open the barrow, Em," he cautioned. "And when we do, we may find nothing of interest. You should be prepared for disappointment."

"Oh, well, yes. But the possibility of finding something is exciting, isn't it? And knowing who he is, well, something about him at least, our Gyn, son of Wig, makes it all the more thrilling, don't you think?"

"Yes, it is," he said, tightening his arm round her. She was so sweet; her enthusiasm was impossible to quash. Her fingers on his chest were distracting, too, sending little tendrils of fire south. Having her lovely, soft curves pressed against his side was so enticing and delicious. He could feel his resolve to stop the kisses crumbling by the second.

He could see the glitter of her eyes and the outline of her features in the dark, the alluring curve of her lips as she raised her face to his. She was so close he could feel the warmth of her breath on his cheek.

He wasn't quite sure who closed the gap between them, himself or Em—perhaps it was mutual—but the pressure of her lips against his was that same drugging delight he'd experienced throughout the day and last night. *Kisses are wonderful. At least with Em they are.* Her rosebud mouth was perfectly delicious.

Her hand crept up round his neck and her body slid over his, her breasts pressing into his chest, her legs tangling with his. His cock grazed her hip, and he swallowed a groan, resisting the instinct to buck his hips. His hands ran over her body through her nightgown as he deepened the kiss and dimly realized he'd lost the fight to resist the temptation of kissing Emily.

She moved against him like she had last night, molding her body to his, her hips moving in a sensuous way that had his cock twitching and leaking on his belly; she returned his kisses and made those little noises in her throat that drove him mad. His hands roved over her body possessively, boldly. Her touch was pleasure and comfort. That she wanted to touch him made him aware of how starved of touch he had been and how grateful he was for it. He pulled her closer, burying his face in her neck and breathing in her scent. "Em," he murmured. "My lovely Em."

"Deo?" she said breathlessly, squirming against him. "Please?" she whispered, reaching for him. *What is she begging me for? More kisses, more . . .* With blinding insight, it hit him that he had managed to relieve himself after their heated passage of kisses last night, but she had not. And here he was compounding the problem.

"Em?" His hands ran over her squirming body, unable to resist touching her as her mouth rained kisses over his chest and her fingers grabbed at his shirt as if she couldn't get close enough.

"Deo, please!" she said breathlessly. He kissed her again, deeply, wanting to give her whatever she desired. She reacted like tinder set alight, her legs straddling his thigh as she pushed her mound against it, her hips moving in sensuous rhythm. He could feel the dampness through her gown. *Em! Oh, Em!*

He deepened the kiss and wished he knew more about what to do to please her.

Kissing Emily was the most delicious thing he had ever experienced. He was hot and hard, but he ignored that, concentrating on her as she writhed on him, her breath coming in short pants, and little mewling noises escaping her as their kisses became more and more demanding and frantic.

Going purely on instinct, he rolled her over into the pillows, swapping his left leg with his right against her body. Continuing the deep drugging kisses, occasionally veering off to kiss her neck, her throat, her chin, her ear, and back to her mouth, his cock throbbed, leaking against the sheets. He ignored it. This wasn't about him.

He shifted his body, so that he could pull her nightgown up and slide his hand beneath. His questing fingers slid over smooth thighs and found the treasure nestled between them. With tentative touches he teased her damp curls, and then with his index finger, parted her lips. Em's exquisitely soft, satiny flesh, so wet and warm against the pad of his fingertip, made him groan with delight.

"You're so wet!" he moaned. He pressed his groin harder against her thigh to prevent himself moving his hips in response.

She jerked under his touch and whimpered.

He stilled his hand, alarmed. "Did that hurt?"

She shook her head. "No." Her voice was breathless. "It feels delicious."

Encouraged, he slid his finger up and down the channel of her lips, watching her face for reactions in the dim light. He lost himself in delight, observing her changes in expression, listening to her ragged breathing, mewls, and moans, and feeling her body writhing under his touch.

What could he do to bring her relief? She was a virgin, so he hadn't a clue if putting his fingers inside her would hurt, break her hymen, or be pleasurable for her. Deciding against risking it, he moved his fingers upward to that sensitive spot that seemed so critical to female pleasure and explored tentatively.

He could feel a raised nub of flesh, and when he touched it, Emily practically leaped off the bed with a cry.

"I'm sorry!" he said, retracting his hand. "Is that painful?"

"Not exactly," she said, panting.

He reached again gingerly and swirled around the spot, his fingers plenty slippery with her arousal. This time her reaction was to moan and arch her body. Much better. Concluding he must be doing something right, he continued the pattern of steady swirling and watched utterly fascinated as Emily became completely frantic. Her hands clutched randomly at the sheets, her head, his arm; and her hips writhed in increasingly sensuous rhythm. Her breathing became erratic, punctuated by moans and whimpers, and as he sped up his movements, outright groans. Her body stiffened suddenly on a deep groan, her head flung backward in the pillows, her neck and upper body arched, and her legs trembled uncontrollably. She uttered another long, drawn-out moan and her body collapsed in a panting heap back onto the mattress.

And that, he thought with satisfaction, was how to make his woman come. Rather pleased with himself, he waited until she opened her eyes to ask, "Was that pleasurable?"

She smiled in a lazy sensuous way that made his cock leak painfully and nodded. "Oh, yes," she said softly.

He smiled in return and, leaning down, he kissed her gently. "Go to sleep," he recommended. Because he absolutely needed to do something about the state of his cock, and he'd rather she not witness it.

"Oh." She cast him a slightly puzzled look and bit her lip. She ran a hand up the back of his neck and kissed him. "Are you sure?" she asked, husky voiced.

Oh, God! When had Em turned into a siren? I have to resist. I really do!

"Yes, go to sleep, sweetheart," he murmured, unable to resist pressing a soft kiss to her forehead.

She sighed, her eyes closing, then she kissed his neck and snuggled into him like a confiding kitten.

He lay there with his cock throbbing, listening to her soft breathing, torn between the pleasure of having her snuggled into him and the agony in his groin. When he was sure she was asleep, he eased out from under her and crept to the dressing room to sort himself out.

Ten minutes later he returned to the bed, waved Kes up, and slid back under the covers. Miraculously, Em didn't wake. She really was a sound sleeper.

Chapter Sixteen

D EO WOKE WITH Emily still curled into him and his cock hard
as an iron bar. The sun was up, just. The events of last
night played out for him as he lay there, staring at the canopy of
the bed, and he smiled with a small amount of smug satisfaction.
He had brought Em pleasure, so he wasn't a complete failure as a
lover after all. And the prospect of being able to do it again—and
more—was very enticing. But how much more? Temptation was
a slippery slope—*no pun intended*, he snorted to himself.

Em moved, pressing her face into his chest, and he looked
down at the top of her head. His chest felt full and tight, warm
with an emotion he was not familiar with. It made him want to
gather her up and squeeze her, stroke her, kiss her, bring her
more pleasure. The sun was a candle to Em's smile. It lit up his
world.

He would do anything to make her happy, to protect her and
make her his. *She is mine, isn't she?* The niggle of doubt over the
marriage contract wouldn't let him be. He needed to make sure
everything was right between them before he took the irrevocable step of consummation. But further than that, he needed to
secure her affection, for without that, the marriage would be a
hollow shell.

A cold wash ran over his skin. She seemed well-disposed

toward him, but what did it mean? He was woefully ignorant of emotions, his own and others'. How should he read her behavior? What did it mean? A kind of desperate panic seized him. *How to ensure she cares for me and will continue to do so?*

Kes interrupted his train of thought by jumping down off the bed and going to the door. With a sigh, he gently eased himself out from under Em and rapidly pulled on breeches, boots, shirt, and jacket to take Kes out.

By the time he got back, he was no nearer a solution to his problem beyond continuing down the path he had begun last night to bring her pleasure. *Perhaps if I give her enough of that she will come to care for me a bit?* For the hundredth time he wished he knew more about females. He had never learned anything about the art of courtship, concluding that such a path was not for him.

When he had placed the advertisement, he had not anticipated the need for courtship. The whole point of the ad was to avoid the necessity. He would contract himself a wife, and they would somehow rub along all right. He hadn't thought through the ramifications of physical relations with his wife. He hadn't anticipated that he would desire her, desperately. That he would want to please her. And if he thought about all the complications of emotions and marital relations too much now, he would start to panic.

He needed to focus on the problem of the tree at the base of the mound. That was a physical problem he could tackle. *Much more comfortable than thinking about Em and how warm and soft and lovely she is . . .*

Tree, Deo! Tree, Deo!

By the time he was washed and dressed again, Em was stirring.

"Deo?"

He turned to the bed, she blinked at him, prettily tousled, and he couldn't resist walking toward her and perching on the side of the bed.

"Good morning. Did you sleep well?" he asked.

She stretched, which thrust her nightgown-covered breasts outward and caused him a rush of heat that stained his cheeks and filled his breeches. "Yes, I did." She smiled shyly and took his hand. "Thank you for last night."

He flushed deeper and smiled. "My pleasure." He raised her hand and kissed it.

She sat up and put her arms round his neck. "I had no idea it would be so—wonderful!"

His smile became a grin, but before he could say anything, she leaned in and pressed her lips to his. As always, the touch of her mouth swamped his senses, and he lost focus on anything but the connection between them. Putting an arm round her waist, he drew her closer and kissed her thoroughly. Kissing Em was definitely his favorite thing to do.

She tugged at him, and the temptation to press her flat to the pillows and—*Tree, Deo!*

He put out his hand to stop her tugging him down on top of her and broke the kiss.

"I'm sorry, Em. As much as I want to, we need to locate the entrance to the tomb today so we can clear the barrow before it rains."

"Oh!" A flicker of disappointment in her eyes smote him in the chest. "Yes, of course." She made an effort to smile. "I was forgetting. Yesterday was such a perfect day. But we do have lots to do, you're right. I'd best get up."

He got up and went to the door. "I'll ring for Jenny for you. I'm going down to speak with Emrys about the most efficient way to locate the entrance."

IT WAS A long day. All the men, even Kenrick and Bidenden, were roped into helping with excavating the rest of the base of the mound in an effort to find the entrance, while the women, under

Emily's direction, sieved the dirt removed by the men. Kes had been confined to the house along with the children.

By mid morning they had cleared the base on the north and south sides with no sign of the entrance, which left only the east side, guarded by the tree. Which was what Deo had said he hoped wouldn't happen.

"What are we going to do?" Emily asked.

Pausing in his shoveling of dirt, Deo mopped his face and took the water flask Emily passed to him. "Thank you." He wiped his mouth and pointed at the earth at his feet. "We should have found the entrance by now if it was on the west, north, or south sides. It must be on the east side as I feared."

Emily looked up at the tree looming over them. It was a grand old oak, quite gnarled and twisted. "Do we have to remove it?" she asked.

"I don't see a way round it if we're to gain access to the entrance. The tree is practically on top of where it must be. She must be several hundred years old and has been guarding this tomb for a long time. Our *comes* has been well protected by it."

Smiggens came over to them. He had obviously heard their conversation. "You can say a prayer for the tree, my lady, if you like, to thank it for its service and apologize for hurting it. It's an old Celtic ritual. You'll need a white ribbon and a libation of honey and water to pour at its base."

Emily turned to Deo. "Could we? It seems awful to remove it with no mark of respect."

Deo nodded. "It's an ancient tree. It seems fitting to observe ancient ritual."

Drawn into the conversation, the other ladies agreed. "I have a length of white ribbon," said Lady Ashford.

"I shall go to the kitchens and fetch a libation of honey and water," said the duchess. "And I know just the receptacle to put it in," she said with a conspiratorial smile.

So everything stopped until the items were fetched. Then Lady Ashford tied the white ribbon around a large, low branch of the tree with a murmured prayer for its forgiveness of what they proposed to do, and Emily and the duchess held the carved, stone urn covered in a Celtic knot design and poured the libation at the foot of the tree.

"Thank you, great oak, for your service in protecting the dead," said Emily. "We honor you in turn for your silent vigil through the centuries, and we are sorry to disturb your rest."

"Amen," murmured everyone, gathered in a circle around the mound to witness the ritual. Emily wiped a tear from her cheek and exchanged a look with Deo, who squeezed her hand surreptitiously.

With the ritual complete, the men began discussing logistics with Smiggens about how to bring the tree down safely.

"We need to remove the lower branches first," said Smiggens, "to be sure they don't do any harm to the barrow in the felling. Once they are removed, we can move on to the tree itself and then the removal of the stump."

Each man was assigned a task, whether it was chopping or sawing off branches or catching them to lay them carefully aside. They worked methodically over the great twisted tree, slowly revealing its structure as the branches with their foliage were removed with chop, crack, and the rustle of leaves.

Em knew she should be sieving, but she was mesmerized by the sight of the men systematically destroying this magnificent old tree. All of them were working in shirtsleeves and breeches. Even Lord Bidenden. Absentmindedly, Em noticed he had stopped to drink some water. She had never seen him look so disheveled. His dark hair curled slightly with the sweat from his brow and gave him a vaguely Byronic air. He caught Emily's gaze on him and smiled. She looked away hastily, lest he misinterpret her looking at him as some kind of interest in his person.

Deo's voice broke into her introspection. "You had best step back, Em. I don't like you being so close to the tree. We're being careful to catch any falling branches, but these are large, heavy limbs, and I don't want you hit by any inadvertent slips."

She grimaced. "I shall not be at ease until you have finished this exercise. It is fraught with danger. I do not want any part of the tree to fall on you, either."

"I don't want it to fall on anyone," said Deo frankly. "Have you found anything of interest in the sifting?"

"A few unmarked pottery sherds and some coral beads, a couple more coins—these ones seem to be King George and one that is perhaps Elizabethan. Nothing Celtic, Roman, or post-Roman yet."

He nodded and picked up his axe. Taking this as a signal to retreat, Emily went back to her sieving. The women had set up at the base of the mound on the north side, several feet clear of the estimated reach of the tree's canopy should anything break off and plummet to earth. Deo's comments had not reassured Emily at all, and as she worked, she was constantly looking over at them and checking the stability of the tree.

The men worked steadily all morning and by lunch time the lower canopy of the tree had been removed and the large branches lopped off.

Staring at the twisted remains of the bared trunk, Smiggens said, "The main problem is going to be avoiding it falling forward onto the mound, my lord."

Deo nodded, frowning. "We don't want that. How do you propose we avoid it?"

"We'll notch the trunk on the far side, of course. But we should also use ropes, my lord, on the topmost portion of the trunk. A tug at the right time should nudge it in the right direction, but it will be dangerous. Timing will be crucial."

"Well, that will be this afternoon's problem. We should all break for lunch and reconvene at one o'clock."

Over luncheon, Deo addressed the company. "The next step will be the actual felling of the tree itself. Because of the angle, it will be difficult to persuade it to fall in the direction we want. Smiggens has suggested we use ropes to guide it, but that timing will be crucial."

"Well, you're certainly giving us some good exercise, Deo," said Emrys with a grin.

"I think it might be advisable for the ladies to remain at the house this afternoon, don't you, Deo?" said the duke.

"Oh, no!" protested Emily, echoed by the viscountess and the duchess.

"You are not leaving us out of the fun, Robert," said the duchess firmly. "We won't get in the way, will we, ladies?"

Emily and Annis agreed that they would not.

"Indeed, Deo, you cannot make me stay behind," said Emily boldly. "I won't be left out of this—it's my excavation, too. You said so!"

"It is your excavation. The duke has a point about safety, though. I cannot stress enough how dangerous this is. Ladies, you must promise to remain well clear of the possible trajectory of the tree."

"We will," said Emily with a smile for the other women.

After luncheon was concluded, Deo went ahead with the duke and the viscount to meet Smiggens, who had taken his lunch in the field with the lads.

The ladies redonned their hats, and set out at a more leisurely pace. They were joined shortly by Lords Kenrick and Bidenden. Bidenden contrived to slide into place beside Emily and said quietly, "It is a great pity that I did not know of your passion for antiquities during our courtship. I could have engaged you in conversation on the topic."

Emily goggled at him. "You have an interest in antiquities, my lord?"

"My father is a renowned collector of ancient artifacts. He dragged the whole family to Egypt in my youth. We explored temples and tombs the like of which you cannot begin to imagine."

"Egypt?" said Emily faintly, her picture of Lord Bidenden undergoing a revision. She had read of the wonders of Egypt and indeed devoured the volumes of the *Description de l'Egypt* she had seen in Hatchards bookshop. She couldn't afford to buy them, of course, but she had reverently paged through the volumes, appreciating the pictures and dipping into parts of the text. It had fired her imagination and longing to visit such an ancient and exotic locale. "How—how wonderful."

"Had you accepted my suit, we could even now have been on a trip to visit it. If you had so desired, of course."

The way he said *desired* with a meaningful look in his dark eyes made her shiver and reminded her forcefully why she had rejected his suit. His overt desire for her made her uncomfortable in a way that Deo's did not. She was beginning to realize that Lord Bidenden did seem to desire her now, although she was still convinced he wouldn't have looked twice at her if it weren't for her fortune.

"It's a moot point, my lord; I did not accept your suit."

"You still could, if—"

"My lord, this is nonsense! I am a married woman!" hissed Emily, flushing. "A happily married woman!" she added for emphasis.

"But your 'husband' would seem to be less sanguine about the marriage than you," he said.

Emily's color deepened as a wash of shame flooded her body. *Has Deo said or done something to make Bidenden think that he doesn't wish to be married to me? Or is it just that disastrous conversation that Bidenden overheard?* Recalling Bidenden's insinuation that Deo preferred men to women, she lifted her head and said quietly, "You are mistaken in your assumptions, my lord. My husband is most content."

Bidenden changed color. "Do I understand from this that your condition has changed from the other day?"

Emily clenched her hands tightly together and spoke through her teeth. "Firstly, my lord, I have not given you permission to address me so familiarly. Secondly, this is not a proper topic of conversation between us. And thirdly, it is none of your business!" And she quickened her pace to get away from him.

BRYSON WATCHED HER walk away with a frown, seriously rattled by her words. He had been keeping the pair under close surveillance, and as far as he had been able to detect, there was no high degree of intimacy visible between them in company. The earl treated Emily with courtesy, but he was not demonstrative. Rather a cool customer in Bryson's opinion. Of course, they were sharing quarters, which meant that anything could have happened in the intervening days since his arrival. But he had been confident of his conclusion that the earl preferred men, reinforced, if anything, by his manner toward Emily in public. For there could be no other explanation as to why he would have refrained from immediately consummating the marriage to Bryson's way of thinking.

Bryson's desire for Emily wasn't altogether feigned. She was not a classic beauty, and if she weren't possessed of a large fortune, he probably wouldn't have taken an interest in her in the first place. But having done so, he found her initially intriguing, precisely because she held him at arm's length. He wasn't used to that. As a handsome man with a title, he was used to women throwing themselves at him. And since his arrival here and the opportunity to observe her in a quite different milieu, away from her dominating mother, he was more attracted to her.

But if the earl had done the deed and made her his wife in actuality, there was nothing to be done. The marriage could not be annulled then and would stand. He found the notion that the earl had taken Emily's maidenhead quite disturbing. The sooner her parents arrived, the better. That would force things to a head, and he would know where he stood.

And if this damned burial proved to have nothing of value in it, and Emily was out of his reach, he would have to find another way of financing his lifestyle, in both the short and long term. Not for the first time, he cursed his sire under his breath.

Chapter Seventeen

EMILY HURRIED AHEAD to the excavation site, her peace cut up by Bidenden's insinuations. She arrived somewhat breathless and agitated, which didn't help when she learned just how dangerous the next phase of the tree removal was.

The tree had taken root at the base of the sloping ground, and its trunk was twisted and angled in such a way that the main trunk lay more or less parallel with the slope of the mound itself.

The morning's work had pared the tree back from the mound. For this part of the operation, guy ropes braced the main trunk that would assist them in bringing the rest of the tree down in what was intended to be a controlled fall. Emily, watching from a safe distance with the other women, fervently hoped they would.

Smiggens, being the only one of them with experience in felling trees, was going to make the cuts into the trunk that would bring it down, and the men would manage the guy ropes that should guide its descent.

Smiggens began his chopping on the east side of the tree, the side away from the barrow. He made a wedge-shaped cut in the trunk with his axe. Then he moved to the side and Deo and Kenrick stepped forward with the double ended saw that would cut through to the hinge from the barrow side of the tree, as Deo had explained over lunch. Smiggens's job was to tell them when to stop. Because of the lean of the trunk and its being butted up against the sloping ground of the mound, they were forced to work in a difficult position, one foot higher than the other and bent to get to the base of the trunk under the curve.

Fortunately, both men were extremely strong. Em watched the sweat bleeding through Deo's shirt as his massive shoulders worked to pull the axe through the wood of the old tree. It took some time, but eventually Smiggens held up his hand and said, "Stop!"

With visible relief, the two men pulled the saw free of the trunk and stepped back. Now came the most dangerous part of the endeavour. The three men scrambled clear of the tree and took up the guy ropes on one side of the tree. The duke, the viscount, and Bidenden held the ropes on the other side.

"Ready, gentlemen?" called Deo.

"Aye," came the chorus of replies. "On a count of three, tug firmly," he said. He paused and then began the count. "One. Two. Three. Heave!"

The tree wavered a bit on its base and the women held their collective breaths, holding each other's hands for support.

Then it began to fall at a south-easterly angle. This was in the opposite direction from Deo's position on the north-east side, thank God, but it was heading dangerously in the direction of the other three men. As it was on the other side of the mound from Emily's position, she couldn't actually see the men who were standing on that side, but horror built as the hinge cracked through, and the great tree wobbled, slid off its base, and crashed to the ground in a cloud of dirt, leaves and debris, to the accompanying shouts of the men and an agonized cry. *Someone has been caught in the fall!*

"Oh, God, Rob was on that side!" cried the duchess.

All three women, released from their position, picked up their skirts and raced around the base of the mound. The branches of the tree took up a lot of area, and they had to edge round them to find the spot where the men were clustered.

One of the men standing there was the duke, obviously unharmed.

"Rob!" the duchess hurried toward him with a cry of relief, and he received her with an arm round her waist. "Thank God! I thought it was you!" she said, pressing her face to his chest.

Emily, on her heels, barreled into Deo who was also standing there, grubby and sweaty but unharmed. "Deo! Who—?"

Deo turned to catch her with his arm, sleeves rolled up to the elbow.

"It's Bidenden. We pulled him out."

Emily put a hand to her mouth in shock and peered around the bodies of Kenrick and Ashford, who were bent over the prone form of Lord Bidenden. Smiggens was kneeling beside him and checking him over for injuries.

"Possibly bruised or broken ribs, I think," he said. "If someone can give me something to bind his chest, I'll wrap it to stop any movement until you can get him to the house and fetch a doctor."

Emily removed her sash, "Here, will this do as a bandage?"

"Aye, thank you, my lady."

She edged forward to kneel beside the fallen man. He was ashen pale, and it was obvious he was in a deal of pain, his breathing was labored, and his face was sheened in sweat. And like all of the men, he was generously daubed with dust and dirt. His eyes were closed. Ashford produced a flask and said, "Take a drop of this, old chap."

Bidenden opened his eyes and Emily leaned forward to hold his head while he took a mouthful of the flask's contents, even that slight movement caused him to gasp with pain. "Thank you," he said huskily. His eyes flickered to Emily, and she saw surprise in his eyes as they rested on her. His mouth twitched up in a wry smile. "Damned tree got me; I wasn't quick enough to get out of its way."

"Smiggens is going to bind your chest until we can get a

doctor to you," she said, using a handkerchief to wipe his brow.

"Thank you," he said again, his eyes closing.

Emily got to her feet, moving out of Smiggens's way as he went to work on Bidenden.

She returned to Deo's side and said quietly, "I have never been so terrified in my life. I was convinced that tree was going to crush you."

Deo looked down at her, his expression strangely blank. "I was fine," he said shortly. He moved away from her to inspect what was left of the tree stump. Emily, left standing there, watched him walk away from her, her heart contracting with pain. *What is wrong?*

DEO STARED BLINDLY at the stump of the tree embedded in the embankment of the rising mound, but it wasn't what he was seeing. He was playing over in his mind's eye the sight of Emily kneeling beside Bidenden and wiping his brow! *Why would she do that?* His muscles were shaking with fatigue, he was grubby and sweaty, and all the elation of success in getting the tree down had drained out of his toes at the sight of Emily tending to Bidenden, who lay like some fallen hero on a battlefield.

He swallowed against a too tight throat and realized he was desperately thirsty. He turned abruptly and went in search of the water flasks.

Smiggens had bound Bidenden's ribs and the duke and Kenrick were carrying him back to the house.

He turned back to the mound and, seizing a spade, he began shoveling and scraping away the dirt round the base of the stump. Only half the job was done—they had to get the stump out now. The other men joined him after having drinks, and he assigned each a spot to dig round the stump, including the duke and Kenrick once they returned from the house. They all worked solidly for an hour to expose the tangle of roots around the stump and hack the main arterial roots connecting the stump to the mound. Then with ropes tied around the massive stump, they tried to pull it out backward down the slope. But it wouldn't budge. Eventually they figured out it was secured to the earth by a massive central root. Once Deo hacked that away, the stump came out with a shower of soil and debris and the strong scent of damp earth.

A cheer went up from the men, with a round of applause from the ladies and calls of "Well done!"

At that point, the duke wiped his grubby face with an equally grubby handkerchief and said, "I think we've done enough for today."

The viscount put his hands to his back and stretched. "I'm with you there, Rob. My back is killing me."

"Beer and a bath," said Kenrick with a grin. "In that order."

Deo nodded. "Thank you for your help. We couldn't have done this without you. Particularly you, Smiggens," he said, offering his hand to the older man.

Smiggens flushed and murmured, "Glad to be of help, my lord."

The duke and the viscount collected their wives and headed off followed by Kenrick.

Deo turned back to the raw earth embankment they had exposed in this side of the barrow. They had dug down and into the barrow several feet now.

The entrance to this damned tomb must be here somewhere. He should leave it until tomorrow. He was exhausted and flat now with anticlimax, all his pleasure in getting the tree off the mound without destroying the barrow dissipated by the sight of Em bent over Bidenden like a ministering angel.

"Deo?" Em touched his sweaty, bare forearm. The touch of her fingertips sent a shiver over his skin and an ache to his chest. "Haven't you done enough for today?"

He swallowed, shoving his spade in the dirt viciously. "I want to find this bloody entrance," he said through clenched teeth. "It must be here somewhere."

"Deo, what's wrong?" She shifted into his line of sight.

"Nothing. I'm just—tired."

"All the more reason to stop," she said with perfect logic.

He closed his eyes and leaned on the shovel. "Go back to the house, Emily, and look after Bidenden!" He straightened and shoveled more dirt.

"Oh."

He scraped some more dirt and shoveled again, expecting her to move away. She didn't. The silence stretched as he scraped and shoveled some more.

"Deo," her voice was soft, and he couldn't resist looking at her. There were tears in her eyes, but she was smiling wryly. "You're jealous?"

He huffed, getting ready to deny it, but what came out of his mouth was the opposite. "Yes, damn it!" He shoved the spade in the dirt and straightened, turning toward her, his hands clenching and unclenching in agitation. "Em—"

She flung herself at him, making him stagger on the uneven ground, her arms going round his middle and her face buried in his damp shirt. "Oh Deo! It was you I was worried sick about all afternoon. Didn't I say so?"

"Yes," he admitted reluctantly, his arms going round her, but he was hesitant to touch her gown with his grubby hands. Her broad brimmed hat was stuck in his face, so he ripped it off her head and kissed her hair. "I'm sorry," he mumbled. "I'm an idiot."

She lifted her head, and he kissed her. The rush of bliss from her mouth on his made him forget momentarily where they were. Then, Smiggens's voice instructing his boys to pile some of the cut branches into neat bundles, reminded him of the impropriety of kissing his wife in front of the servants, and he let her go reluctantly.

Energized by her kiss, his earlier elation came flooding back, and he said, "I'm sure the entrance is here somewhere—it must be. I want to find it, don't you?"

"Of course, but you must be exhausted."

He shook his head. "I'm fine, we have at least another two hours of good light."

She bent to pick up her hat that he had tossed away. "All right, but let me help you," she said, shoving it back on her head. "I can rake the dirt away," she nodded to the pile of garden implements supplied by Smiggens, "as you dig it out. Won't that be quicker?"

"Yes," he admitted with a grin. *God, she is wonderful!*

He dug steadily for half an hour, until the muscles in his back and shoulders were screaming. After the work he'd already done that day, he was pushing even his strength. He would have to stop soon. He shoved the spade in the dirt one more time, and it jarred on something hard. He stuck it again and got the same thing. He shoveled the dirt away, working at revealing whatever his spade had hit.

"Em, I think I've got something." She stopped raking and came to stand beside him as he worked to reveal the top of a flat stone.

Ten more minutes revealed the edge of the large flat stone and a bit more digging under it revealed another stone set beneath the top one. This one was inset, he soon discovered, in dry stone walls of smaller flat stones on either side. It was a lintel over an entranceway, he was sure of it.

With about a third of it uncovered, he stopped, sweating and panting, his muscles trembling with fatigue.

"We found it," he said with a grin. "And I'm done in. Enough for today."

She wrapped her arms round him. "You're magnificent!" she said, looking up at him with such unmistakable warmth and pride in her eyes, his chest felt full and tight. No one had ever looked at him like that before.

He wrapped an arm round her and kissed her. "I couldn't have done this without you."

"And all the men who helped with the tree," she pointed out.

"Yes, and them. I will have to thank them properly later. Come on, I need a bath so badly!"

She grinned, and they gathered up their personal belongings and headed back to the house. Smiggens and his lads had left them some time ago.

Chapter Eighteen

D EO LAY DOWN on the bed with a groan. He'd had a long, hot bath and then accompanied Em down to dinner where he had tried to express his gratitude to the other men for their help and was told to stow it. Bidenden had been attended by the doctor but did not appear for dinner. A circumstance Deo was glad of, despite his conscience twinging him. After all, the man had helped as much as the others and been injured for it. Even so, Deo hadn't gotten the image of Em bent over the other man solicitously out of his head.

"What hurts?" asked Em, climbing on top of the covers with him.

"Everything," he admitted.

"Would it help if I rubbed your muscles?"

He opened his eyes and blinked at her. "That—that sounds wonderful."

She smiled. "I have some oil somewhere. Just a minute." She got off the bed and went into the dressing room. She emerged a moment later with a little brown bottle and got back on the bed. She was dressed in her nightgown and robe. He had donned a nightshirt.

"It smells of lavender, will you mind that?" she asked. "I use it for headaches."

His lips twitched. The prospect of Em's hands all over him was too enticing to pass up. *If I smell like a garden afterward, who cares?* "No, I don't mind."

"Good. Take your shirt off," said Em in that direct way she often adopted. He had noticed that she was a mix of timid and bold depending on the circumstances. It was another of her endearing qualities. He should be concerned about her seeing him completely naked and the behavior of his cock, but a part of him was too eager for her to touch him to care. He sat up and removed his shirt and collapsed back onto the pillows again.

She ran her eyes over him in silence, unconsciously biting her lower lip, and something in her gaze—*covetous?* As if she had just spied something she wanted to eat—made him flush with desire. He stifled a groan as his traitorous cock stirred.

"Hmm," murmured Em. "Roll over. I'll do your back first. I imagine that and your shoulders and upper arms have taken the brunt of the strain."

Relieved to hide his wayward organ, he rolled onto his stomach and closed his eyes.

Em rustled about, getting into position, and he heard the soft clink of her putting the glass bottle down on the bedside table, then her oiled hands were on his back and shoulders, gliding over the skin, her fingers pressing into the sore muscles.

He groaned from the sheer pleasure of it.

"Does that hurt?" she asked.

"No. It's wonderful!"

"Good." The note of satisfaction in her voice wasn't lost on him. He subsided into the pillows and mattress, soaking up every stroke and rub of her fingers as she worked over his body, beginning at his shoulders and upper arms, then down his back. No one had ever touched him like this before—well, no one had touched him at all really. Even his mistress's touch had been minimal, at his request. *But I can't deny myself this pleasure. Em's touch is too exquisite.*

When she reached his buttocks, he instinctively tensed up at the intimacy of it, his cock stiffening beneath him.

"Relax!" admonished Em, gently, and he did his best to obey. Her touch was hypnotic, and he gradually relaxed to the point he was almost dozy, as she ran her hands from his shoulders all the way down his back and up again.

Then she started on the backs of his thighs, her oiled hands sliding over his hairy skin easily enough. But when her thumbs rubbed his inner thighs and grazed his ball sack it woke him sufficiently to make him jerk, his groin filling with heat. *Did she do that deliberately or was it accidental?*

She continued on down his legs to his calves and then his feet, and he relaxed again. Even so, the heat in his cock did not subside, and he moved his hips a bit to get the engorged member into a position that was a little more comfortable.

By the time she finished rubbing his toes, he was all but asleep.

"Do you want to roll over so I can do your front?" she asked in his ear, her warm breath a caress that sent tingles down his spine.

"Hmm," he murmured. *God, she is an angel.* With an effort, he heaved himself over onto his back, not bothering to open his eyes. He was too relaxed, too close to sleep. He had never felt like this before, especially in the presence of another human.

Her fingers spread oil on his chest and reached behind the back of his neck to massage the tendons there. She worked over his chest and his forearms and hands, his thighs and shins. Occasionally her fingers grazed near his stiffened cock, but she didn't touch it. He wasn't sure whether to be miffed or grateful for that omission. She transferred her attention at last to his face and head. Her fingers pushing through his hair and massaging his scalp was so delicious it was almost sexual. When she tugged his hair gently, he actually groaned.

"Where did you learn to do this?" he asked drowsily.

"My mother suffers from tension headaches. I would massage her head, shoulders and back for her."

He was awake now, and his cock was hard and hot against his belly.

She leaned forward and kissed his mouth, and his hands came up to capture her and hold her, discovering she had shed her robe and gown. He drew her closer so he could kiss her properly, deeply. *How do I thank her for that wonderful experience?*

She slid down beside him. As his hands roved over her naked form, he groaned again and kissed her some more.

"Em," he murmured, rolling to pin her to the bed and kiss her deeply. His hands found her small breasts and massaged them. His fingers found her nipples and she arched under him, whimpering, her body pressing up into his and squirming against his thigh.

He knew what to do about this, and he moved his hand down to spear her satiny lips and stroke. She gave a very satisfactory moan. "Oh, Deo!"

He grinned against her neck and murmured, "Em! I want to see you unravel, Emily."

She moaned again, pushing up into his touch, moving her hips, as he stroked her repeatedly, her breathing disjointed and her hands clutching at him. He sped up his touch gradually, giving that special place a lot of attention, careful to imitate what he had done before that seemed to work so well the first time.

"Deo! Ohh!" Her back arched, her head flung back into the pillows and her whole body shuddered. A long, drawn-out moan followed, her hips giving little jerks as she pressed into his fingers and uttered soft grunts. These gradually dissipated, and she slowly collapsed into the mattress, her body still moving in a slow sinuous fashion on the sheets.

He watched all this in fascination. Her reactions had been different this time, similar but different. He wondered if that meant it felt different? *Probably?* He knew from his own experience that orgasms were different in intensity and sensation depending on how he achieved them and what frame of mind or condition he was in. *I suppose it is the same for women?*

"Good, Em?" he asked, anxious for feedback.

"Hmm," she murmured, bringing her legs together, still moving her hips. She rolled into him and nuzzled her face into his chest, pressing her damp mound against his thigh.

His cock jumped, leaking liquid, and he was reminded of his own tumescent condition and the heated ache in his groin. He pulled her close against him and said with a helpless sort of moan, "Oh, Em." *God, I want you! When will that damned letter arrive from the solicitors?*

She was pressed against him, skin to skin, her hand roaming over his chest and worse yet, her hand moved down until it encountered his engorged cock.

He lay very still as her hand touched him ever so lightly. He swallowed a groan, not wanting to startle her, and waited to see what she would do next. His cock was quivering, and more liquid leaked out the eye. Her oiled fingers stroked him, and he couldn't restrain the groan.

"Can I help?" she asked breathlessly. "Show me what to do?"

Wordlessly, because he didn't think his vocal cords would work at this point, he took her hand and wrapped it around his hard shaft, moving it up and down slowly. After a stroke or two he moved her hand up and showed her how to smear the moisture over the head, pulling the foreskin fully clear of the crown.

"Like this?" she said, moving her hand up and down slowly from crown to base.

With his eyes closed, he nodded. Finding his voice, he croaked, "It's most sensitive on the head."

"I see," she said, concentrating her hand over the crown and the place just below it, moving it up and down more rapidly. He groaned again; it was so exquisite. Her hand was small and felt very different to his own, but the whole notion of her doing it was so arousing he didn't think he would last long. He knew a momentary panic at how she would react to his seed spilling all over his belly, but he had reached the point of overwrought arousal where he didn't think he could stop.

His hips pumped up into her grip with increasing speed and his grunts and groans became positively animalistic. He managed to refrain from swearing aloud. But the words formed in his mind as he hit the point of no return, the hot rush of pleasure seized his body and his cock erupted, jerking in her grip and spilling hot come all over his belly.

Panting, his body slumped back against the pillows, and he lay with his eyes closed, waiting for her exclamation of disgust. When there was none, he opened his eyes and watched her let go of his cock slowly and raise her hand to her mouth and lick a drop of his seed off the back of it. She closed her eyes as she tasted it and smiled. "It's slightly salty and slightly sweet."

Her reaction, so far from disgust, made his throat tighten.

"Emily," his voice was husky.

"Was that all right?" she asked anxiously.

"Emily!" He scooped her up against him and hugged her tight.

"I gather it was then?" she said.

He nodded, unable to speak.

"Well then," she said with such a note of satisfaction he was tempted to laugh. He used his shirt to wipe the mess off his belly. Discarding the shirt, he settled himself back against the sheets, drawing her close against him.

"Sleep," he murmured against her hair, and she nodded, nestling in.

He lay for a bit trying to fathom the events of the evening, but sleep overcame thought, and it was morning before he knew it.

Chapter Nineteen

THE NEXT MORNING, Deo surveyed what he had uncovered last night, flanked by Emrys and Rob, who had been very excited to learn over dinner that he had found the entrance at last.

"Well, let's get cracking, shall we, old chap?" said Emrys.

In some ways, Deo wished that he and Em could keep this to themselves, but the whole household was invested in this discovery now, and he nodded. "We shall."

With crates and boxes to store things in, paper and cloth to wrap them, as well as brushes, water, and cloths to clean them, if required, Em and the ladies were set up to receive the items they might find once the entrance was clear and the tomb opened. Deo had ensured they had lamps to see by and trowels, scrapers, and brushes for uncovering delicate items. There would be no crude spade work once they gained access to the tomb.

Em had her sketch pad, too, so that she could draw what they found in situ before it was moved.

Smiggens and the groundsmen had done a good job of clearing away the dismantled tree so there was room to work now on the east side of the mound.

The men began by digging out the entrance completely, which took about two hours. The women sieved the earth that the men dug out, looking for anything of interest. They had quite a collection of coins, lots of pottery fragments, and a few beads, pins, and one metal belt tip. But nothing that Deo thought related to the probable contents of the barrow.

They had to dig around some of the severed roots that were still in the soil, and as they dug, it became clear that a few of them had penetrated the wall on this side of the barrow, displacing some of the stones, but the damage was less than Deo had feared it would be.

The entrance—when finally, fully revealed—was set within the dry stone walls on either side and measured about three and a half feet in height and approximately three feet in width. It was entirely blocked by a single flat stone that appeared to have been carved to fit.

"We may be very lucky. Our tomb appears to be not only intact and undisturbed, but hopefully weatherproof, too. If that is true, the level of preservation may be higher than would otherwise be the case," said Deo with satisfaction. "We may even be lucky enough to find the remains of the deceased."

The viscountess shuddered. "Really? Wouldn't even the bone have decomposed by now?"

"It depends on the type of soil. Some seems more favorable for preservation than others. Also, damp and air circulation seem to play a part as well," Deo said, examining the entrance stone. "Our next challenge, gentlemen, is how to get this stone out of the entryway."

"It must weigh several tons!" objected the viscount.

"I think we might be better off trying to remove the lintel stone. It's fairly large in area, about three feet by four I would estimate, but less than a foot thick, and we can get at its edges as it overlaps the plug stone beneath it on all sides that we can see," said the duke.

"I agree," Deo said. "I'll just need to fully uncover the rear side of it. It must be covering a short entry space. We might be able to haul it off with a team of draft horses."

"I'll go see my head groom about getting the horses," said the duke. "You dig out the stone."

Deo grinned at Emrys and the two of them clambered up on top of the mound that was still covered in soil and began digging out the rest of the lintel.

An hour later, the team of four horses was assembled and harnessed and ready to drag the lintel off the top of the plug stone. They looped rope around the lintel on both exposed edges, and those ropes were harnessed to the team.

Once secondary ropes were used to tie the loops to each other across the top of the lintel in two places to stop the ropes slipping off, and with everyone well clear of the area, the duke's groom, Hastings, encouraged the team to pull. Initially nothing happened. But persistence eventually caused a shift in the great lintel stone and with a loud scrape and much dust and debris, the stone inched forward on its platform.

Having gained the momentum, the horses moved forward more rapidly. The stone slid forward with a loud scraping noise and toppled to the ground with a *thunk* in front of the plug stone, edge down. The horses, after a momentary stop, pulled it clear, and with a final plop of dust, it settled flat side down in the dirt, and Hastings brought his team to a halt.

A cheer went up from the company, and Hastings waved and took a bow with a grin in his rusty colored beard.

"Now we will see what's what!" said Deo with a grin at Em. He headed for the mound, climbing up the earth covered cairn to the gap revealed by the removal of the lintel and peered inside. Stone-lined walls and an earth packed floor met his gaze along with some debris that had fallen in with the removal of the lintel.

He turned as Em joined him and leaned over to look inside. He grabbed her, fearful of her toppling in she was so eager to see what was revealed. It was, he thought, roughly a five-foot drop to the bottom, considerably less than his own height.

"Pass me down a lamp," he said, easing himself down and over the lip of the stone into the gap, which was about three feet wide and four feet long. He was right about the height; it came up to his chest.

"What can you see?" called the duke as Deo crouched down.

"A stone lined chamber, roughly rectangular in shape with a roof that slopes. There are some dark shapes, but I don't know what they are yet." He took the lamp passed down to him by Em and set it on the ground, before reaching up to help her down into the hole with him. With his hands on her waist, he set her on her feet and squeezed. "This is it, Em!"

She nodded, her face alight with anticipation. She picked up the lamp, and he crouched to pass under the stone roof, with her following stooped beside him. The light from the hole and the lamp penetrated the darkness. The chamber was roughly six feet wide and he estimated nine feet long, and once they passed into the chamber, the roof was approximately a foot higher than the entry area, allowing Em to stand upright but he still had to duck his head. The smell of damp earth and stone met his nostrils and a musty smell. He almost didn't know what to look at first—the dry-stone construction of the tomb or its contents. The draw of the contents won out as Em exclaimed, "Look, Deo, what is that?"

A roughly rectangular depression in the ground in the center of the chamber, partially filled with debris, was illuminated by the lamp.

"Do you think that is the burial?" she asked.

"Yes, most likely." Deo squatted beside the edge of the depression. "I think the space was dug out to lay the body in and a wooden lid placed over the top, most of which has disintegrated, and other debris has fallen in on top."

He glanced around the chamber. The floor was uneven, and a layer of debris covered everything. The shapes he had seen from outside as he'd looked in from the entry, resolved themselves as blocks of stone that seemed to have fallen from the roof. Or perhaps they were just leftovers not used by the builders. He couldn't see any gaps in the roof where stone could have fallen from. The stone they had put back into place the other day plugged the only gap he could see.

"What shall we do first?" asked Em.

"Fetch your sketch pad. We should record everything, including measurements. I have a leather measure for that, with string for long stretches. Come on, the others will be busting to know what we are seeing." He headed back to the entrance, trailed by Em.

The duke, the duchess, and the Ashfords had gathered round the entrance, looking down into the hole from above. Deo addressed them. "We have found what we think is the burial, a depression in the ground. Pass down Em's sketchbook and pencils and my measuring tape—it's the leather coil—and also the ball of string on the wooden spindle. Once we have recorded the basics, we will start excavating the burial."

"Is there room for the rest of us down there?" asked the duke.

"It will be a bit crowded, but yes, I suppose. Hand down the stepladder for the ladies."

At this point a "Hoi!" from further afield brought Deo's head around, as Kenrick hove into view with Bidenden. The latter appeared no worse for wear from his ordeal, he had apparently only sustained bruising.

"Thought we'd come and see how you were faring," said Kenrick with a grin.

"Deo says we've found the burial, but we will have to excavate it yet to find out what is in it," said the duke. "We were just about to pop down and have a look."

With the addition of the two men, it was agreed they would come down in pairs. So, the duke and duchess came down first, and the duke helped Deo with the measurements while the duchess recorded them, and Em sketched the interior of the burial chamber.

"I should have thought to sketch the entrance before we removed the lintel," she said.

"Can you do it from memory?" asked Deo, stretching his leather measure along the long side of the burial depression.

"I can try, but it won't be as accurate."

With the preliminaries taken care of, the duke and duchess vacated for the viscount and his lady, who brought down with them the digging tools and an extra lamp.

The viscountess clutched her husband's hand and shivered. "I don't know what it is, but tombs always give me the shudders."

"The ghoulies won't get you, Annis, I won't let them," said Emrys, putting an arm around his wife's waist.

She smiled up at him fondly and said, "I know, it's all nonsense. I shouldn't be afraid."

Emrys kissed her forehead and Deo looked away at this blatant display of affection, even as he wondered if he and Emily would ever behave like that.

"So can we help?" asked Emrys, coming to crouch down by Deo who was kneeling on one side of the depression. Em was in position on the other side.

"Not with the digging, old chap, but you could pass up the buckets of debris we pull out for the ladies to sieve through."

"Happy to," said Emrys with cheerful agreement. The viscountess went back up to join the duchess with the sieving, and Emrys passed the buckets of debris up to the duke. Kenrick and Bidenden clambered down to have a brief look at operations, and Deo was annoyed to see Bidenden crouch down by Em and speak to her. As Kenrick and Emrys were having a conversation at that point right beside him, he couldn't hear what Bidenden and Em were saying. But Em nodded at his ribs, as if asking him how he did. He seemed to make light of it and ask something to do with her sketchbook, because she held it out to show him some of the pictures in it.

Deo clenched his teeth and, restraining his dog-in-a-manger instincts, forced himself to look away from them and pay attention to the conversation going on next to him. Shortly after that, Kenrick and Bidenden withdrew, and Deo was able to relax and concentrate on the job at hand.

Many so-called excavators were nothing more than grave

robbers in Deo's opinion, their methods rough and ready, looking only for the most valuable items and oblivious to the historical data to be gleaned from careful, painstaking clearance of a tomb. He was not of their number. He believed that good records and careful removal were essential to recovering and preserving as much of the find and its historical significance as possible. Therefore, he and Em took their time removing the debris in layers with small trowels and checking each trowel's contents with a quick sort of the fingers, before dumping it in the buckets.

An hour later they had got through the debris layer and the fragments of wood from the lid and that was when the real finds began to reveal themselves.

"Deo?" Em's excited tone made him look up from his careful sifting of a trowel full of dirt in which he thought he had detected a faint glint of gold. "Look!" said Em, pointing with her trowel at something. She picked up her brush and dusted it over the object. She was working at the western end of the grave and he at the eastern end, nearest the entrance.

He kneed up closer to see what she was working on, and as she brushed, something green-tinged began to emerge. At first a round knob and then, surrounding it, a convex disk of metal about nine or ten inches in diameter revealed itself. The outer rim of the disk was layered with a strip in which hints of a design were visible through the green corrosion on the object.

"It's a bronze shield-boss, I think," she said excitedly. "Of Celtic design, you can see a hint of the knot work in the outer strip." She looked up at him, her face alight with joy at the discovery. "Oh, this far exceeds anything I thought we would find!"

He grinned as delighted as she. *This is what we went through all that pain for, and it was worth every minute of it!*

The viscount climbed back down with an empty bucket at that moment. "You've found something?"

"Yes!" Em waved at her find, and continued carefully brushing away the dirt surrounding it as the viscount came to crouch beside her and look. "It's bronze. The green corrosion should clean up. I can't wait to see what it looks like restored. Oh, this is marvelous."

"What is it exactly?" asked Emrys.

"A shield boss!" said Em, grinning at him. "And I think it has a Celtic design. Deo, this confirms our burial is an Anglo-Celtic warrior, yes?"

"It would seem likely, Em. We need to try to identify the names if we can. But it is strongly suggestive, I would say,"

Emrys fetched the duke, duchess, and viscountess down to watch Em carefully clearing the shield boss and its surrounds.

"The wooden shield it was attached to has rotted away, but if we're lucky we might find the metal bar grip if this is from a round shield. The later ones had leather straps and were shaped like kites." Her brush swept wider and found something else. "Deo!" Her excited cry had him moving closer.

"Deo, I think there is an outer ring from the shield! Look!" She dusted furiously and revealed a concentric ring of metal about four inches wide surrounding the inner boss about eight inches farther out. "Oh, I have to sketch this!" she said, removing the last of the debris from the top of the find. The outer ring was also corroded green and hinted at some sort of pattern embossed into the surface.

Deo returned to his careful removal and dusting and was rewarded a few minutes later by a find that took his breath away.

"Em—"

She looked up from her sketchbook. "What have you found?"

"I think," he said, dusting carefully, and trying not to let his voice shake, "I've found an Anglo-Saxon drinking horn with silver mounts."

"No!" Em got up and came round to his side to look as he sat back a bit to show her. The conical shape of the horn was clear, and the darkly tarnished mounts hinted that they were silver. "Celtic and Anglo-Saxon finds in the one burial?"

He nodded. "It certainly suggests our fellow could claim

descent from both. He must be a Briton or a Saxon with a significant British heritage."

"But for the British elements to have survived Roman occupation in this area suggests a strong influence of some kind."

"It does. Or connections to the north or west which were still firmly under British control at that time." He delicately dusted round the horn, which appeared to be lying on more fragments of disintegrated wood. He looked around at Emrys standing behind him. "Can your wife draw? I think we are going to need more than one artist to capture these finds."

"She can," said Emrys. "I'll fetch her."

The finds came thick and fast after that, and Deo and Em were unwilling to leave the tomb for luncheon, so the meal came to them. They sat on a blanket by the mound and ate, then the whole team resumed working.

The remains of the body were found beneath the plethora of finds that included weapons and jewelry, glass cups, and even a fragment of cloth, mineralized by being attached to a brooch. Amazingly, a more or less complete skeleton was recovered from beneath the grave goods that had been piled on top of him.

By Deo's estimation, the presumed male was approximately five foot eight inches tall. The skull was proportional to the body with most of its teeth intact, if a little worn, indicating that the man was probably middle aged. A break in the cranium, consistent with a blade, seemed a likely indication of the cause of death.

Noting this, Em said, "So he is a warrior!"

"Yes, it seems so." Deo smiled at her excitement.

But the prize find was discovered last, buried beneath the body. They almost missed it.

It was growing dark by the time they removed the last of the bones and placed them carefully in labeled boxes. Em was scraping the bottom of the burial pit for any more fragments of wood or bone when her trowel hit something. She scraped at it and revealed a gleam of gold.

"Deo!" she squealed, using her brush to sweep the dirt away from the object.

Deo turned back from the entrance and, stooping over, he came toward her.

"What—" He stopped, stunned.

Almost speechless with excitement, Em waved at the convex curve of gold revealed by her brush. It took another ten minutes of careful brush work and digging to reveal the item and remove it from its earthen bed. It was a gold goblet, with a flared base and globe shape, like a large marble, between the base and the cup part of the goblet. It was plain and smooth, no decoration. But despite being buried in the earth for hundreds of years, it gleamed like new, which meant it had to be solid gold.

After wrapping it in cloth and transferring it reverently to a box while the others looked on in awe, Deo carried it to the surface. It was almost dark now.

Weary but happy, the excavation party loaded the boxes and baskets onto a cart and wheeled it carefully back to the house, where the items were carried reverentially into the library and laid out on the big trestle tables that had been set up there for the purpose. Deo and Em had days of careful examination and recording ahead of them.

But for tonight, a bath, dinner, and sleep were high on the agenda. Over dinner, the excavation party entertained Kenrick and Bidenden with tales of what had been discovered. Deo let Emrys and Rob do most of the talking. He was done in—and content. They had uncovered and captured a major find. He would get plenty of opportunities to address the Antiquaries Society on the topic and write papers about their *comes*. With Em's help. He was determined she should fully share the credit for the discovery. Which would no doubt put several learned gentlemen's noses out of joint, who thought women weren't good for anything except having babies.

He glanced at Em and caught her yawning behind her hand. The emotions of the day, coming on top of yesterday's drama, were no doubt exhausting.

He thought about sweeping her off upstairs to bed, to pick up where they had left off last night. But they were both so tired that further amorous adventures might have to wait. But a man could dream, couldn't he?

Chapter Twenty

BRYSON TOYED WITH his wine glass as the servants cleared the last of the meal away and Pendrell and Emily announced they were retiring immediately. When the ladies also withdrew, the duke offered to show his brother, Ashford, and Bryson the new finds, which had dominated the conversation over dinner.

"Sure, why not?" said Kenrick. Bryson, whose ears pricked up when told of the treasures that had been recovered from the tomb, followed them to the library. *Perhaps my insurance policy will pay off after all.*

The duke led the way. "It was most exciting to see each item revealed from the dirt. They don't look like much at the moment, but I am assured by Deo that when they are properly cleaned and displayed, they will look quite spectacular. Aberdeen will want them for the museum, of course, as is proper."

"You won't keep anything for yourself, Your Grace?" asked Bryson, closing the library door behind him as he was the last to enter.

"Deo and I agree they belong in the museum. Although I'm a little surprised he doesn't want to keep anything for his own collection."

"The items were found on your land, Your Grace. Don't they belong, by rights, to you?"

The duke shrugged. "Technically, but I'm a firm believer that our heritage should be shared in the public domain. If the body belonged to an ancestor, it might be different, but this fellow seemingly predates the Layne occupation of this land by several hundred years."

"Deo and Emily have tentatively dated him to the sixth century, I believe," said Ashford, who had accompanied them.

The duke turned to the large trestle table set up in the middle of the room upon which rested a number of boxes and crates. He took the lid off one box and invited them to look at the contents. Nestled in the cloth within was an elegant gold goblet that would not look out of place on a modern dining table. "This is probably the piece that will draw the most attention."

"The Holy Grail, eh?" said Kenrick with a raised eyebrow.

"Well, it could be, for all we know," said the duke with a smile that indicated he didn't for a minute think it was.

"The fellow was buried under a Celtic cross, was he not?" asked Bryson, betraying he had been paying more attention than he was wont to show.

"Aye," said Ashford. "I'm fascinated to hear what theories Deo and Emily are going to put forward about this burial and its occupant. My wife has a few of her own. You can take the governess out of the schoolroom, but you can't take the schoolroom out of the governess!" He smiled with a peculiar pride. Bryson couldn't see that admitting your wife was a former governess was anything to boast about.

The duke put the lid back on the goblet and moved onto the other items. The shield and the drinking horn seemed to Bryson to be potentially the most interesting items historically. Unless of course the goblet really was a candidate for the Holy Grail? *Could I manufacture a tale to give that credence? If so, the goblet would become almost priceless . . . Something to consider there.*

The other items of interest included a square-armed cross in gold and rubies and a silver brooch with sapphires. There was also a belt buckle in bronze, tarnished like the shield, but it should clean up nicely. The rest were of less interest. A set of green glass cups, three iron daggers and the remains of an iron sword, two wooden buckets identified only by their surviving corroded metal rings and handles.

Leaving the treasures to join the ladies, Bryson pondered what his next move would be. Best to leave the treasures where they were for the moment, at least until they had been cleaned and fresh drawings done of them. With the sketches, he could send off a letter to his broker to approach his father for an offer on the items. Then it would be a simple matter to appropriate them and disappear. But not before Emily's parents arrived. He wanted to wait and see if he had any hope of snatching her from Pendrell.

If he was to remove the items before he left, where would he put them? He needed somewhere secure that no one would find, and which no one would associate with him if they did, by some mischance, find them.

⭻⭻⭻⭻

EMERGING FROM THE dressing room in his nightshirt and robe, Deo expected to see Em curled up in bed, but there was no sign of her. He went through to the sitting room and found her bent over the rubbing of the cross spread out on the desk.

"I thought you'd be in bed; you were yawning so much earlier."

"I got to thinking about this rubbing," she said. "I was sure I remembered there being a fragment of another line of text, and I was right. Look," she pointed to the bottom of the rubbing. "The cross is broken off at an angle; there must be another piece. Do you think we can find it?"

"We can certainly look," he said, wrapping an arm around her waist and tugging her back against him. "But not tonight. I'm exhausted, and so are you."

"Yes, but I'm so excited I don't know how I will sleep."

"I can think of one way," he said, husky voiced, kissing her neck. He had been conscious of her all day, even throughout all the excitement of the finds, but trying not to think about it. Her rosewater scent reminded him of how delicious she was. Yes, it was unwise to continue their bed games, but the temptation was more than he could withstand.

Today's events had consolidated in his mind the certainty that Em was his partner for life. He couldn't imagine going forward now without her by his side. She was his perfect match, and he adored her.

He nuzzled her neck, and she said with faint delight, "Deo."

He scooped her up and carried her into the bedroom, deposited her gently on the bed, shed his robe, and climbed in with her. There was still the matter of their actual marital status to work out, but that was hard to remember when she was here in his arms. Kes jumped up on the bed and made himself comfortable on their feet.

"Em, today would not have been anywhere near as wonderful without you," he said, sliding his arms round her.

"Oh, Deo, I feel the same. You made the day wonderful for me," she said, snuggling into his chest. A warm satisfaction and contentment spread through his body, making his normally tense muscles relax.

He let out a faint sigh and settled back into the pillows. "Em, there is something I've been meaning to ask you," he said hesitantly.

"Yes?" she looked up at him.

"I understood your reluctance to go home when you explained how you were treated, but I wanted to ask if your parents made a practice of that sort of thing?"

"Starving me, you mean?" asked Em, with a quirk of her lips.

"Well, yes, that is an outrageous example. But I meant any disproportionate punishment."

"Oh yes, starving me was one of Mama's favorite tactics,

although she had never imposed it for that long before, or so ruthlessly. Generally, it was just missing a meal or two. But in this case, the servants were forbidden to speak to me or help me on pain of dismissal without a reference." She said this quite matter-of-factly.

He was appalled. "Em, that is outrageous. The worst kind of abuse!"

"It's no worse than the way you were treated, Deo. In fact, I think it is far less dreadful. I did receive some affection, you know. It was just conditional on doing what Mama wanted."

"What about your father? Was he kind to you?"

She shrugged. "He is far too afraid of Mama to stand up to her for me. He wanted a son, you see. He needed an heir, and he was stuck with me, a useless girl, instead."

"You are not useless!" he said fiercely and squeezed her tight.

She squeaked and giggled. "Well, no, I don't feel useless after today, but I used to feel—oh, I don't know! As if I didn't fit anywhere. Mama was forever nagging me to be something I'm not—sit up straight, smile, curtsy, dance, converse on the stupidest topics, try to be pretty and desirable to gentlemen—when all I wanted to do was read and study antiquities. And talk to someone who understood!"

"Exactly!" He swallowed the sudden lump in his throat. "That is exactly how I felt."

She burst into giggles. "Deo, I cannot imagine you curtsying!"

He stared at her for a moment and then his lips twitched, and he burst out laughing. Which made her laugh harder until there were tears streaming down her cheeks and she collapsed on him, gasping for breath. "Oh, please, stop, my ribs hurt!" she said, going into another fit of giggles.

"Emily Frances, you are delightful!" he kissed her forehead and wiped at the tears on her cheeks with his thumbs.

"Mama only called me Emily Frances when she was angry with me," she said with a sigh. "Which was a lot of the time."

"I cannot wait to make your mother's acquaintance," he said

a little grimly. "I shall disabuse her of the notion that you are anything less than perfect."

"Oh, Deo!" She flung her arms round his neck and kissed him. Which put paid to conversation for a while as he forgot all his vows of continence and pushed her back into the pillows for a thorough kissing.

EMILY SQUIRMED BENEATH him, her body set alight instantly by his kisses. *Will he make me his wife indeed tonight?* It would be the perfect cap to a perfect day. She wanted him quite desperately, she had come to realize over the previous days, and she was a little puzzled by his insistence that they wait on the solicitor's letter. What difference did it make? He had already said they would repeat their vows if necessary, and if he took her, then Bidenden would stop this nonsense of trying to claim her as his.

She had felt sorry for him when he was injured by the falling tree, but she had no interest in him compared to Deo.

There was no doubt in her mind that Deo was the man she was meant for, and she wanted so much to be able to say she belonged to him and only him in every sense, forever.

Deo tugged at her nightgown, so she sat up to help him get it off over her head. And she was so pleased when he removed his nightshirt and settled back onto her body with nothing between them. *Yes!* She exulted. It seemed she was to get her wish.

Deo resumed their kisses, his hands roving over her body, cupping and squeezing her breasts in a way she found delightful. Her breasts were small, and she had worried that they were inadequate, but Deo didn't seem to find them so.

Deo ran his lips down her neck, which set tingles off on her skin and the heated ache between her legs intensified. "You're so delicious, Em. I can't get enough of you," he murmured, and she grinned with pleasure.

"So are you," she whispered, her hands roaming over his big body. His mouth continued south and when his lips closed over one of her nipples, she arched her back with a cry, as a bolt of aching heat shot to the place between her thighs. His tongue worried at the nipple and his mouth suckled in an extraordinary way that had her writhing with need and whimpering like a puppy.

"Em," he said breathlessly, transferring his mouth to her other nipple and continuing to fondle the damp one with his fingers. The double assault made her buck under him. The ache between her legs demanded something, some pressure, *something!* She moved her legs, tangling with his and pushing up into his thigh when it came down between hers.

She made a sound between a moan and grunt, grinding herself shamelessly on his leg. She could feel the hot, hard length of his member pressing into her belly.

Will he take me now? Please, Deo! She panted, trying to move her legs to spread them for him, but he seemed oblivious of her efforts. Instead of repositioning himself between her legs, he moved his mouth down to her belly in a series of damp kisses, moving slowly lower until his mouth was pressed to the crinkly hair covering her mound and the merest inch from the place that ached so ferociously.

In the next instant he moved a fraction lower and set his mouth right on that spot.

She bucked in shock. "Deo!"

He pressed her hips down with his hands and did it again with a muffled sound that was part groan, part expletive, she thought.

Then his lips parted, and his tongue touched her, just there! It was the lightest of touches, but its effect was devastatingly pleasurable. She groaned and gasped. "Deo!"

He did it again, and again, until he was lapping her flesh in a way that had her writhing and moaning helplessly. It was the most intense pleasure she had ever experienced, and her breath came in gasps, her pulse thundering in her ears as the pleasure wound up and up into a tight ball and exploded, sending a cascade of intense tingles through her body in waves to her very extremities.

"Ohh!" she moaned, her body going gradually lax as a pleasurable lethargy took hold of her.

Deo sat up on his haunches and grinned at her, wiping his chin with his shirt.

"You liked that," he said with such a self-satisfied air that she laughed.

"Yes, yes, I did."

"Good. I wasn't sure, but I couldn't resist tasting you." He leaned over her, resting his weight in his hands on either side of her shoulders. His hard member was pointing straight at her. She reached out to touch it, and he jerked and groaned.

"Em!"

"Are you going to do something with this?" she asked boldly, hoping he would say yes.

"If you'd like to stroke me, I wouldn't say no," he said, panting a bit.

"Wouldn't you rather put it inside me?" asked Em, stroking him gently with her fingers, running her thumb over the head, where moisture was gathering.

He bucked his hips with a groan, his eyes closing. "God, Em, you'd tempt a saint!"

"You want to?" she said, rubbing her sticky thighs together and continuing to stroke him.

"Of course I want to!" he panted. "I've thought of nothing else for days!"

"Well—"

"No." He opened his eyes and visibly gulped. "I promised you all the proprieties would be met. We will be married properly before—oh God, Em!" His voice became strangled as she rubbed the crown of his member with her fingers.

"How do you know we are not?" she asked.

"I am almost certain we are not. I did not get your father's permission. You are underage, Em. Oh fuck, woman!" His eyes closed again. "Finish me, please?"

She regarded him with a mixture of frustration and affection. And inspired by what he had done for her, she slid down the bed until she was positioned so that she could get her mouth on his member. Leaning her head up, she swallowed the head.

"Fuck, Em!" His eyes flew open, and he stared down at her, his hips jerking in reflex. She grasped his length and sucked on the large bulbous head; it was the most extraordinary feeling to have it in her mouth. It made her core pulse and ache. She could taste the salty sweetness of that fluid, as she moved her tongue against the hot, hard flesh.

"Em!" his voice took on a desperate note. "Your neck might get sore in that position. Move back up to the pillows."

She agreed and elbowed her way back up the bed and sank into the pillows. He kneed closer to her, until she could take him in her fist and her mouth again.

Straddling her body with his knees, he grasped the headboard of the bed to keep his balance. With his great thighs on either side of her head, she was enveloped in the musky scent of his maleness, and it made her body pulse in response.

"Hold your fist against the base," he panted. "That will stop me choking you."

She nodded, moving her fist to the base of his member and taking more of him into her mouth. She loved the feel of it filling her mouth. Was this something like how it would feel to have him inside that other part of her body? She couldn't fathom how; it was so different, surely. Yet she still found this arousing. Heat was gathering between her legs.

"I'll pull out before I—" His voice broke on a groan as her tongue swirled round the head, and she sucked, imitating as best she could what he had done to her nipples. They were smaller, but the principle seemed the same.

He swore again. She had never heard Deo swear before; that was three times in as many minutes. He was clearly deeply affected. She smiled round his member, pleased to have such an effect on him.

Then he drew back his hips and thrust forward into her mouth and she tightened her grip on the base, allowing him to use her mouth for his pleasure. She glanced up at him. His eyes were closed, and his expression was twisted in an almost feral expression of desire. She had never seen him so aroused, and a heated pulse of desire throbbed between her legs. His breathing was audible, and his grunts and moans told her he was close to losing all control as the thrust of his hips got deeper and more frantic, forcing his member almost to the back of her throat with each stroke.

He groaned loudly and wrenched backward, clear of her mouth, and she watched fascinated, as his member jerked, and gobs of opaque fluid spurted out the eye in several shots. It was hot and sticky. A dob landed on her chin, and the rest daubed her breasts in streaks and blobs. She watched as the organ pulsed, disgorging the last of its load, a final drop landing between her breasts.

Deo leaned against the headboard; his eyes closed as he got his breath back.

Emily traced a finger through the rapidly cooling puddle on her breasts and was in the act of raising it to her mouth to taste it again, when he opened his eyes and gazed down at her, his expression going from relaxed to horrified.

"Oh God, I'm sorry!" he said, his face flushing.

She raised her eyebrows in surprise. "For what?" she asked, sticking her finger in her mouth and grinning. "It's still salty-sweet, what a treat!" She scooped up a bit more, and he just goggled at her, his jaw dropped.

"Here, let me," he reached for his night shirt and wiped up the mess swiftly.

"Yes, I suppose I can't eat it all," she said, disappointed.

"Oh, Em!" He slid down beside her and pulled her close, tucking her face into his shoulder.

"What?" she said, slightly bewildered by his reaction. "Did you enjoy it?" she asked anxiously.

"Yes—yes, of course I did!" his voice sounded oddly thick, and she pulled her head back to look up at him. He blinked, but it didn't disguise the tears in his eyes.

She put up a hand to his face, alarmed. "Oh, Deo, what's wrong?"

"Nothing!" He swallowed visibly and sniffed. "You are the most perfect woman in the world," he said, his voice cracking. Holding her tight, he buried his face in her hair.

She wrapped her arms round him and whispered, "You are the most perfect man."

"No," he sniffed again. "No, but you make me feel like one."

She nuzzled into him, and he shifted to make her more comfortable. She yawned, the day's activities suddenly catching up with her.

"We should try to find the rest of the cross tomorrow," she murmured.

"Yes, we should. Go to sleep, sweetheart," he murmured back.

She relaxed on a breath, and very soon sleep took her.

DEO HELD HIS wife—*because, damn it, she is my wife in spirit if not in fact*—and listened to her breathe. *I love her. I love her so much it hurts.* He was ashamed of his past weaknesses. His stupid embarrassment that had held him hostage for so many years. Em's reaction to being covered in his seed was so natural and delightful he wondered how he could have been so afraid of something so silly for so long. *I didn't think I knew how to love, but she has taught me by the example of her sweet caring spirit. Does she love me? She hasn't said so, but then neither have I.*

That letter from the solicitors must arrive soon. Then we can settle things, and I can say how I really feel and hope she feels the same.

He swallowed down his irrational fear that he was inherently unlovable. *If my parents didn't love me, who would or could?* He pushed the painful thought away and took comfort from Em's warm body pressed against his. It seemed she *could* and *did*, if her behavior was any indication. It would be nice to hear her say so, but he needed to be brave enough to tell her how he felt first. It was the man's privilege and pain to risk rebuff. He had thought to avoid all the messy complications of emotions, but he now saw how hollow and empty that was beside the richness that his connection with Em offered. When they made their second set of vows, as he was now convinced they would need to do, it would be in a very different spirit from the first time.

He sighed and closed his eyes.

Chapter Twenty-One

D EO HAD AGREED with Em that he would try to find the other half of the cross this morning, and they would spend the afternoon working on the finds from yesterday. Learning over breakfast of their intention to find the rest of the text, the viscount offered to help Deo dig. Em had been torn between wanting to be there if they found the cross and wanting to work on the finds, but in the end she decided to stay at the house and work on them. So it was himself and Ashford prosecuting the search for the broken base of the cross.

"If it is here at all, it must be buried, but hopefully not too deep. It must have been broken in antiquity. I am beginning to think, deliberately," said Deo, digging his spade into the soil around the base of the stone tomb. The plan was to work outward from the base in a six-foot radius, with exploratory digs every square foot or so, down to the depth of a foot.

"Did he fall into disgrace with some ancient king?" offered Emrys, digging cheerfully.

"It's possible. That could explain the partial erasure of the names and title. But somehow, I don't think so. If that were the case, the tomb would have been desecrated, too. We are damned lucky it wasn't robbed in antiquity. It must have been forgotten. For which I can only assume the damage, breaking, and burial of the cross was responsible."

"What's your theory then?" asked Emrys, stopping to wipe his brow with a handkerchief. They were working on the west side of the tomb, Emrys on the southern and he on the northern end, moving toward each other. They had completed two concentric rows so far and found nothing. Deo surveyed their little holes and mounds of earth, *like the work of so many moles!* He smiled in whimsy. He missed Em's presence. Without her, things seemed less vibrant. She injected such enthusiasm and delight into everything. A lick of heat raced through his blood at the memory of last night's antics. They really should stop; it was dicing with the worst kind of temptation. Yet it was so addictive he didn't know *how* to stop.

"Theory, Deo?" prompted Emrys.

Jerked back to the present, Deo stuck his spade in the ground and said, "My theory is that the cross was damaged because of the struggle for supremacy between the Celtic and Catholic versions of Christianity that raged during the sixth and seventh centuries. The Celtic flavor was the older version, endemic to Ireland and Britain, the Catholic version came from Rome. King Oswy of Northumbria was raised in the Celtic faith in Dál Riata, the Irish settlement in Scotland. The chief proponent of the Catholic doctrine was Bishop Wilfrid. He and Oswy fell out and Oswy had him banished by all accounts. But Wilfrid got his way in the end and the Celtic doctrine was all but stamped out eventually."

"So, our fellow was Celtic Christian then?"

"The cross would seem to indicate he was, yes." Deo stuck his spade in the ground for a second go at this particular hole, and it hit something hard. "Ah!" he exclaimed, and did it again with the same result. Scraping up a shovelful of earth, he dumped it aside and dug again. "I might have something."

Emrys stopped digging, and came over to him, while Deo dug out around the irregularly shaped object in the ground.

"I think this might be it!" He grinned at Emrys, and knelt to scrape around the shape with his fingers. The earth was cool and damp. He rose and exposed more of the object with his spade. He had initially uncovered what seemed to be the square, stone base of the cross, apparently tipped over on its side. A bit more digging revealed the rest of a shaft with an angled, uneven end. He knelt again to scrape more earth from around the shape and Emrys joined him.

With the earth clear, they could get their fingers underneath the heavy stone but couldn't dislodge it from its bed.

"I think we need some rope," said Deo.

"I'll get it," said Emrys, springing to his feet and heading over to the coils of rope still lying by the side of the mound. They looped the rope about the shaft and hauled it upright and, from there, manhandled it out of the hole to lay flat on the grass, with the text side up.

"Go fetch Em, will you? She won't want to miss this. And tell her to bring the paper and charcoal for rubbing," said Deo, heading over to fetch the brush, cloths, and water to clean the surface of any earth still clinging to the cross.

"On my way!" said Emrys and trotted off toward the house. He returned twenty minutes later with Em, just as Deo had got the text cleaned.

"You found it!" said Em, dropping to her knees beside him. "Is the text—oh yes, it is! How marvelous!"

"It's a little damaged because of the break, but the blow seems to have been made from the other side of the shaft, and most of it is legible, I think," said Deo.

"Let's see what we can get with the rubbing, shall we?" Em placed the paper she had brought over the stone and applied the charcoal. In a matter of moments, she had the text rendered in charcoal on the paper. "This is so exciting, Deo," she said, lifting the paper up.

Deo nodded. "Take it back to the house, Em. We will decipher it there. Emrys and I will just tidy up here."

She smiled and set off with her prize, and Deo watched her go with a besotted grin. He wanted to say to Emrys *Isn't she adorable?* But reticence stopped his tongue.

"Yes," said Emrys.

"What?" said Deo, startled.

Emrys grinned at him and punched him on the shoulder. "Go on, admit it."

Deo flushed scarlet. "Admit what?"

"How much you adore her. It's written all over your face, man."

"Hmm," mumbled Deo. "I've been meaning to thank you for the idea of advertising. Best thing I ever did." He swallowed and cleared his throat. "You're right, I do adore her. She's—" words failed him, and he shook his head.

"I know," said Emrys quietly. "I feel that way about Annis."

Deo looked at him and smiled. "We're lucky devils."

"We are. Rob too. Just Jerome left now."

"He's a hard case," said Deo, gathering up the equipment, while Emrys recoiled the rope.

"I don't know," said Emrys. "I think there is more to him than he lets on."

"I used to envy him," said Deo. "The way he could talk to women, have them fall at his feet. Now?" He shook his head, grinning and thinking of Em. "I wouldn't be him for anything under the sun."

DEO AND EMILY spent the afternoon working on the finds in companionable accord, interrupted by bursts of discussion on several points. Emily had wanted to work on deciphering the text from the cross straightaway, but Deo had suggested they leave that until after dinner. So she went back to cleaning and sketching. She didn't think it was possible to be so happy as she was now. She couldn't resist glancing up every now and then to look at him, bent over the big desk in the library, compiling notes for a document that would record the process of the excavation and their finds. *It will be our first joint paper. I will get my name on a paper!*

She knew how fortunate she was that Deo was prepared to share the credit with her. Many wives in this field of endeavor did not get such consideration from their husbands, irrespective of their contributions. Deo had made it clear he respected her input and wanted to ensure it was recognized in full.

When she thought of the misery of her existence a mere few weeks ago, it seemed incredible that her life could change so dramatically and for the better in such a short time. To think she could have been preparing to marry Bidenden at this very time. Her stomach swooped at the notion, and she had to resist the urge to get up from her seat and kiss her husband just to reassure herself all of this was real.

It had been extremely real last night. Their shared passion was another revelation to her. She wished that dratted solicitor's letter would arrive so that Deo would allow them to progress to full intimacy. She was very much looking forward to that. She grinned to herself. Then she would feel like a real wife, and they would be bonded properly. It all felt a bit in limbo at the moment.

She certainly hoped that she had convinced Viscount Bidenden to abandon his ridiculous notion that she would give up Deo for him. She would never do that in a million years. The idea was absurd. She would live with Deo in sin before she would contemplate marriage with anyone else.

The afternoon flew by and they joined the others for dinner, where the conversation still revolved mostly around the finds and speculation about who the mysterious occupant of the mound was.

As soon after dinner as they could politely excuse themselves, they made their way to their sitting room, and Emily got out the rubbing. Spreading it on the desk beside the other one, they matched up the two where the break was. The letters of the first word of the new bit of text were interrupted by the break, and there wasn't much to go on. But the rest was more legible than the original part of the text.

_____ IN P_____IO APUD BEDDEIGYR CECIDIT

"This second to last word must be a proper noun—a location or a name, I think," said Emily. "Why does it sound familiar?"

Deo chewed his lip. "It's hard to make out, but I think this first missing word is *qui*—who. See the upper part of the curve of the Q is visible on the original piece and the curve of the bottom of the U and a fraction of the downward stroke of the I is visible on this piece."

"Yes, I agree. So, this portion definitely relates to our *comes* mentioned in the first line of text!"

"This part—*cecidit*—is clear; that means 'fell.' And if this partial word is *proelio* for 'battle' or 'fight,' it refers to someone who fell in battle."

"So—the Battle of Beddeigyr!" finished Emily, bouncing in her seat. "*HIC IACET something-GYN COMES DE CAERLYR FILIUS WIG-something QUI IN PROELIO APUD BEDDEIGYR CECIDIT.*"

"Here lies Something-gyn, Earl of Caerlyr, son of Wig-something, who in Battle at Beddeigyr fell."

"I do wish we could work out what their full names are," she sighed. "What and when was the Battle of Beddeigyr? And why does that name sound so familiar?"

"I'm not sure, but we can find out," said Deo, getting up and going to a pile of books on the side table.

"Oh, why can't I think? I'm sure I know this!" said Emily, frowning at the part of the text she had written out on the parchment in front of her. *Eigyr*.

"*Eigyr* is a personal name that means maiden!" She bounced up excitedly. "*Bedd* is Welsh for grave and *Eigyr* means maiden. So, grave of the maiden!"

"What is *Eigyr* in English? I feel like I should know." Deo said. Then answered his own question. "Igraine?"

"*Beddeigyr*. Bedeigraine."

Deo paused in his sorting through the pile of books and straightened slowly. "Igraine is Arthur's mother."

Emily's eyes widened and her mouth fell open. "Oh, gosh yes, you're right. King Arthur! But—we can't have stumbled across anything to do with him, can we?"

Deo shook his head. "Unlikely. He's considered by many scholars now to be more legend than real—"

"True, but even so, surely there is a man behind the legend. Someone real who may not have performed all those fabulous feats, but who was impressive enough to change history. Someone remembered as Arthur, King of the Britons."

"Yes, certainly. I agree with that. I think there was such a fellow," Deo conceded. "A Dark Age king who held back the Saxon tide for a generation or more."

"Then isn't our *comes* too late for Arthur?"

"Not really, Em. Most of the tales associate Arthur with sixth century British kings like Urien and Cador."

"Oh!" Emily sat down abruptly, her legs giving out.

"Are you all right?" he said in alarm, coming to her side.

"Yes, yes! It's just—overwhelming! I mean Arthur! The greatest king in British history!"

"Hold on a minute, Em. We don't *know* it's anything to do with him at all, the name may just be a coincidence."

She took a breath and let it out slowly. "You're right, of course. I'm getting ahead of myself. But oh, Deo, I've got tingles, what if it *is*?"

"Only one way to find out. We need to comb through the Arthurian texts to see if we can find anything pertinent. I've got Geoffrey of Monmouth here, but Rob will have the others in his library, I'm pretty sure. I'll go fetch them; you take a look at Geoff." He handed her a copy of the *History of the Kings of Britain* by Geoffrey of Monmouth and headed downstairs.

It was a translation from 1718 by Thomson and contained a gazetteer and index at the back, she was pleased to see. She started to comb through the entries. By the time Deo came back, she was beside herself.

"Deo! Look, this must be where the identification of Caelyr with Leicester comes from. I found it in the gazetteer at the back. But the really exciting bit? I've found his name! The spelling is a bit different, but that would be the variation between Welsh and English, I think. He's actually mentioned in the text!"

She showed him the passage.

"It gives a list of leaders gathered at one time—consuls—and gives a name, Jugein of Leicester. And there is another reference—possibly a variant spelling—here with Jonathal of Dorchester, commanding the third division of troops at the Battle of Suesia! It must be him; don't you think?"

"The Battle of Bedegraine isn't the Battle of Suesia," objected Deo.

"No, it's a different battle, but it shows he *was* a battle commander. *And* that he fought for Arthur!"

Deo nodded slowly. "Perhaps," he said cautiously. "But is the name similar enough?"

"*Gyn* could be a variant of *gein*, couldn't it? And we know that part of the name is missing so couldn't the first part be *Ju*? His father's name is *Wig* something. Couldn't it be *Wigein*? *Jugein* and *Wigein* are just variant spellings of the same name, aren't they?"

He smiled ruefully at her. "You make a good argument, Em. Now if we could locate Bedegraine . . ."

"Which books did you get?"

"Bede, Wace, Layamon, and good old Mallory. Which did you want?"

"Mallory! Bedegraine sounds to me like something that he would use."

He nodded, handing over the volume and sitting down with the rest.

Emily took Mallory and thumbed to the back, looking for an index and was gratified to find one. "Got it!" she said a moment later. "The Battle of Bedegraine in the forest of Bedegraine!" She looked up, grinning. "And here, oh my gosh, Mallory says '*After this Merlin departed from his master and came to King Arthur, that was in the castle of Bedegraine, that was one of the castles that stand in the forest of Sherwood."'*

"Sherwood is close to here, north of the river Trent," said Deo, putting down his book but keeping a finger in it to mark his place.

"Oh, Deo, this does sound like it might be something that actually happened."

"Maybe. Though you need to remember, Em, there have been a lot of forgeries over the years associated with Arthur."

"But don't you think—?"

"I don't know, Em. It's very tempting," he admitted.

"But you're not convinced? Surely if someone were going to manufacture a forgery, they would do it about someone famous, like Bedivere or Cai? Not an obscure commander no one has heard of. The cross was broken and buried a long time ago . . ."

"It does look persuasive, Em. I'm just wary of claiming something that is so closely associated with Arthur. Particularly Mallory's Arthur, who is much more fable than fact. The names in Mallory's work are largely fictitious, whereas the ones in Nennius, Bede, and even Geoffrey are much closer to history."

She sighed.

"Don't look so cast down. I'm inclined to think you might be right. I've just found this in Wace. It echoes Geoffrey on our Jugein fellow and there is a variant spelling of Vigenin and," he paused and grinned at her. "And I've found a third variation: Iuegyn,"

"Oh Deo!" She sprang up and flung her arms round his neck. "It is our man, then?"

"I think the order of probabilities comes down on the side of yes," he temporized.

"Just say yes, Deo," she said, leaning in to kiss him. He pulled her close then, and there was no more talking for a bit.

"Bed," he murmured a while later, kissing her neck.

"Yes, I think we've earned it," she said, and he scooped her up and carried her into the bedroom, where clothes got scattered, and they fell into bed.

DEO RAN HIS hands over his wife's lovely body and remembered with a guilty start that he hadn't taken Kes for his walk. Poor fellow was getting neglected. He would take him out, but after he had finished pleasuring his wife.

As she had said, they deserved it. The joy of doing what you love and sharing it with someone you love—there was no greater felicity, and he hadn't known it was possible to be this happy. His somewhat dreary and tightly controlled former existence seemed grey and foggy in comparison to the vibrancy that Em brought to everything. The intensity of feeling, the visceral pleasure of her body, and the unmitigated joy of her presence colored everything.

It was a shock to realize how quickly it had happened. In a matter of just over a couple of weeks, his life had been transformed. All thanks to this lovely woman beneath him. He cupped her small breasts in his great hands and kissed her with passion and tenderness. It was getting harder and harder to resist the inevitable. Fortunately, he was well-disciplined in self-restraint, or he would have given into temptation long ago. If Em had her way . . . The fact that she wanted him brought him undone in ways that he couldn't have fathomed a week ago.

He slid sideways and murmured, "Em, turn on your side."

She threw him a puzzled look and rolled toward him.

"No, the other way," he said.

She rolled away. "Like this?"

"Yes," he said, pulling her back against his front and spooning her tiny frame with his large body. He ran a hand down her belly to the place between her legs and stroked her softly.

"Oh, Deo," she sighed, squirming her lovely bottom into his

groin. His cock, already hard, caught between her buttocks, and he groaned. He moved back a fraction and used his hand to adjust the position of his cock. Sliding it instead along the channel of her wet lips, between her thighs.

"Deo," she gasped.

He kissed her neck and nuzzled her ear, sliding a hand under her to reach a breast, while his other hand continued to stroke that place he knew gave her the strongest pleasure. He moved his hips a bit and found that sliding his cock along her flesh was just about the most pleasurable thing he'd ever felt. "You like that?" he asked huskily.

"Yes!" She moved with him, and he groaned again. He wasn't going to last long in this position, it felt too good. He sped up the stroking of his fingers between her legs and tweaked her nipple gently, encouraging her to reach her peak before he lost control. The pleasure was building rapidly in his groin, as his cock slid backward and forward in the hot slippery hollow between the tops of her thighs and the satiny lips of her sex.

Perhaps it was the novelty of it that made it so erotic—he'd certainly never done anything like this before. He was getting quite inventive with ways to pleasure Em without taking her fully.

"Em, come with me!" he begged, panting, his hips moving faster of their own volition. She squirmed, her thighs tightening, and gasped.

"Deo!" her choked cry cut off and her body shook, and he lost the last vestige of his control. The pleasure spiked in a hot rush of heat and bliss, as he came hard, his cock shooting its load onto the sheets in front of her.

He groaned with the release and pulled her tight against him as the throbs of pleasure slowly died away. He got his breath back, listening to the heavy beat of his pulse in his ears and feeling it in his chest as it settled. He hugged her and kissed her neck in wordless joy.

She twisted in his embrace to face him and, wrapping her

arms round his neck, she kissed him. "The perfect end to another perfect day," she whispered.

"Yes," he murmured, kissing her again. Their legs tangled, and they lay together in silence for a few minutes in contentment and shared accord. This was what he had dreamed of and never thought he would have. The best that he had aspired to was the notion of a companion who would share the work with him. He never thought that their communion would run so deep or extend to such physical passion.

Kes who had been lying by the fire, chose this moment to paw at the bed.

"All right, old fellow," he mumbled. "I'll have to take Kes out," he said, disentangling himself reluctantly from Em.

She nodded and smiled. "Hurry back. I'll miss you," she said whimsically, reaching for a handkerchief to wipe the sheets.

He dove back to kiss her again. "I will." He stroked her nose and got out of bed to pull on his clothes. The days were getting warmer as they edged toward the height of summer, but the nights were still chilly. Going through to the sitting room, he let Kes out, and he escorted the dog downstairs and through the drawing room double doors to the north lawn. He paced while Kes ran about sniffing and finding a suitable spot to do his business under a shrub.

Reentering the house, he closed and locked the French doors and went back out into the front hall. He crossed the hall and ascended the stairs with Kes by his side. He couldn't wait to crawl back into bed with Em where it was warm and comfortable.

HIS HEART POUNDING in his chest, Bryson watched the Earl climb the stairs through a crack in the library door.

When he was sure Pendrell had reached the second floor and his bedchamber, he slipped out of the library, closing the door carefully behind him. With his prize tucked under one arm while he carried his candle, he made his way quietly back to his own room.

Once there, he lit a full candelabra on the desk and sat down to thumb through Emily's sketchbook and select the images he wanted. He then drew paper, pen and ink from the drawer and began the planned letter to his broker. An hour later, he had the letter copied out fair and, adding the sketches, placed the lot in a large envelope. He would slip into town early to post it.

He wondered what to do with the sketches he had not used. *Should I return the book with the remaining sketches? Burn it?* He decided against either. The former because it would alert Pendrell that someone was after the items whose pictures were missing, and the latter because they were Emily's drawings, and he might get an opportunity to win her favor by "finding" and returning them to her. He was fonder of her than he had thought was possible. If only he could find some way to drive a wedge between her and Pendrell and turn her heart toward him.

Well satisfied with this night's work, and contemplating different scenarios in which Emily became his, he undressed and crawled into bed.

Chapter Twenty-Two

D EO ROSE EARLY as was his wont and took Kes out while Em slept. Returning to the house, he was approached by the duke's butler, Creighton.

"A letter has arrived for you, my lord." He held it out on a silver platter and Deo took it with thanks and a sinking stomach. Slipping it into his coat pocket, he made his way upstairs with Kes. Entering the sitting room, he sat down at the desk strewn with papers and books from last night and drew the letter out. He looked at it for a moment, dreading and yet anxious to know what it said. Taking a deep breath, he broke the seal and opened the sheet.

My Lord,

I regret to inform you that in the event that you have not obtained the lady's father's permission, her being underage does invalidate the marriage.

Following your instructions, we have written to Viscount Efford on your behalf to secure his permission, but have not, at the time of this writing, received a response. The matter of the lady's name on the marriage license being different to her birth name does not have a material bearing on the validity of the marriage from a legal standpoint.

However, in order to rectify the situation, and ensure that the marriage is legally binding, we recommend that once you have obtained Viscount Efford's permission, you apply for a new license and exchange your vows again with the lady in question, should you wish to do so, of course.

In the event that you do not, you cannot be held legally responsible for the lady or the state of her reputation. In particular because she deceived you in the matter of her age.

I remain your obedient servant,
Charles Armitage, Esq.

Deo sat staring at this missive for some time, prey to a mix of emotions, not the least of which was indignation at the notion he was not responsible for Em or the state of her reputation. Of course he was. If not legally then morally. Both of which considerations were irrelevant anyway, as he wished to be married legally to Em. The fact that he wasn't made him feel rather sick.

Especially in light of the way they had been carrying on intimately for the past several days in particular. He was just thankful he had resisted the temptation to consummate the marriage fully. He knew it was a technicality, but his sense of honor was somewhat assuaged by the fact.

His impulse was to leave for London immediately to confront Viscount Efford and obtain his permission, but the fact that his solicitors had already written to him probably made that moot. He may very well receive a response almost on the heels of this letter he now held.

He could not think that Efford would withhold his consent in the circumstances. It wasn't as if he was a bad match for Em. On the contrary, he was an excellent match on paper. He was possessed of a title, significant independent means, a clean reputation, and a healthy body and mind. The fact that Em was an heiress made no difference to him—his own income was sufficient to make it a nice bonus, but not one he had looked for. He would take Em if she were penniless.

The door opened and Em appeared in her robe, her hair tousled. She hadn't plaited it last night. He reflected that once, not very long ago, the notion of seeing a woman in such disarray would have embarrassed him. Seeing Em like that gave him a flush of a different kind. *She is my wife. Except she isn't.* She came toward him.

"What is it, Deo? Is that the letter?"

He nodded.

"What does it say?"

He held it out, and she took it with visibly trembling fingers. She read it, twice he thought, before she met his gaze. She looked a trifle pale. "What will you do?"

"What it says. Wait to obtain your father's permission and secure a new license."

"You want to do that?"

"Of course I do!"

"Are you sure? It says you don't have to," she pointed out.

"I am sure," he said stiffly. "If you are?"

Her face crumpled and she said tearfully, "Of course! But what if Mama won't consent?"

He frowned and pulled her into his lap, wrapping an arm round her. "Your father has no say in the matter?"

"Mama always gets what she wants," said Em, sniffing.

"I really don't anticipate that will be an issue, Em. I'm quite eligible, you know. In any case, if your parents should withhold consent, it could be deemed unreasonable in the circumstances. I don't need or want your fortune, Em. Unlike Bidenden, I couldn't give a toss how much money you have."

"Oh, Deo." She flung her arms round his neck, and he squeezed her.

"We will sort it out, Em, don't worry. But I'll sleep out here tonight."

"Why?"

"Because I am more determined than ever to do the right thing by you. The law may have scant regard for your rights, but my sense of honor will not allow me to compromise you further than you have already been compromised."

"But my reputation would be past saving at this point, Deo, if people knew the truth."

"That's irrelevant. I *do* know. Don't argue with me, please, Em, I am fixed on this, and you won't change my mind."

"Very well," she said meekly and leaned in to kiss him. He kissed her, unable to resist; the temptation of her was overwhelming. He broke the kiss and tipped her off his lap, determined to do the right thing if it killed him.

"Go and dress. I'll see you at breakfast," he said gruffly.

She nodded, moving toward the bedroom door. She paused and looked back. "Thank you," she said softly and slipped from the room, closing it behind her.

He sighed, closing his eyes. He loved her so much his chest ached with it. This would all be sorted in a couple of days. Then they could be comfortable.

⊁⟫⟩⟨⟨⊰

AFTER BREAKFAST THEY repaired to the library to continue their work on the finds, and it took Emily all of five minutes to notice her sketchbook was missing.

"Deo, did you move my sketchbook?"

"No," he looked up from the desk. "Where did you have it last?"

"I'd swear I put it here," she said, pointing to the pile of papers in the middle of the trestle table at which she was working. "Annis's sketches from the excavation are here, but my sketchbook with all my drawings in it isn't."

"It must be here somewhere," he said, rising to help her look. "Perhaps it fell on the floor and a servant picked it up and put it somewhere when they were cleaning?"

Half an hour later they were still unable to find it.

"Perhaps Annis or the duke took it to look at something?" offered Em, feeling very frustrated and a little put out.

"Unlikely, but we will ask," said Deo, heading for the door.

They found Emrys and Annis in the schoolroom with the children. Neither had touched her sketchbook, and they were concerned that she couldn't find it.

The duchess they found in the parlor with the housekeeper going over daily accounts and menus.

Deo said, "Sarah, can we have a word?"

"Of course, we were just finishing up anyway. Thank you, Mrs. Williams." The housekeeper curtsied politely and left the room.

"What is wrong?" asked Sarah.

Deo frowned. "I'm not sure, yet. But Em's sketchbook has gone missing."

"Oh, that is odd. Do you think the servants might be responsible?

"I hope not. It may just have been misplaced, but so far we haven't been able to find it."

"Do you want me to ask the servants?"

"Not yet. I don't wish to accuse anyone of anything without evidence," said Deo.

"It truly may have just been misplaced. Perhaps I've misremembered where I put it," said Emily.

"Rob wouldn't have taken it, would he?" asked Deo.

"He didn't mention anything, but we can ask him. Did you ask Emrys and Annis?"

"Yes, we've already spoken to them."

"Well, let's go and ask Robert. He's in his study with his steward this morning." The duchess led the way, and they burst in on the duke in a group.

Rob looked up, surprised. "Good morning, my love. To what do I owe this delegation?"

The duchess went around to his side of the desk and murmured something in his ear.

His eyebrows went up and he shook his head. "No, I haven't." He waved to the man on the other side of his desk, "Giles, can you give us a moment, please?"

"Of course, Your Grace." He rose and left the room, shutting the door behind him.

"This is most peculiar," said the duke.

"I may have misremembered where I put it," said Emily, blushing. She was starting to feel uncomfortable about the fuss she was causing. "If I can't find it, I can redo the drawings of the items. It will just be the ones from the excavation that are lost."

"But still, it is worrying," said the duke, frowning. "I'm very reluctant to think any of the servants could be responsible. Most of them have been with us for years, and anyone new we employ always comes with excellent references."

"Indeed, we don't want to accuse anyone, do we, Deo?" said Emily quickly.

"Not without cause, no. Where are Kenrick and Bidenden?" he added.

"Creighton will know," said the duke. "Out, I should think. Neither showed for breakfast."

Lords Kenrick and Bidenden were indeed out.

"Lord Bidenden had business in Leicester this morning, I believe, and left the house before eight," said Creighton. "Master Kenrick took his horse for a gallop at about ten o'clock. I am in expectation of them both returning for luncheon however."

Emily and Deo returned to the library, and she sat down at the table. "I shall just have to do new drawings, Deo, and we will hope the sketchbook turns up. Oh, wait! Perhaps I took it upstairs last night?"

"Wouldn't you have remembered?"

She shrugged, "I was a little distracted last night. I was very excited! I'll just go and look. It won't hurt to check."

He nodded and went back to his desk, while she raced upstairs to check the untidy mess of papers and books on the desk and side table in their sitting room. She tidied everything up carefully as she made a thorough search of the room but didn't find her sketchbook. A little dejected, she returned to the library.

"No luck?" he said, taking in her expression and the fact that she was emptyhanded.

"No. I wish I could remember—" She broke off. "You came in here last night to get those books, didn't you?"

"Yes." He frowned. "I don't remember anything out of place, but I wasn't looking at the trestle table. I went straight to the shelves."

She sighed and sat down. "Well, I'd best get started on a new set of sketches then."

Lord Bidenden didn't return for luncheon, but Kenrick did. When asked about the sketchbook, Kenrick said quizzically, "No disrespect to your artistic skills, Emily, but I've little interest in such things. Unless of course," he added with a cheeky look at his brother, "that goblet turns out to be the Holy Grail after all!"

Deo cast a puzzled look between the brothers. "No one has suggested it is, to my knowledge."

"We made a joke to that effect last night," said the duke.

Emily leaned forward eagerly. "Did Deo tell you that we have identified our man as a commander who fought under Arthur?"

"What?" said the duke, dropping his fork.

"Em!" protested Deo. "It's not a positive identification. It relies on Mallory for goodness' sake!"

"Only for the Bedegraine bit," remonstrated Emily. "His actual name appears in Geoffrey and Wace and Layamon. You showed me those last night."

"Whoa! Hold on!" said the duke, leaning forward. "You found this fellow's name in *History of the Kings of Britain?*"

Deo sighed and threw Emily a frown. "We did."

"Along with the identification of his location, which appears in the cross inscription," added Emily, defiantly. "So, we know it's him. It has to be. He is from Caerlyr, which is Leicester, and Geoffrey, Wace, and Layamon *all* give him as Jugein of Leicester or some variation of the spellings we have on the cross. And

Geoffrey says he was a commander at the Battle of Suesia. The inscription tells us that he fell at the Battle of Bedegraine. Which, according to Thompson's translation of Mallory, was located in Sherwood Forest, just north of here."

Emily sat back, beaming.

The duke and the viscount exchanged looks, and Emrys said with a grin, "And when were you going to tell us this, Deo? You didn't breathe a word of it at breakfast. How could you sit on a discovery like that?"

Deo visibly squirmed and shook his head. "I'm still trying to make up my mind if I believe it," he admitted. "It just seems too fantastical to me."

"If it's true, it's the find of the century, surely?" said the duke.

"Potentially. But there is a lot more century left, Rob. I wouldn't count chickens."

"You're a conservative old stick, aren't you?" said Emrys, still grinning.

Deo shrugged. "With a scholarly reputation to protect, one tends to be."

Emily squirmed at that. *Have I gone too far? But surely there is no harm in sharing our discovery with Deo's friends?*

"So, it might be the Holy Grail after all?" said Kenrick.

"No!" said Deo. "There is no evidence for that."

"I don't know about that," said Kenrick. "It was found in a Christian burial of a Knight of the Round Table. Sounds like the perfect candidate to me!"

"This is precisely why I didn't want to talk about it!" said Deo, going almost as red as his hair.

"Steady on, old chap," said Emrys, "Kenrick's just teasing you."

Kenrick chuckled, leaning back in his chair. "Sorry, couldn't resist."

"But is he, though?" asked the duke. "Seems to me there might be some truth to that?"

"Not you too!" said Deo.

"No, I'm serious," the duke said. "You should consult Aberdeen, see what he thinks."

"That's the most sensible thing you've said yet," said Deo.

"Good. We'll write to Aberdeen then, after luncheon."

Deo nodded reluctantly.

AT THE CONCLUSION of the meal, Deo and the duke left the dining room together, heading toward the duke's study. Emily, several steps behind them, faltered when Deo didn't acknowledge she was there.

"Deo?"

He turned and looked at her soberly. "Keep working on the sketches, Emily. I'll join you later."

"Oh." She swallowed, feeling like he had pierced her chest with a dagger. "All right." She turned and walked with dragging steps back to the library.

It was the first time Deo had not included her in something to do with the excavation, and she was hurt and puzzled as to why he was so annoyed with her. There was no doubt he was annoyed, quite angry in fact, and Emily entered the library to sit and stare at the artifacts, but she had no heart for the work. Her throat tightened and tears welled up and rolled down her cheeks and she sobbed into her handkerchief.

Annis found her a few moments later. Emily hadn't heard her enter, being too engrossed in her own misery. "Oh, my dear," said Annis, drawing up a chair and putting an arm around her.

Emily was startled and embarrassed to be discovered crying. She generally did so in private, for her tears were never tolerated by her mother. She stiffened and tried to stem the flow, but the sobs kept coming. She couldn't get Deo's expression of disappointment out of her head, and it was breaking her heart.

"It's all right, my dear, have your cry out. Men are insensitive sometimes. And even the most placid temperaments can get grumpy."

Emily wiped her eyes and blew her nose, trying to swallow her sobs. "You—you m-mean the viscount gets grumpy, too?"

"Occasionally," admitted Annis with a soft smile. "He is the dearest man, but even he succumbs to bad temper occasionally."

Emily blew her nose again. "Deo used to be quite bad-tempered when I first met him, but he has been much less so lately. I was taken by surprise, I suppose." She swallowed and added, "Oh, it hurts when he looks at me like that! And the worst part is I don't know what I did wrong!"

"He didn't take Lord Kenrick's teasing well at all, did he?"

"No." Emily kneaded her damp handkerchief in her hands. "He is of a rather serious disposition. I used to think he didn't have much of a sense of humor, but lately—he has been much more cheerful and lighthearted."

"Yes, I have noticed the difference. That is due to you."

"Is it?" said Emily wistfully.

"Of course it is! It is plain to the meanest intelligence that he adores you."

"Not at the moment he doesn't. Oh, what did I do wrong?" wailed Emily. Tears started down her cheeks again.

"I think he did not wish the possible Arthurian connection spoken of."

"Yes, but why?"

"Well, for precisely the kind of reaction it provokes. People jump to conclusions."

"Yes, he doesn't like that. He is always counseling me to be cautious in my interpretations. But in this case, the evidence is so strong—" She broke off, shaking her head. "I wish I hadn't said anything now. But how was I to know he didn't wish it spoken of? He didn't tell me not to say anything. If he had, of course I wouldn't have said it."

"I'm sure he will explain his reasons later when he is more rational," said Annis.

"I suppose so. I do not wish to be a bad wife, Annis. Am I?"

"Of course not. It is natural to have disagreements occasionally, even in the most harmonious of relationships. I have found that the secret is always to communicate one's feelings—but in a rational way, when the emotions are less engaged." Annis smiled softly. "I am fortunate to have a husband who agrees with me on that head. He was married before, as you must know. He has brought what he learned from his first marriage to ours, and it helps a great deal. Deo doesn't have that experience, my dear, so try not to be too hard on him."

"Oh, I wouldn't! He has been—" She stopped and swallowed. "Oh, if you only knew how wonderful he is! I love him so much!"

"Of course you do. And your shared happiness has been a delight to witness for all of us."

Emily smiled down at her lap. "Have we been so obvious?"

"Emrys and I think so, but then we know what love looks like."

"He does love me, you think?"

"Without a shadow of a doubt," said Annis firmly. "You should see the way he looks at you. He is very proud of you, you know."

"Oh!" Emily blushed with delight.

"Now I shall leave you to your work, for Emrys and I have promised the children an outing this afternoon while this wonderful weather holds," she said, giving Emily a hug and rising.

Emily sprang up and hugged her back. "Thank you so much. I'm not accustomed to having friends. Especially female friends. You are most kind."

Annis blushed faintly and said gruffly, "You may always count us as your friends, Emily. You're like family to us, for Deo is a brother to Emrys in every way that counts."

"Then you are like my sister? I have no siblings or even cousins," confessed Emily, her heart swelling with affection.

"I have no family either, except a brother I never knew growing up, so it has been the greatest felicity to have Emrys's family as my own. And before him, the duke and duchess treated me like family, too. Robert and Sarah are the kindest and most generous people. I was the duke's sisters' governess, you know, before I married Emrys."

"I do know. That sounds like a very romantic tale."

"It is," acknowledged Annis with another faint blush and a soft smile. "I will tell it to you one day. Emrys was my knight in shining armor. Now I must go—the children will be waiting for me."

Left alone, Emily took a deep breath and sat down at the table, determined to get on with the task at hand and wait patiently for Deo to reappear, so that she could apologize and perhaps understand why he was so upset with her.

AFTER AN HOUR spent composing a letter to Aberdeen with Robert, Deo left the duke's study to return to the library and to face Em. He had been very annoyed with her, but his temper had cooled in the intervening time, and he couldn't rid his mind of the image of her hurt expression as he and Robert left her in the hallway.

He pushed the door to the library open and stood watching her work. She was seated at the trestle and working on a sketch of the now cleaned up shield boss and its outer ring.

All his love for her welled up, and he stepped into the room, determined to apologize for being a grumpy tyrant and try to explain why he reacted the way he did. She must have heard him, because she turned.

"Deo—"

He was shocked to see the redness of her eyes. *She has been crying! I am a brute to upset her so!* He crossed to her side and dropped to his knees by her chair.

"Em, I made you cry! I'm so sorry." He took her hands and kissed them.

"No! I'm sorry I made you angry. I didn't mean to, Deo," she said quickly.

"My darling Em." He took her in his arms and kissed her gently.

She leaned her head against his shoulder and said, "I confess I don't completely understand what I did wrong."

"You didn't do anything wrong, precisely."

"You were annoyed with me."

"Yes." He stopped and took a breath. "It's not your fault, Em. You're so intelligent and well informed, I forget sometimes how young you are, and how much experience of the world you lack. The academic world is harsh, Em. You will be aware that I have a reputation of some standing—"

"Yes! You are well respected, a leading authority, in fact. That is one reason I was so flattered you were prepared to accept my application initially. I couldn't believe my luck," she admitted with a smile.

"I've built that reputation over years of careful and meticulous research."

"Of course."

"Don't you see, Em? Claiming something so—so outrageous as a connection of any kind to King Arthur is—well, it will lay me open to all sorts of criticism. I could lose my reputation over it."

"Oh. I see—even if the evidence is persuasive?"

"Even then, yes. It's not incontrovertible, you see. If it were, the situation might be different. But the fact is there will be men who will shoot holes through the evidence we put up and try to take me down for it. The field is competitive, and the barbs slung by opponents can be nasty. Naturally, I'm protective of my own reputation, but I'm also protective of yours. As a female it will be difficult enough to establish you as a respected authority in your own right. This could ruin your chances before you are even established. I don't want that for you."

"Oh, Deo." She flung her arms round his neck. "I'm so sorry. I didn't understand."

"I know, and I'm sorry I made you cry. I'm a brute to do that." He cupped her face and kissed her. "It's not all doom and gloom, however. Provided we manage this carefully, it could all turn out well. Aberdeen's support will be crucial. Robert's support as patron will help. He is known as a man of exemplary honor. That will disarm any attempts to paint this as a money grab or a forgery. Rob would never be party to anything shady, and everyone will know that. And if we can pull it off . . . well, it may make, rather than break, your reputation." He smiled as her expression took on a look of awe.

"Really?"

"Yes, really. But we must be patient, Em, and practice rectitude."

She nodded. "I promise, no more blurting things out!"

"Good." He kissed her hair.

"What did you say to Lord Aberdeen?"

He reached into his pocket and extracted a sheet. "I thought you'd want to read it. This is the draft copy. It's got the amendments we made scrawled on it, but you'll get the gist."

She read it and he added, "I didn't mention you, not because I want to exclude you, but because I don't want to prejudice Aberdeen before things even start, and I don't know what his views on female scholars are. If he's set against them, it could damage our cause before it is even formulated properly. When I can sound him out on the topic, I will know how to proceed to include you."

"Thank you, Deo," she said, and her eyes glistened.

Alarmed, he said, "Don't cry, Em. I can't bear it when you cry!"

She sniffed. "I'm not, really!" She buried her face in his jacket and did cry, which had him patting and stroking her back and murmuring helpless words of comfort. Fortunately for his equilibrium, the tears were short-lived. He didn't think he would ever get accustomed to female tears, certainly not Em's anyway, especially if he was the cause.

He remembered vividly from his childhood an instance of his mother in tears and his feelings of helplessness to comfort her. Not that she had wanted his comfort. She had told him to leave the room. Why that scene came back to him now he didn't know. He seldom thought of his mother, and that particular memory wasn't one he'd entertained in a long time. But it went some way toward explaining why he found feminine tears so very hard to cope with. At least Em did want and accept his comfort, as inadequate as it might be.

Em nestled her head into his shoulder and said, "Annis found me crying and she was so sweet, Deo. She said I should count her as a sister, because you and Emrys were as brothers. I've never had a female friend, let alone a sister. It was so kind of her. She is the loveliest person."

"Yes, she and Emrys are well matched, for he's the kindest man I know. I'm glad she did that." He squeezed her. "Emrys, Rob, and Jerome *are* like brothers to me. The four of us would do anything for each other. It's been like that since school. You wouldn't think on the surface that we had anything in common beyond the fact that we're all gentlemen. We don't talk about it much; it's taken as read. All for one, and one for all."

"All for love?" quipped Em with a smile.

"Yes, all for love." He kissed her again, she was irresistible.

A little while later, he said, "We need to do some work, Em."

"I know," she said, flushed and slightly breathless.

He reluctantly let her go and climbed to his feet. Turning away, he rearranged his breeches and headed toward the desk.

The rest of the afternoon passed in companionable accord.

Bidenden was back for dinner, and inevitably the topic of the Arthurian connection came up again, much to Deo's annoyance. He recognized it was like trying to stem the tide, however. The topic was too enticing for people to leave it alone.

Bryson retired to his room early, claiming fatigue after his day in town, his mind buzzing with the dinner conversation. He wished he had known about the Arthurian connection when he sent the letter to his broker. He could send an addendum tomorrow. But given the potential value of the items, it became imperative that he secure them tonight. By his calculations, Emily's parents should arrive tomorrow, which would bring everything to a head.

His actions would be dictated by the outcome of that confrontation. If he was lucky, his long shot would come off. If not, he had this very nice cache of valuable items to fall back on, and the notion of wresting the money for them from his sire, all unbeknownst to the man himself, was a highly satisfying prospect.

He waited until the household was asleep before venturing downstairs to the library, bringing a pillowcase to place the items in for transporting them to the hiding place he had decided to use. He left the boxes, taking only the wrapping. If he took the boxes, it would be immediately obvious the items were missing. It would buy more time if the thefts were not discovered immediately, he reasoned. He had arranged with Kenrick for the two of them to go shooting first thing, and they wouldn't be back until midday or thereabouts, which with any luck, should coincide with the arrival of Emily's parents.

Confident of the hiding place not being discovered, he put into place his last piece of insurance. He had taken the belt buckle also, which was the least valuable of the showy items, but still *looked* valuable, particularly to the uninitiated, as it gleamed like gold even though it was only bronze.

His target for deflection was the gardener, Smiggens. His conscience gave him a slight twinge over that. The man had bandaged his ribs for him initially. But needs must. It was his father's fault. If he hadn't cut him off without a penny, all for a trifling debt of five thousand pounds and a bit of trouble over a lightskirt, he wouldn't be forced to take such drastic steps. But what was a fellow to do? He had to live on something.

He made his way to the storage shed that had a small cottage attached, that housed Smiggens and his grandsons. The shed was padlocked, so he turned his attention to the cottage. All was dark inside. He approached the door and found that it opened easily and, fortunately, quietly.

The first room was a quasi-kitchen cum sitting room. Presumably, the rear room was the bedroom. Sufficient light came through the window to illuminate the space, and the slight glow of coals from the banked fire gave off a faint glow and some warmth. He listened for any sounds of the occupants stirring and heard nothing.

A table and three chairs dominated the kitchen space, and beyond it were a sofa and a storage chest that seemed to be doing double duty as a table. He trod over to it and found that the lid lifted easily. Inside were piles of linen. He slipped the buckle between the folds of the linen, closed the lid carefully, and with a fast-thudding heart, beat a hasty retreat out the door.

Returning to his room, he penned a further note to his broker and retired to bed, once again well satisfied with his night's work.

Chapter Twenty-Three

"I DIDN'T KNOW it was possible to enjoy having intercourse so much without actually having it!" confessed Deo, collapsing in a panting heap on top of Emily. A comfort kiss had led to caresses and fondling and rubbing, and, well, now here they were, naked, tangled up, and sated.

Em giggled. "Is that what we're doing?"

"Yes," he said emphatically.

His plan to sleep in the sitting room had come to nought, because he was weak where Em was concerned. There was no other excuse. That and the fact that he couldn't bear it when she got upset. A hint of tears on her part, and he was giving in.

It had been a near run thing tonight, too. He had come perilously close to slipping his cock inside her as he rubbed it against her lips. The position was erotic as hell and very dangerous. Even knowing their situation now was barely enough to stop him. Perhaps he should just post back to London and see her father? They really couldn't go on like this.

He pulled her close and she snuggled into him. He did love that. It was impossible to imagine his life without her now.

AFTER BREAKFAST THE next morning, Deo accompanied Emily straight to the library to continue where they had left off yesterday. Emily went to the table and he to his desk.

"Deo." Something in Em's voice made him turn from the desk, where he was about to sit down, with a presentiment of fear.

"What—" He took a step toward her.

"Deo, it's gone!" She was staring at a box. "The goblet! It's gone!"

He stepped closer and saw that the box was empty.

Em put out a hand to him, and he steadied her with his arm as she staggered. "Where . . . how?" she said helplessly, as he eased her down into her chair.

"I don't know, Em," he said grimly and began checking the other boxes. "The shield, the broach, the cross, and the drinking horn are also gone. And the belt buckle. Everything of obvious value. Clearly, we should have taken more precautions. There is a thief in the house. Stay here. I will alert the duke."

He left the room, going in search of his host. He found him in his study. Ten minutes later, Deo, Em, the duke, Emrys, Annis, and the duchess were all gathered in the study.

"I will ask Creighton to assemble the servants immediately," said the duke.

"Where are Bidenden and Kenrick?" asked Deo.

"Gone shooting, I believe; I heard them organizing it yesterday," said Emrys.

"The first thing we need to do is organize a full-scale search. For which we will need a fair few people," said Deo.

"Surely whoever took the items will have absconded with them immediately?" said Emrys.

"As much as it pains me to do so, we must question the servants first, I think," said the duke. "I will ask Creighton to assemble everyone in the ballroom. I will address them. The rest of you, watch everyone's faces, if anyone is guilty or knows something, their expression may reveal it. I am going to put the fear of God into them anyway. I cannot believe—" He stopped, clearly profoundly affected by this apparent betrayal by people he trusted.

He left the room, and the duchess wrung her hands, tears starting to her eyes. "This is so upsetting!"

Annis put her arm round her. "I know. I cannot believe it either."

Shortly, the duke came back into the room with Creighton, who looked around at the assembled company and then at the duke. "Your Grace?"

The duke shut the door. "Creighton, I need you to assemble the household. *All* of the household—outdoor and indoor servants, no exceptions—in the ballroom immediately."

Creighton's eyebrows went up, and he visibly fought the impulse to ask why. After a moment he bowed. "Of course, Your Grace, at once."

"He's well trained," remarked Emrys, as the door shut on the butler.

Within thirty minutes, everyone was assembled in the ballroom. The chatter died down as the duke and duchess entered with Deo, Em, Annis, and Emrys. Deo estimated there were between forty and fifty people gathered in the room.

The duke and duchess took their places at the front of the room and the rest of them positioned themselves so that they could see everyone's faces. They were clearly puzzled as to why they had been assembled. Creighton and Mrs. Williams, the housekeeper, were doing a head count. Smiggens and Hastings, as the most senior outdoor servants, nodded at a question from Creighton.

Creighton turned to the duke. "All the servants are present as requested, Your Grace."

"Thank you, Creighton."

As soon as the duke began speaking, the silence in the room was absolute. People even stopped shuffling. All eyes were trained on the duke. Sarah stood beside him, her face impassive, but her clenched hands were an indication of her distress.

"Firstly, I would like to thank all of you for your years of faithful and excellent service to us. Many of you have been in our family's employ for decades. And those who are relatively new have come to us with exemplary references. On the back of that, what I have to say now pains me deeply." He paused. Deo, scanning faces, saw smiles and frowns and worried glances, but nothing that he would characterize as guilt per se.

"You would all be aware of the enterprise that has been going forward over the last week or so, led by the Earl of Pendrell and his wife." All eyes turned to Deo and Em. "The excavation has been a successful one, providing much valuable information and, as you would also be aware, valuable items. It never occurred to me or the duchess that those items might be at risk in this house, such strong faith did I have in the honor and integrity of my household." The duke's voice deepened. "I am devastated to discover that my faith has been misplaced."

A gasp of horror went round the room and Deo scanned rapidly, looking for anyone turning pale, frightened, or likely to bolt. There were shocked expressions aplenty. He couldn't see every face in the room, but of the ones he could see, either they were very good actors, or they were not guilty.

"The responsible party will be found," the duke continued. "They will be arrested and charged. The likely consequences are transportation or hanging for a theft of this magnitude."

The servants began to shuffle and murmur.

"I am, however, as you know, a compassionate man. I will give you a moment of amnesty. If the guilty party will step forward now and offer up the location of the stolen items, I will show leniency. You have five minutes." He took out his watch. "Starting now."

The next five minutes were agonizing, as they all waited. No one stepped forward or spoke. At the end of the five minutes, the duke put his watch back into his pocket and said, "You leave me with no choice. Until the miscreant is found, you will all remain here while a search is conducted of the house and grounds."

The murmurs rose at this, and the duke waited until they died down. "Before we commence that task, I will ask you all one last question."

He paused and waited again for the noise to subside.

"Does anyone have any information that might assist us in our search? Has anyone seen or heard anything suspicious or untoward?"

There was a pause and then Creighton spoke. "Your Grace, if I might say something?"

"Of course, Creighton."

He bowed. "Thank you, Your Grace. I am truly shocked by this occurrence, and I hope that you know you have my unswerving loyalty. I will do whatever I can to assist you in the recovery of the items in question."

"Thank you, Creighton."

Creighton bowed again, then he turned and addressed the crowd behind him. "You all know the duke and duchess are generous and kind employers. We are privileged to work for them and the envy of our peers. Do not squander that good fortune. If anyone in this room knows anything at all, speak now, for you know the consequences if you do not." His tone of voice sent a visible shiver through a number of their ranks.

The next twenty minutes were chaos as Creighton's word let loose a torrent of protestations of innocence and avowals of loyalty from the servants, none of whom seemed to know anything to the purpose, but who were all keen to establish their own innocence of any wrongdoing. If there was a thief among them, they were playing a deep game and were far more hardened than Deo would have thought possible for an opportunistic criminal. This argued for someone with the ability to cooly plan such a theft and the sangfroid to remain calm in the face of discovery and deflect suspicion from themselves. Were any of these people capable of that?

He was about to ask the duke who their newest servant was,

when the duke managed to restore order by requesting in a carrying voice, "Silence, please."

The noise stopped abruptly. "The servants' quarters in the attics will be searched by the Ashfords. Mrs. Williams, you will accompany them as you have the keys to all the rooms. Creighton, you will accompany myself and the duchess and search the cellars and servants' rooms in the basement. Hastings and Smiggens, you will go with the Pendrells and search the outdoor servants' rooms. The rest of you will remain here until the searches are complete. I regret the necessity to do this, but I have no other choice. If you are not guilty, you have nothing to fear."

Murmurs greeted this, and they all dispersed to their appointed places of search, with the instruction to report back to the ballroom when done, or if anything was found.

Deo and Em followed Hastings and Smiggens out of the house. "We will search the stables first, I think," said Deo.

"Certainly, my lord," said Hastings, leading the way. "The grooms sleep above the stables, your lordship. But I and my wife, who is the cook in the house, have a two-room cottage attached to the back. You'll wish to check those quarters?"

"Yes, Hastings, thank you for your cooperation," said Deo.

"Shocking business, my lord," replied Hastings. "You're welcome to look all you like. The missus and I have nothing to hide, and if any of my men are responsible, I'll tan their hides this side of Sunday for betraying the duke. Served this family all my life, I have. Never heard of such a thing!"

Deo nodded, feeling acutely uncomfortable.

"Aye, it's a shocking thing," corroborated Smiggens. "There has never been anything like this before. My father was born on this estate, my lord. The Laynes are the kindest and most generous family in all of England. I would die for them." He shook his head, stumping along beside them.

A thorough search of the stables and grooms' accommodations showed up nothing, and they moved onto Smiggens's shed and the cottage attached that housed himself and his grandsons.

The shed was padlocked, but Smiggens hurried to unlock it for Deo to enter and search. Again, there was nothing that you wouldn't expect to see in a garden shed. Smiggens then led them to his cottage.

"You'll forgive us if it's not as tidy as it should be, your lord and ladyship," he said apologetically, holding the door open for them to pass within. "Three males in a house tend not to be as house-proud as a woman would be."

The first room, which was both kitchen and sitting room, was sparsely furnished. A pantry in the corner offered the only storage that Deo could see. He checked that and then went through to the bedroom where three cots each with a chest at its base took up the entirety of the room. He searched the chests and the mattresses. And returned to the main room where Em stood by a chest he hadn't noticed before.

"What is in there?" asked Deo.

"Linens, my lord. You're welcome to look," said Smiggens.

Deo knelt and began lifting out the folded linen. Something heavy slipped from the folds and fell with a ding to the stone floor.

Em gasped, and he looked down at the belt buckle by his knee. He dropped the linen back into the chest and picked it up.

"What's that?" asked Smiggens, peering at it.

"One of the missing items," said Deo, watching him closely. They had been careful not to mention what exactly had been stolen.

Smiggens went white as his shirt. He looked at Deo with horror in his eyes. "No! I've never seen that before. I didn't—I wouldn't. God in heaven, not one of my boys—" He swallowed, visibly sweating. "My lord, I don't know how that got there, but I swear on my Esmie's grave I didn't take it. I never go in the house, my lord, unless I'm summoned like today. You have to believe me!"

Hastings, who had remained outside while they searched the

cottage, presumably hearing sounds of distress, pushed the door open and stepped inside.

"What's happening?" he asked, taking in the tableau as Deo rose to his feet slowly.

He wanted to believe Smiggens, he really did, but the evidence was damning. He passed the buckle to Em who cradled it in her hands.

"We found something," said Deo, his eyes still on Smiggens, who was visibly trembling. Tears ran down the man's face, but he said nothing further as Deo turned to the other man. "We need to search again, thoroughly."

Hastings, who had gone white with shock when he realized what was happening, nodded. He flung a look of disbelief at Smiggens. The two men must have known each other all their lives. This would be almost as great a shock to Hastings as it was to Smiggens.

He and Deo turned the cottage upside down, but found nothing else. Throughout it all, Smiggens stood silently weeping.

Deo and Hastings escorted the stricken man back to the ballroom where they found everyone else waiting.

The duke took one look at Smiggens's face and said, "Good God, what—"

Em held out the buckle mutely.

"Pendrell, what happened here?" he asked, his eyes on Smiggens.

"We found the buckle in a chest in Smiggens's cottage," said Deo.

Smiggens dropped to his knees before the duke. "I didn't—I swear I didn't!"

"Grandad!" His grandsons rushed forward.

"Grandad, what's wrong?" asked the eldest.

"Hush, lads," he said, wiping his face. "Let the duke speak."

"What explanation have you for this, Smiggens?" asked the duke.

"None, Your Grace. I don't know how it got there, but I

didn't put it there, I swear on my Esmie's soul I didn't, I wouldn't, and the lads wouldn't either. Boys, you haven't seen this before, have you?"

The lads shook their heads.

"Your Grace," Annis stepped forward. "Whatever the explanation for this, I'd swear black and blue Smiggens isn't responsible." She put a hand on the older man's shoulder as she spoke and squeezed.

Smiggens gave her a grateful look over his shoulder and murmured. "Thank you, lass."

Before the duke could respond to this, there was a great clanging of the doorbell.

Creighton looked to the duke, "Your Grace?"

The duke sighed and rubbed his face. "You'd better answer that, Creighton, but the duchess and I are not at home to visitors." He turned to the rest of the servants and said, "You may return to your posts, and thank you for your patience."

The servants began to file out of the room, many of them casting curious or pitying looks at Smiggens, who had risen to his feet after a gesture from the duke and stood with an arm round each of his lads. When they had cleared the room, the duke opened his mouth to say something and was cut off by strident tones filtering up from the ground floor.

"Stand aside, you clodpole!"

Chapter Twenty-Four

E M CHANGED COLOR. "Mama!"

Her parents are here? Deo put an arm out to steady her. When Em changed color, she had a tendency to faint, in his experience. But if her parents were here, that was a good thing. He had several things he wanted to say to her mother, but they would have to wait until he got the requisite permission from her father.

"Em—" he began, but she evaded his touch and ran out to the landing overlooking the stairs to the entrance hall. He followed. Below stood Creighton, manfully attempting to protect the entryway, but despite his experience, it seemed he was no match for Emily's mama. A short, slightly rotund woman in a bonnet and pelisse, had barged her way into the house, followed by a man of medium height with a thickened waistline. He removed his hat, revealing a thinning crop of brown hair going grey.

"You have my daughter here! Produce her at once!" demanded Lady Efford, striking poor Creighton in the chest with her reticule.

"Madam," said Creighton, in arctic accents, stepping back a trifle to avoid her blows, "if you will just tell me your name, I will endeavor—"

"Mama—" Emily ran down the stairs, and Deo followed at a more sedate pace.

"Emily!" This dramatic exclamation was followed by an embrace that gave the lie to Em's tales of starvation and punishment. "My baby! Where have you been? We have been worried sick!" lamented Lady Efford.

"I'm sorry, Mama—" Emily said, emerging from her parent's effusive embrace. This was just the sort of display of affection her mother would show in front of others, Deo surmised. He was sure that the presence of other people was all that stood between Emily and a thorough roasting.

"Lady Efford!" The door being open still, Lords Bidenden and Kenrick could be seen coming through the entrance. The hall was getting quite crowded, Deo decided.

From the balcony above, the duke said, "Drawing room, Creighton."

Creighton bowed and said firmly, "Lady Efford, if you will step this way?"

Just at that moment, Kes appeared at the top of the stairs and with a loud bark, his ears madly flopping, lolloped down them past the duke and duchess and the Ashfords, who were also coming down the stairs. Of Smiggens and his boys there was no sign. *What has Rob done with them? And who the hell let Kes out?*

As Kes landed in the hallway just then, still barking and making a beeline for his legs, he didn't have time to entertain that thought.

Lady Efford caught sight of Kes and screamed. "Help! Who let that great hound in the house?"

"Kes, heel!" he snapped, and Kes stopped cavorting and barking and sat panting at his feet.

"Drawing room!" said Creighton. "This way!" He tugged Lady Efford, and her spouse chivvied her from behind, so that she was forced in the direction of the drawing room, trailed by everyone else, including Kes.

"Thank you, Creighton," said the duke quietly as he entered

behind Deo.

"Tea, Creighton, please," said the duchess. Creighton, who really was an excellent butler, bowed and shut the door on Kenrick, who was the last to enter. As the members in the room sorted themselves out, Kenrick leaned against the wall, crossing his arms and grinning. "This looks like it will be entertaining."

Deo ignored the comment. Kenrick's sense of humor was wildly inappropriate at times. Trailing a now quiet Kes, he joined Emily, who was attending to her mother, taking her bonnet and getting her seated. She was flanked, he was irritated to see, by Bidenden, who was bowing over Lady Efford's hand.

"Lady Efford," said the duke, coming forward, "I don't believe you have met my wife, the Duchess of Troubridge. Sarah, this is Emily's mama, Lady Efford, and her father, Viscount Efford. You are most welcome to our home, my lord."

"Oh, Your Grace!" said Lady Efford, springing up and dropping into a deep curtsy. "You are most gracious. Delighted to make your acquaintance, Duchess," she said gushingly. Deo winced internally and glanced at Em, who was looking mortified.

Emily's father offered his hand to the duke, ignoring his wife's effusiveness. "Thank you, Your Grace."

"Have you met Lord and Lady Ashford?" asked Sarah diplomatically.

When those introductions were made, she added, "And Lord Kenrick Layne, my husband's brother."

Lady Efford inclined her head graciously and then eyed Deo. "And who is this gentleman?"

Sarah looked startled. "I assumed you were already acquainted with the Earl of Pendrell, Emily's husband," she said.

Deo judged it was time he took a hand in proceedings and stepped forward. "I have not had the pleasure of making Emily's parents' acquaintance yet. We omitted to mention that we, err, eloped!" he said awkwardly and felt himself flushing faintly.

Emily's mama was staring up at him, stunned. "Emily, is this true?"

"Yes, Mama." She sidled up to Deo and took his hand, which immediately made him feel better.

"Are you aware, my lord, that my daughter is not of age?" asked Lady Efford.

"I am now," said Deo, incurably truthful. "I was not at the time of contracting our alliance."

"Which means that, according to law, the marriage is not valid!" said Bidenden.

"Oh!" Lady Efford staggered backward and fell dramatically onto the sofa behind her. "And you contracted this 'alliance,' as you call it, without our consent, when she was already affianced to another! You stole our girl away from us. Right out of our home. How you did so, I do not know but—"

"He didn't!" interrupted Em. "I ran away!"

"Oh, you wicked girl!"

Em flinched at that tone from her mother and Deo put a protective arm around her, and his temper flicked up in her defense. *No one, least of all her mother, is going to be mean to my Em!*

"No more wicked than trying to starve her into accepting a proposal that was distasteful to her!" he said, looming over the prostrate Lady Efford.

Lady Efford gobbled like a turkey at this for a moment and then, getting a hold of herself, she sat up and said, "Edward, you are not going to let him talk to me like that, are you?"

But before her spouse, who was looking anywhere but at his wife, could respond, Bidenden stepped forward and said smoothly, "Never fear, Lady Efford, I shall not let him speak to you that way. Retract that statement, Pendrell," he said, turning to face Deo.

Deo, who was almost a foot taller than him and considerably broader in the shoulders, stared down at him in disbelief. "This is none of your affair, Bidenden. Stay out of it."

"I believe it is my affair, as I am the gentleman to whom she was affianced, before you stole her."

"He didn't steal me," said Emily indignantly. "I told you; I ran away!"

Bidenden turned an accusatory gaze on Deo. "And how does she come to be in your company, Pendrell, masquerading as your wife?"

"There is no masquerade! She *is* my wife!" said Deo, itching to punch Bidenden in the face. "At least she will be, once I obtain her father's permission and we take our vows again."

"At the risk of being indelicate," said Bidenden, leaning forward. "Has the 'marriage' been consummated?"

"Yes!" said Em, flushing scarlet. "I am Deo's wife in every sense that matters!"

"Oh!" Lady Efford's moan cut across Em's words. "Edward, she is ruined!"

"Em!" Deo said in an agonized voice. He took a breath and turned to Lady Efford. "Madam, I can assure you that your daughter is not ruined!"

"Ah, I knew it!" said Bidenden. "I heard him confess the marriage had not been consummated the day I arrived. There can only be one reason for that!"

Deo flushed and clenched his fists.

"Deo, please." Em's voice penetrated the fog in his head.

Jerked back from a murderous desire to shut Bidenden up permanently, he turned to her and said gruffly, "Em, you know it's not true."

She smiled and he kissed her hand.

"Lord Bidenden, do I understand," said Lady Efford faintly, "that despite all, you are still prepared to take Emily to wife?"

"I am," said Bidenden with a triumphant smile.

"No!" said Emily.

"Over my dead body!" growled Deo.

"Edward!" Lady Efford said shrilly. "We must get her married to Bidenden straightaway."

All eyes turned on Lord Efford, who raised his eyes from his cuff and said quietly, "No, Beatrice. It is clear that the man Emily wants is the Earl of Pendrell."

Lady Efford gasped, staring at her husband in shock.

"I'll sue you for breach of promise!" said Bidenden to Lord Efford, through his teeth.

"I think not," said the duke quietly. "A gentleman, Lord Bidenden, would retire quietly from the lists. It is plain the lady doesn't want you."

Bidenden flushed and bowed stiffly to the duke. "Forgive me, Your Grace. My passionate desire for Emily had led me to extremes. I apologize. I shall remove myself to the local hostelry. It is clear I am no longer wanted here."

The duke nodded. "I also trust to your discretion in this matter? It is clear to me that your passion for the lady is more to do with her fortune than herself. You wouldn't wish me to have a word with your father, would you?"

Bidenden went white and then red. "I understand you perfectly, Your Grace. I will leave forthwith." He bowed and left the room.

⟫⟫⟪⟪

EMILY WATCHED AS Mama was staring at Papa as if at a stranger. "Oh, Edward!" she said faintly, tears running down her cheeks.

"Yes, my dear?" he said.

She dabbed at her cheeks and sniffed, turning her attention back to Emily. "I suppose an earl is almost as good as a marquess."

"He is better, Mama, because I love him!" said Emily, squeezing Deo's hand and looking up at him with adoration.

Deo jerked at her confession, going adorably red. "Em!" he said softly.

She blinked at him, tears threatening. It had been a very emotional day.

He kissed her hand, squeezing it tightly.

She turned to her father. "Papa?"

"Yes, Emily?"

She let go of Deo's hand and flung herself at her father, which made him stagger backward. "Thank you, Papa!" she hugged him and kissed his cheek.

"You're welcome, my dear." He looked at Deo over Emily's head, and Emily turned to look at Deo as he spoke. "I gather you do love my daughter, Pendrell?"

"God, yes," said Deo, his eyes on Emily as he said it.

Completely forgetting that public displays of affection were unladylike, Emily flung herself at him then. "Deo."

And Deo kissed her in front of all those people. It was delicious but all too brief. Cut off by the round of applause that greeted it from the assembled company—begun, she suspected, by Kenrick, who had peeled himself off the wall to shake Deo's hand and kiss her cheek.

"Congratulations. Quite a romantic tale. My sisters would have loved to see this!"

Creighton arrived with the tea tray at that point, and the duchess served tea while Deo and Emily received congratulations from the Ashfords.

Emrys clapped Deo on the shoulder, "Well done, old chap."

Annis hugged Emily, and Emrys added to Deo, "I'll take you into Leicester tomorrow to see the bishop. We'll get you another license and I daresay Rob will let you use his chapel for the wedding."

The duchess looked up from serving tea and handing around cakes to say, "Yes, of course! You will be the third of us brides to be married in the Chapel, and I will be delighted to dress you!"

Emily flushed with pleasure. "Thank you, Sarah."

She took a cup of tea and a plate of cakes over to her mother and offered them. "Mama?"

Mama sat up, stuffed her handkerchief into her reticule and took the proffered tea and cakes. "Well, I suppose it's all turned out rather well in the end. But Emily, *how* did you meet him? You never said."

Emily sat down beside her mother and said, "I answered his advertisement."

Mama stopped with a cake halfway to her mouth. "Advertisement?"

Emily flushed and smiled in memory. "He advertised for a—an assistant. He's an antiquities scholar, Mama. I thought the advertisement was from a woman. A female scholar. I was rather shocked when I discovered he was a man."

Mama took a bite of her cake. "How extraordinary. Then what happened?"

"Well, he proposed. You see, he was looking for a wife who could also be his assistant."

Mama took a sip of tea. "Most peculiar. He's quite a well looking fellow. Why did he have to advertise?"

She looked over at Deo who was still talking to the Ashfords.

"He's shy," she said with a soft smile. "And he wanted a wife who was also interested in antiquities."

"So, all those fusty books you read helped you find a husband?"

"Yes, Mama."

"Hmm." She took another sip of tea. "An earl no less."

"Yes, Mama."

"Well, all's well that ends well then."

"Yes, Mama," said Emily with a smile.

"He's rather big, isn't he?"

"Yes, Mama, he is. You should see him without his shirt on!"

"Emily!" But Mama was smiling. Emily felt a surge of relief. Mama would never change, but now Emily didn't need to deal with her everyday and—she glanced at Deo across the room—she thought her husband would be equal to Mama in future.

Emily joined her husband as Deo turned to the duke. "By the way, Rob, what did you do with Smiggens?"

"I sent him back to the cottage under Hastings's supervision. We will have to decide what to do about him. I can't believe he took the items."

"He didn't! I'd swear it," said Annis staunchly.

"But someone has," said Deo. "We should search the rest of the house and post a watch tonight."

"Agreed," said the duke.

Once tea was completed, the duchess conducted the Effords to a suite, where they planned to rest until dinner, and the rest of the company dispersed.

Alone at last, Emily turned to Deo and walked straight into his arms.

"You meant it, what you said to Papa?"

"Of course!" he said gruffly, hugging her tight. "Did you mean it?"

"Deo, I've been in love with you since we left London, I think." She frowned in an effort of memory. Everything was a bit of a blur. "I think when I discovered you loved Gothic novels, too, it was, oh, just the icing on the cake. You were my perfect match. My soul's mate." She smiled up at him, misty eyed.

"You're mine too, Em. I couldn't imagine my life without you now. I was certain of it the day we cleared the tomb, but even before that I knew I wasn't prepared to let you go for anything. I'm sorry it took me so long to figure it out. Emotions are not something I'm used to dealing with. But I've been wanting to tell you I love you for several days now. I don't know how I kept it in. It felt so overwhelming sometimes. Like I couldn't breathe, it hurt so much."

"Oh, Deo!" she sighed and buried her face in his great chest. "I'm so happy!"

"Me too!" he said and kissed her.

The kiss, as always, was delicious, and she lost herself in it for several minutes until he finally broke it and murmured, "I'll have to sleep elsewhere tonight, now your parents are in the house. We will get the license and be married in the chapel as soon as possible. I can't wait to make you my wife properly, Em."

"I can't wait either," she said.

He let her go with obvious reluctance. "In the meantime, we

need to search the rest of the house and grounds. Our treasures are still missing."

She nodded, frowning. "Do you think Smiggens did it?"

"Not really, but we have no other lead at this point."

"Deo, do you think—" She stopped because the enormity of the idea took her breath away. "Do you think it could have been Bidenden?"

He stared at her very hard. "I did wonder fleetingly, but I thought it was just that I disliked him so much because of his persistent pursuit of you. Why?"

"Well, I always thought his interest in me was mainly motivated by his desire for my fortune. Although,"—she broke off flushing—"I do have some proof he desired me."

"Do you?" asked Deo grimly. "What did he do?"

"Oh, nothing more than I've told you, I think. But when he grabbed me and tried to kiss me in the anteroom after lunch the day he arrived—"

"I didn't know he'd done that!" Deo's expression became quite ferocious.

"Oh, didn't I tell you? Anyway, he—well I—I could feel that he wanted me, if you know what I mean," she said, blushing.

"Yes, I know what you mean, and I'll string him up by his neckcloth!" growled Deo.

"Well, anyway, I do think it was mainly my fortune. I accused him of it that day and he denied it. His father is quite wealthy, so he shouldn't be short of funds, but perhaps he is? And he did mention to me that his father has a strong interest in antiquities, too. He's quite a collector, apparently."

"God, yes! Why didn't I make that connection? His father is the Marquess of Malmsbury." Deo headed for the door. "I need to speak to Rob about this. We let the fellow go! If he's taken the items, he could be halfway to London by now."

Chapter Twenty-Five

Having assembled the duke and duchess and the Ashfords in the duke's study, Deo said, "We believe we may have identified the thief."

"Who?" asked the duke.

"Bidenden. I didn't make the connection before—his apparent complete disinterest in the work we were doing threw me off—but his father is a collector of antiquities. Em?"

"He told me so, the day we moved the tree. I think he was trying to imply that he understood my passion for antiquities, but I didn't believe him. And since his father is very wealthy, why should he be so keen to marry an heiress?"

"Unless he were in some kind of financial trouble," finished Deo.

"Hmm, I wonder if Kenrick knows anything?" said the duke. Going to the door, he opened it and addressed Creighton. "Do you know where Lord Kenrick is?"

"In the billiard room, I believe, Your Grace."

"Thank you." The duke came back in a moment with Kenrick, who ambled through the door after his brother.

"What's this, a council meeting?" He shut the door casually behind him, looking at the assembled company with a raised eyebrow.

"Rick, you may not be aware, unless the servants have told you, but we discovered that the valuable items uncovered by Deo and Emily were stolen overnight."

Kenrick raised both his eyebrows. "Have you found the culprit?"

"Not yet. Do you know if Bidenden is in any financial difficulty?"

Kenrick pursed his lips. "I know there was some dust kicked up by his father over a few trifles. But Bryson never asked me for money or indicated he couldn't pay when we played. I knew he was pursuing a lady, but I wasn't aware, until this afternoon, that the lady was Emily." He nodded to her and smiled. "He seemed genuinely cast down when his suit didn't prosper though, so I had concluded he was attached to the lady. However, the fact that he continued to nurse hopes in your direction, Emily, once he knew you were married, is a mystery to me. That does smack of desperation."

"How well do you know him?" pressed the duke. "Would you vouch for him?"

"We were friends at Eton. Not close like you fellows," he indicated with a wave of his hand. "But I'd have counted on him to stand as a friend, yes. I've never known any ill of him, by my standards, which may not be yours, Rob." For once, he didn't look flippant or amused. "Don't tell me you suspect he may have had a hand in this theft?"

"Unfortunately, we do. Were you aware his father is a collector of antiquities?"

"No, but then my interest in such things is about as high as my interest in female fripperies. In fact, less," he added. "The only reason I had any interest at all in this endeavor was because it was on our land and you fellows were doing it." He frowned. "He was a little off his game this morning, but I thought it was due to lack of sleep. He admitted to me that he hadn't slept well."

"Damn!" said Deo. "And we've let him get away! If he has the items, he will have absconded as far and as fast as he could by now."

"He said he was going to spend the night in town," remarked Kenrick.

"He did," corroborated the duke.

"Surely that was a pretense. What possible reason could he have for lingering?" Deo took a pace round the room; he was having difficulty containing his emotions.

"It really depends on where he has stashed the items," said Emrys thoughtfully. "If they are somewhere he couldn't retrieve them in daylight—"

"He would need to remain until nightfall to collect them," finished Emily.

"He must have hidden that belt buckle in Smiggens's home to deflect attention," said Annis. "I knew Smiggens wasn't guilty of theft. That was probably Bidenden's biggest mistake. If he had planted the item on one of the newer servants, it might have been more plausible."

"I shall send my valet, Bridges, into town to ascertain if Bidenden is still there. Bridges is very discreet and can be trusted," said the duke. "Once we know if he is still in the vicinity, we can plan a trap for him."

"Otherwise, we will need to give chase," said Deo, clenching his fists in agitation. It was infuriating to have to wait, but he could see the sense in the duke's proposal. "If he is still here, the items must be somewhere on the estate."

"It might be better if I went," said Kenrick. "It would be nothing unusual for me to go into town and call into an inn for a heavy wet. If I saw him and convinced him no one suspected him, it would embolden him to come and collect the items, wouldn't it?"

"Perhaps," said the duke slowly. "But it might make him suspicious."

"You insult my acting abilities, Rob." Kenrick grinned. "I might be able to glean something from him, too."

Seeing that Robert was still reluctant, he said seriously, "Let me, Rob. I feel responsible. After all, I invited him here. If I'd even suspected—well, I wouldn't have, is all I'll say. I know you think I'm a feckless fribble with no moral fiber, but this is an insult I can't overlook."

"I don't think you're a feckless fribble!" said the duke roughly.

"Just lacking your high moral standards," said Kenrick with an ironic smile. "In Papa's name, let me do it. You know he would say I should, if he were here."

Robert stiffened and then nodded. "Very well."

"Good." He clapped his brother on the shoulder. "I'll not let you down, Rob," he said gruffly, his usual insouciance completely absent. He left the room and Deo said, "I still think we should make a push to find the items. We only checked the servants' quarters. There are a hundred places he could have put them, if he hasn't already taken them."

"True, but I'd like to set a trap for him, catch him red-handed," said the duke.

"We can still do that. But if we know where they *are,* we can concentrate our trap on that location. Not knowing where they are will make it extremely difficult to trap him. Forgive me for stating the obvious, but this is a big estate, Rob. They could be anywhere. Somehow, I doubt they're in the house if he is planning to come back for them. I think if they were, he would have taken them with him. After all, everyone was in the drawing room at the time."

"You think he's buried them?"

"It seems the most likely to me, yes. Digging them up will take time. He wouldn't have had that, leaving in daylight. And he wouldn't have wanted to risk being seen by the outdoor servants, depending on where he put them."

Robert nodded. "Any idea where to look first?"

"What about the piles of dirt we pulled off the burial mound?" said Em. "He will have known we haven't had time to start the restoration process yet. It would be the easiest and quickest place to hide them and virtually undetectable, because the earth is in piles as we left it. Not tamped down and undisturbed, which would be obvious, if anyone were looking for a place he could have buried the items."

"My God, Em, you could be right," said Deo with an admiring smile that made her blush with pleasure.

"Would he have just dropped them back into the barrow itself?" asked Emrys.

"Possibly, and if so, that would be easy to check. Which is why I don't think he will have done it. Too easy to find them. I think Em's theory is the most plausible," said Deo.

"Let's go check then," said Emrys with a grin.

All six of them traipsed out of the house and across the lawn toward the burial site, taking a lamp with them.

"I'll check the inside of the barrow first," said Deo. "Then I think we should survey the site for any clues before we just start randomly digging. If we want to trap him, we don't want to tip him off we found the items."

On arrival at the site, Deo climbed the mound and jumped down into the entryway. Reaching for the lamp, he ducked his head and ventured inside.

"As I thought, they are not here," he said, reemerging a minute later.

"No signs that he has dug up anything in there?" asked Emrys.

"No, it's as we left it," said Deo, hauling himself out of the hole. They fanned out and inspected the piles of dirt. The tools they used, shovels, mattocks, a digging bar and trowels were still there.

"I suggest we use the digging bar to prod the mounds and see if there is anything inside them," said Deo, picking up the six-foot-long heavy iron bar with a chisel end.

The duke nodded, "Good idea. That will disturb the earth the least and make it easy to disguise that we have been looking."

There were a dozen sizable piles of earth scattered around the base of the denuded mound. Deo began a careful search of each using enough force to push the bar through the earth but not so much that it would cause damage to the items if he encountered them—he hoped. He checked eight of the twelve without finding anything of note. A couple of bits of tree root initially gave him false hope. He was beginning to think this theory was wrong, or he'd missed the items altogether, when he poked the bar into the pile on the south-eastern side of the mound nearest to the fallen tree and thought he detected something. In fact, some of the branches were lying on top of this particular pile.

He prodded carefully and Em came closer, "Have you found something?"

"I think I might have. Fetch me a trowel, will you?"

A trowel was fetched, and the others gathered round to watch him carefully remove some of the dirt from the pile to uncover a dirt covered cloth. He put his hand in and felt the cloth. "Yes," he said with a grin. "I can feel the shape of the drinking horn. All right! Do we leave it here, or dig it out, rebuild the mound and let him dig it up and find nothing?"

"I think it will help the magistrate get a conviction if we leave it there and let him dig it up. There will be no doubt of his guilt then," said the duke grimly.

"We can trap him nicely here, I think. We will discuss the details back at the house. Let's find out what Kenrick has gleaned. If we are right, Bidenden will still be in the vicinity unless he's decided to give up and flee."

Deo was a little reluctant to leave the precious items there, having found them, but the duke's argument made sense, so he spent another ten minutes ensuring his invasive tactics were camouflaged, and they made their way back to the house, where they met Kenrick returning from his errand. The duke dispatched a footman to stand guard over the mound, while the rest of them assembled back in his study to hear Kenrick's news.

"He's staying at The Red Lion. He's claiming he was too upset by the way things had fallen out with the Effords to travel today." Kenrick threw Emily a look. "He is playing the rejected suitor to the hilt. If I didn't know better, I would have been inclined to believe he is truly heartbroken. I made much of Smiggens's apparent guilt and my shock over it, saying that you, Rob, were deliberating what to do and how to force him to reveal the location of the remaining missing items. I said Smiggens was still claiming innocence. I made it sound like we didn't believe him."

"Right," said Robert. "Well, we know what to do now. I shall send a note to the local magistrate, Sir Gerald Kingsley, immediately. I've set a footman to keep watch on the mound for the next few hours. And someone had better let Smiggens know and put the poor man out of his misery. I shall apologize to him personally tomorrow when all this is settled, and make it widely known that we never suspected him. I don't want his reputation tarnished in the local area for this."

"I'll tell him," said Annis. She wiped her cheeks. "I'm sorry, but he has always been like a father to me. The notion that he might be guilty of something so heinous—I couldn't bear it." Emrys squeezed her shoulders. "We'll tell him together, love. Come on."

DEO AND THE duke sat down to plan an ambush for Bidenden, and Emily went to check on her parents. It was imperative they not let her mother find out they suspected Bidenden of treachery; she couldn't be trusted not to gossip.

Emily was still reeling from her father coming to her defense. He had never done such a thing in her life. She wanted to find a chance to tell him how truly grateful she was. As it transpired, Mama was asleep and Papa was perusing the paper in the sitting room of their suite, a pot of ale by his elbow.

Closing the bedroom door quietly on her sleeping mother, Emily went to him and dropped to her knees by his chair.

"Papa, thank you!"

He lowered the paper and looked at her over the top. "What for, my dear?" he asked, putting the paper aside.

She opened her mouth and closed it when her throat locked up. Blinking back tears, she said, "For speaking up for me."

He looked uncomfortable. "No need for tears, Emily. It was obvious where your preference lay, and even a blind man could see the earl loves you."

"Oh, Papa!" Emily cast herself on his chest again and sobbed. He patted her awkwardly. "Your mother gets notions fixed in her head, and she seemed very set on you marrying Bidenden, but it made no sense when you were already hitched to Pendrell. It would have caused a huge scandal if you had married Bidenden instead. I was also concerned when I learned that Malmsbury had cast Bidenden off."

"Has he?" she asked, sitting up and wiping her eyes. "What for?"

"I'm not sure, but the story was circulating in the clubs. Must be pretty serious for a father to cut off his heir. Of course, your mama knows nothing of that. I couldn't tell her, and it was worrying me no end. Couldn't have my girl hitched to a fellow with that kind of reputation. But all's well that ends well, my dear," he said, echoing his wife's sentiment from earlier. "You ran off with Pendrell instead. Not sure how you accomplished that or even how you made his acquaintance."

So, Emily repeated her story to him, adding, "I fainted in his arms, Papa, when I arrived at the house. I was so shocked. I thought the advertiser was a woman, and after hardly any food for a week—"

"What?" he interrupted. "What are you talking about?"

"Mama was trying to starve me into accepting Bidenden's suit. I thought you knew?"

Her father stared at her, horrified. "No, I did not. Why didn't you come to me?"

"If you recall, you weren't there." She looked down at her clenched hands, acutely uncomfortable. "In any case, you have never been prepared to stand up to Mama for me before. I—I just assumed you knew." She shrugged. "I know you were disappointed I wasn't born a boy."

"Oh, God in heaven, Emily, I am so sorry!" His voice cracked, and she looked up to see his face twisted in grief, tears tracking down his cheeks. "Your mother had so many miscarriages. At least one we knew for certain was a boy. Your birth was difficult, Em. After it, well, your mother never conceived again."

He wiped his face, as she stared at him in shock.

Seeing her expression, he took her hand. "I think we were both guilty of resenting you a little for surviving when he didn't."

She withdrew her hand and went to stand before the fire, trying to digest what he had told her. "I see. Well, that explains why neither of you loved me," she said matter-of-factly. Her heart was breaking, but she felt numb.

"No!" He rose from his chair and went to her. "That isn't true. Of course I love you. I don't think either of us ever quite got over the grief. Your mother felt as if she had failed me and she took it out on you." He stopped at a loss. "I'm so sorry, Emily. This is hard to forgive, I can see that."

"Yes, it is," she swallowed the lump in her throat. "But at least things make sense now."

He scrubbed his face and thinning hair. "I'm sorry," he said again. "I'm sorry I let your mother get away with—" He stopped and cleared his throat. "Did she make a habit of punishing you like that?"

"Withholding food?"

"Yes."

"She would do it quite often, and threaten the servants with dismissal if they disobeyed her and brought me food. That is why I thought you must have agreed with her. It was usually just a meal here or there. But this last time was the most sustained period. Previously, I usually gave in after a day or two. This time I wouldn't, although I was close to doing so when I got Deo's letter."

"Your mother's behavior is abominable. I will be having a word with her about that."

She sighed. "Thank you, Papa, but I think it is a little too late."

"I know," he said hollowly.

She wiped her face, and he tentatively held out a hand to her. She hesitated a moment and then went to him and let him hug her. She couldn't remember him ever hugging her in her whole life. It hurt, but it was a kind of strange comfort too. *Can I forgive them?*

"You were the tiniest thing when you were born, you know," he said over her head. "But you were a fighter." He cleared his throat again and sniffed. "I hope you never have to suffer the pain of losing a child, Emily. It is the most horrendous thing in the world. It's no excuse, but—"

"I understand now, Papa," she interrupted him, lifting her head to look at him. "It helps to know. I wish you'd told me; I wish someone had told me. It might have helped."

He nodded and, cupping her face, kissed her forehead.

"You're a good girl, Emily. I'm proud of you."

She nodded, tears edging down her cheeks again as a burst of warmth broke through the pain in her chest. "Thank you, Papa."

Chapter Twenty-Six

D EO WAS ON edge. The waiting was unbearable.

Deo, the duke, Emrys, and Kenrick, waited in the lee of the ruins with Kingsley, the magistrate. The ladies, of course, had wanted to be involved, but had been confined to the drawing room—the gentlemen had been unanimous and adamant on that point. The last thing Deo needed was to be worried about where Em was and whether she was in danger. While he didn't believe Bidenden was an inherently violent man, he did think he was a desperate one. And desperate men could do unpredictable things.

Emily's parents were asleep and would hopefully be none the wiser as to what transpired that night.

As it was almost pitch black, the cloud cover obscuring the moon and stars, there was no danger of their quarry seeing them. Several of the duke's men, along with Kenrick, were scattered in a ring around the mound out of sight. If Bidenden made a run for it, he would be cut off, whichever direction he chose.

The magistrate had counselled them to wait until the accused had the treasures in his hands before revealing themselves. As the items were found on the duke's property, he was technically the owner and would bring the charges.

Deo's role was to identify the contents of the cloth wrappings as being the stolen items and vouch for their value.

Emrys was to act as a witness.

Deo's nerves were stretched to breaking point by the time a figure carrying a lamp emerged from the trees bordering the open field in which the site was situated and began walking toward the mound. As everything was shrouded in shadow, the lamplight stood out like a beacon as it bobbed along, flashes of the figure holding it illuminated by its glow.

The air was crisp and cool, a light breeze was rising, and the clouds promised rain before dawn, although they had been fortunate that so far it had held off.

The figure drew closer. He was wearing an overcoat, and his face was obscured by his hat. He reached the mound, and looking about with the lamp held high, he located the pile of tools. After collecting a spade, he moved around the side of the mound to the pile near the tree. Deo's heart thudded hard in his chest as he watched the man begin to dig through the pile of dirt. It only took a few moments. He bent and pulled a sack free of the dirt and shook the debris off of it—that was what Deo had felt when he put his hand into the hole. He set it aside and began to scrape and shovel the dirt back into a pile.

A signal from the magistrate indicated that they should begin to move. Emerging from the ruins, they moved quietly toward their quarry. If he looked up, he might see them as moving shadows. But they had the advantage of being able to see him quite clearly because of the lamp at his feet, whereas they were in darkness.

As Bidenden was engrossed in what he was doing, he appeared oblivious to danger until Deo's foot came down on a twig which cracked. It was enough to cause Bidenden to look up and around. Deo froze and assumed his compatriots did likewise. He couldn't see them in the darkness.

Bidenden returned to shoveling dirt quickly into place. Then he bent to pick up the sack and with that in one hand and the lamp and shovel in the other, he skirted the mound back to the place where the tools were lying. He put the shovel back and lifted the sack over his shoulder. With the lamp in hand, he struck out in the direction he had approached from.

Deo broke into a run at this point to intercept him, heedless now of giving away his position. As if sensing something—or perhaps Deo made more noise than he knew, as his heart was thudding hard in his ears, making it difficult to discern sounds—Bidenden looked around in alarm and then broke into a run.

"Stop, thief!" bellowed the magistrate.

Bidenden tossed the lamp and ran. In the pitch darkness, Deo blinked and cursed, trying to work out if Bidenden was still heading toward the trees or had hared off in a different direction. Deciding the trees were still the safest bet, he stuck to that course and was rewarded moments later by colliding with the other man.

Bidenden struck out at him with a wild swing of his fist which connected with Deo's jaw as he bent forward to tackle Bidenden to the ground. With the speed of his forward trajectory and his weight, he brought the more lightly built man down easily and landed on top of him as his head spun from the blow.

Bidenden wriggled beneath him, gasping and grunting, and Deo levered himself up and dealt him a blow to the jaw that knocked him unconscious.

Deo clambered to his feet as the duke and Emrys came up to him, followed by the lumbering magistrate, who was puffing hard. Emrys had stopped to collect the lamp, and by its light, they inspected the prostrate body of Lord Bidenden at their feet.

"That him?" asked the magistrate.

"Yes," rasped Deo, shaking his own head to clear it and bending to retrieve the sack.

Emrys bent to check Bidenden's pulse in his neck just as the other man came round. He groaned and blinked up at them. Then, looking around at the sack clutched in Deo's hands, he groaned again.

Kenrick, who had been stationed in the trees, appeared just then and bent over him.

"Why?" he asked simply.

Bidenden fought to his elbows and shook his head as if clearing it. Before he could answer, the magistrate stepped forward and addressed Deo. "Can you verify the contents of the sack, my lord?"

Deo crouched down and opened the sack as Emrys held the lamp up so that he could see the contents. "Yes, these are the stolen items." He put a hand in and felt around for the smaller pieces and withdrew a small cloth-wrapped bundle and unwrapped it carefully. The cross lay in his palm, glinting in the lamp light.

Kingsley turned his attention to Bidenden. "You, sir, are under arrest, for the theft of property belonging to the Duke of Troubridge."

Bidenden closed his eyes. Kenrick put out a hand to clasp his arm and haul him to his feet and repeated his earlier question. "Why?"

Bidenden swallowed. "The usual reason. Money. My father cut me off some months ago." He smiled but it wasn't a happy one. "I planned to sell the items to him for an exorbitant sum anonymously through a broker. It seemed like poetic justice to me."

"Well, you can be as poetic as you like in jail," said the magistrate, clearly unimpressed.

Bidenden ignored him, and addressed himself to the duke. "Your Grace, I am guilty of the worst possible trespass on your hospitality, for which there is no excuse beyond desperation and the addled state of a brokenhearted man. I realize the hope is slim, but I beg you for clemency. You have the items back, no harm done. Might you see your way clear to dropping the charges?"

Deo's blood pressure went up. *The gall of the man!* Before he could say anything, the duke said, "I'm within my rights to bring the full strength of the law against you, Bidenden." Bidenden went white, visible even in the poor light. "But I think I may have a worse punishment than that for you, which will serve our interests better.

"You can cool your heels in our cellar for a few days while I write to your father. I'm sure he will devise a suitable punishment for you. Equally, I am sure he won't want it known that his son is a common thief. As a consequence, none of the events that have transpired here in the past few weeks will be known outside of this group. Will they?"

The duke's tone made Bidenden swallow visibly. After a moment, the man said, "I could almost wish to stand trial in preference to facing my father's wrath, except I am afraid I might hang, and I've no wish to die. I understand you perfectly, Your Grace. No word of what has transpired here shall ever pass my lips, beyond what I may have to say of necessity to my sire. He will no doubt fashion, as you have so astutely concluded, a fitting punishment for my crime." He bowed. "I thank you for your—mercy." He grimaced as he said it.

"Am I to understand, Your Grace, that you do not wish to press charges against this gentleman?"

"You are, Kingsley," said the duke, and he took him aside, no doubt to offer some inducement to soothe the man's ire at being dragged out of bed for nothing and to keep his mouth shut.

Deo wasn't sure how he felt about Robert's decision not to press charges against Bidenden. But he understood the reason for it and most of it had to do with protecting Emily's reputation and Deo's own, for which he could not but be grateful. And he was in the right of it in regard to Malmsbury's ability to make his son suffer to an extraordinary degree. Deo knew from personal experience how cruel a father could be to a son. He could almost feel sorry for Bidenden.

Chapter Twenty-Seven

EMILY, CLOSETED ANXIOUSLY in the drawing room with Sarah and Annis, couldn't sit still, jumping up repeatedly to pace the room.

"My dear, you will wear a hole in my carpet!" said Sarah with a smile. "There is one of Bidenden and a dozen of our men. There is really no need to be so anxious."

"But what if Bidenden should have a gun?" fretted Emily.

"Robert has his pistol, and let me assure you he is an excellent shot," said Sarah placidly.

"That is fortunate," said Annis, "for Emrys, by his own admission, is not. Although he *is* handy with his fists."

Emily turned and smiled wanly. "I suppose I should have more faith in Deo. After all, he is big enough. He must outweigh Bidenden by several stone. But the thought of him being hurt brings me undone!" she confessed.

Just then, sounds from outside the room sent her scurrying to the door and out into the entrance hall, closely followed by the two ladies.

Deo was there with a dirty sack clutched in his hand and with him were the duke, Emrys, Kenrick, and, surprisingly, Bidenden. There was no sign of the magistrate.

"Deo!" She hurried toward him, and he received her into the

arm not holding the sack. "Are you all right?" She examined his face anxiously and detected a slight swelling on his jaw. "You've been hit!"

"It's nothing, Em," he said with a grim smile and held the sack up. "And we have the items."

Behind him, the duke was in conversation with Creighton, and she noticed that Bidenden was standing rather slump shouldered, with his arm gripped firmly by Kenrick. He looked pale and weary beyond measure and his face was starting to show signs of a bruise. *Was Deo responsible for that?*

"What happened?" she murmured to Deo. "Where is the magistrate?"

Just then, two footmen appeared and, taking an arm each, they escorted Bidenden toward the rear of the house, disappearing through the door that led, Emily thought, to the kitchens.

"What—?" she began, and Deo encircled her waist and drew her back toward the drawing room where everyone else was also headed.

With the door shut, the duke said, "I'm sure you're all agog to know what happened. I can see you are surprised to see Bidenden returned with us. He is going to spend some time in our cellar while I write to his father, the marquess. I decided that it serves our purposes better not to press charges against him and instead to let his father deal with the matter. There will be less scandal this way." He turned to Sarah. "I'll address the household tomorrow. I believe we can trust to their discretion, my dear."

Sarah slipped her hand in his and kissed his cheek. "An excellent outcome, Robert. I am proud of you."

Emily turned back to Deo and touched the red mark on his jaw. "Someone hit you!"

Deo rubbed his jaw absently. "Oh yes, Bidenden's fist caught me as I tackled him to the ground." Emily, emboldened by the duchess's display of affection, reached up to touch his jaw gently and then kissed the spot.

"You'll be pleased to know, Em, I knocked him senseless for

his trouble," he added, flushing faintly with pleasure under her kiss and confirming her guess.

"I demand a full recounting of events. Tell us what happened!" commanded Annis, plumping down on the couch. Emrys joined her and they all sat. Each man offered a bit of the tale from his perspective, and it didn't take long to impart.

Emily nestled into Deo's arm and sighed contentedly.

"Well, that has all turned out for the best, then," said Sarah. "We had best retire to bed, for we have a wedding to plan tomorrow." She threw a smile in Emily's direction.

Emily flushed and glanced shyly up at Deo, whose expression softened as his eyes connected with hers. He took her hand and kissed it, saying, "Yes, Emrys and I will fetch the license tomorrow. The duchess, I believe, is going to organize your dress."

"That I am," said Sarah, rising. "The blue room has been made up for you, Deo, and your man has moved your things there temporarily."

"Thank you, Sarah," he said, rising like the other men.

Annis rose too, and both couples said goodnight and left Deo and Emily alone.

The clock on the mantle struck three as Deo took her in his arms. "It's been a long day, Em," he said, folding her close and kissing her hair.

She wrapped her arms round him. "It has, and, oh Deo, I had the most extraordinary conversation with my father. Mama had several miscarriages before me, including a boy. After me, she couldn't have any more." She blinked. "I'm not sure I can forgive them exactly for the way they treated me, but I understand it better now. Papa actually said he loved me. I don't know that I believe him, but it felt so good to hear the words. I think he does in his way, but he was too weak to stand up to Mama. It will be hard to forgive that."

"Em!" Deo hugged her tight, and she buried her face in his chest. Whether her parents loved her or not, Deo did. Her heart was full. She could choose to forgive them in time, she hoped.

"I wish they had told me. It made so much sense of—well, everything!" She sighed, rubbing her cheek against his chest. "They don't hate me, they just wished for a boy and couldn't have one."

"No one could hate you, Em," he said roughly, squeezing her. "You're a ray of sunshine!"

She smiled up at him. "My darling grump!"

He kissed her then, and it was some time before either of them said anything.

"It's only two days, but it's going to feel like forever until our wedding night," he said, husky voiced. "It will be different this time, Em. The words will mean something."

"Yes, they will," she said, snuggling in closer.

"Come on, we had best put these treasures away. I do hope they haven't been damaged with all this mishandling. Then I'll escort you to *your* room, which will be ours again very shortly."

⇉⇇

THE TINY CHAPEL was decorated with flowers and candles, and the scent of incense filled the air. The sun threw a multicolored streak across the stone floor through the stained-glass window above the altar.

Deo was right. It was different this time. And the words did mean so much more. When Emily had uttered those words the first time, she had been preoccupied with worry over the details of her name and age. She had also been thinking that it wasn't a real marriage. They would part company at the end of the project, and she could get on with her life as an independent scholar out from under her mother's thumb.

This time, she spoke the words with all her heart as she stood before the altar in the lovely dress the duchess had lent her. With her small hands in Deo's big, blunt-fingered, freckled ones, she looked up into his dear face. His deep blue eyes blazed with the fire of love and set her heart fluttering.

Mama cried and her father hugged her and wrung Deo's hand. She received the congratulations of her friends with a warm heart, for she truly felt that they were friends now after the events of the past few weeks, and she was charmed to receive the bouquets of flowers bestowed upon her shyly by the Ashfords' youngest daughter and boldly by the eldest.

After the wedding supper and many toasts to their health and happiness, they were finally able to escape to their suite and shut the door on the world.

"You look so delicious, Em, I'm afraid to touch your gown for fear of ruining it," confessed Deo.

"Well, I am not. Help me with the laces," said Emily, turning her back to him.

His fingers pulled at the lacing of her gown and loosened it so that she could pull the bodice free and lift it over her head. Laying the gown down on a chair, she turned back to him in her corset, petticoats, and chemise. "There, now you may touch me to your heart's content, for I certainly plan to touch you," she said, walking into his arms and plastering herself to his front.

His arms enveloped her in a tight hug, and he murmured, "Em, I love you so much."

"I know, I feel the same about you!" She looked up at him adoringly. "Now please, Deo, make me your wife fully before I expire of frustration!"

He grinned and kissed her. "With the greatest pleasure on earth, Lady Pendrell," he said, scooping her up and carrying her into their bedroom.

⋙✦⋘

SETTING EM DOWN on the bed, Deo knelt to remove her shoes and stockings, reflecting that the one advantage of the "practice" they had been having, was that he was remarkably free of nerves at the prospect of consummating his marriage—at last! He helped her stand and turned her so that he could loosen her stays. They fell away to reveal her slender form beneath. He looked at her, his wife, filled with anticipation and love. Two emotions that would have been foreign to him mere weeks ago. His big hands caressed her body with possessive delight before undoing her petticoats and letting them fall at her feet.

She stood clad only in her semi-transparent chemise, and he took a moment to appreciate her. Em had changed his life and him for the better, and he would never go back to the person he had been before, he could not. The old Deo was a stranger to him now. How he had lived his life in such a barren wasteland he didn't know. It was like a life recalled without color, whereas now everything was as brightly painted as a sunrise. Illuminated by the sun that was Emily.

He gathered her close and kissed her. He could laugh at the man who had been afraid of kisses if it weren't so pathetic. Yet he knew Em didn't think he was pathetic. She loved him. It shone in her eyes when she looked at him and filled his heart to bursting. For the little boy whose parents never showed him any affection, Em's love was a precious gift beyond price.

He let her go just long enough to remove his own clothes as rapidly as possible and returned to remove her chemise and bear her down into the bed where he had learned to pleasure her and learned what a true treasure she really was. Beyond their shared passion for antiquities, Em understood and accepted him. There was no greater gift.

Em's hands roamed over his skin, sending tingles of desire to his cock, which was achingly hard. That he wanted to plunge himself deeply inside her was not new, but the notion that he was now free to do so as often as he desired was a prospect that took his breath away. The fact that she desired it as much as he was almost overwhelming.

He kissed her with increasing passion, and she met him every step with equal fervor. He dimly wondered what he had done to deserve such happiness and pushed away the thought. He was not going to allow his old insecurities to ruin this moment.

His hands squeezed and caressed her lovely, finely wrought body. She was a slender reed to his great bulk, yet she was strong, his Em—strong, determined, clever, and loving. He could not have asked for a better combination in a wife. She brought out the best in him and made him feel as if he could conquer nations just to make her happy.

Fortunately, all he needed to do right now was bring pleasure to her body, and he knew how to do that. Stroking her between her legs, he found her deliciously wet in anticipation of their joining, and it made him groan with longing for precisely that.

He had taken the opportunity yesterday to ask Emrys, red-faced, for a tip or two in regard to having a virgin bride and his friend had been most forthcoming on the topic. He applied that knowledge now by pushing a finger inside her, something he had heretofore refrained from doing. Em's reaction was everything he could have desired.

⇉⇇

EMILY SQUIRMED BENEATH Deo's touch, his fingers eliciting wonderful tingles that made her ache, then he did something he'd never done before. Pushed a finger inside her. Her eyes sprang open in shock and her hips surged up into his touch as the delightful sensations compounded her already heightened arousal.

"Deo!" she panted.

"Do you like that?"

"Yes!" She moved in a way she hoped conveyed exactly how much she liked it, and he must have gotten the message, because he then added a second finger, and that was even better. His thumb was also doing delicious things to that spot that sent her over the edge every time. The combination had her breathless and aching for that rush of pleasure she knew he could give her. When he added a third finger, there was a stretch and a pinch that made her gasp.

"Em? Does that hurt?" His worried tone and expression made her clutch at him.

"Only—a pinch," she said. "I know it's supposed to hurt the first time. It's all right, don't stop!"

"Are you sure?"

"Oh!" she moaned in frustration. "Yes! Yes! I want you, Deo, please! No more waiting. You promised!"

He nodded. "All right. Just a little more preparation and—" He let a breath out on a soft groan. "I want you too, so much, you have no idea!"

"I do!" she said, pushing up into his touch frantically. "I really do, Deo. Please."

He pushed a fourth finger inside her and that did stretch and make her gasp with the slightly more than a pinch.

He winced and removed his fingers, kissing her softly. "I'm sorry."

"Don't be sorry, just do it!" said Emily, grabbing his shoulders. He was too big to shake, but she wanted to. *The big lummox! I love him so much!*

He shifted, settling his body between her legs, but taking his weight on his arms. She stared up at him and smiled. He locked his fierce blue gaze with hers and moved his hips, seeking the right place to join their bodies. She felt the blunt head of his cock pressing against her flesh. He pushed and her body resisted. He shifted and pushed again. She moved her hips up a bit, shifting the angle, and he pushed again, harder, and suddenly, with another pinch, he was inside her. She gasped and he groaned, his eyes closing involuntarily.

"Fuck, Em!"

She grinned. She was his now, and he was hers. She wrapped her arms around as much of him as she could reach and moved upward into his downward thrust. It took a few goes, but they found a rhythm and the pinch was rapidly forgotten in the bliss. His face was flushed and his expression grim as he moved his hips with increasing speed. "Em!" he ground out through clenched teeth, and shifting his weight to one arm, he reached between them to touch her and bring her pleasure to its peak.

He rubbed her lightly and fast. "Em, please! I—"

The pleasure built and built between his fingers and the indescribable feeling of him moving inside her. Full, tight, and elementally satisfying in a way she couldn't comprehend, she moved more frantically beneath him, her breathing completely erratic and her heart pounding in her ears.

"Deo!" she cried out as the building knot of desire tightened unbearably and suddenly shattered, cascading through her body in waves of delight.

"Em, Emily, Em," his muttering of her name was accompanied by frantic kisses rained on her face and neck as his body arched and trembled. He gasped and groaned and grunted. And she felt the jerk of his cock and the hot rush of his seed within her. For a long moment his body held still and then slowly collapsed on top of her in a panting heap.

DEO, HIS HEAD buried in the pillow by her head, panted, his body still caught in waves of bliss, slowly falling apart with the lethargy of absolute satiation.

Finally, he turned his head and sought to check her expression. "Em? Are you all right?"

She turned her head and smiled at him lazily. "Yes, Deo, much *more* than all right.'" He levered himself upon one arm and planted a kiss on her mouth.

Then taking his weight on both arms, stroked a curl off her face and said softly, "You are my wife now and no one can take you away from me."

"Or you from me, Deo," she said, framing his face with her hands and kissing. "I love you."

"I love *you*," he responded, with his whole heart.

Epilogue

Cheetham Hall Sussex
Two months later

"FETCH, KES!" SAID Emily, throwing a stick she had found on the beach for Kester. The hound took off after the stick, his paws kicking up wet sand. Emily took Deo's hand again as they resumed their leisurely stroll along the beach. Her feet were bare and her skirts hiked up to stay clear of the splash of the waves washing up around their feet. Deo had eschewed his boots also, and they left two sets of footprints behind them in the wet sand, one large and one small.

It was a fine, sunny day with only a scattering of white fluffy clouds overhead. They'd had a magnificent summer.

Kester came back with the stick, panting happily, and Deo paused to throw it this time, sending Kes careering down the beach three times farther away than she had been able to throw it.

They had been back home for over a month now and Emily was filled to the brim with contentment. They spent their days working on the catalogue of antiquities for Aberdeen, and in between, Deo's book and their nights curled up in each other's arms. *Really, could life get any more perfect?*

They had received another letter from Aberdeen this morning—they would be going up to London to present a paper on the finds from The Castle to the Antiquarian Society and discuss the Arthurian connection. After that, they were going to Cornwall to work on a dig at Tintagel, the supposed birthplace of Arthur, where some farmer had uncovered another Celtic cross. It was too exciting for words.

The breeze tugged at her cloak and her hair, and she shivered involuntarily.

"You're getting cold," said Deo, wrapping an arm round her and rubbing her arm. "We should head back to the house."

"No, no. I'm fine."

"I've thought of something I want to add to our paper," he said, firmly turning them to head back up the beach.

"Oh well, in that case—" she said with a grin.

He whistled for Kes, and they headed back to the house, discussing the addendum he wanted to make.

Settled in their study again, Em remarked, "We will be able to see Emrys and Annis in London and give them our congratulations in person. I'm so happy for them," looking up from the paper she was proofreading, her mind having wandered to the letter she had received from Annis that morning.

"Hm?" Deo pushed his glasses up his nose. "Yes, of course, one more to add to their clan. I swear Emrys is as clucky as a broody hen."

Em peeped at him, a little disconcerted by his comment. The subject of children had never come up between them. Their minds had always been on other things, but she wondered now if Deo even wanted them. Given his own upbringing, it might not be surprising if he didn't. She was conscious of a twinge of disappointment.

She watched his hawkish profile for a moment as he continued scratching away at the sheet of paper in front of him.

"Do you want children, Deo?"

"What?" he looked round, dropping his pen which spluttered on the sheet.

"I said—"

"I heard what you said! Are you pregnant, Em?"

"No, I don't think so. I just wondered. We haven't ever talked about it."

His shoulders dropped. "I should have an heir, but it's not something I—" He stopped. "I'm not sure that I know how to be a father, Em. But I'll try."

"Oh, Deo." She got up and sat herself down on his lap, wrapping her arms round his neck. "You'll be a wonderful father."

His face screwed up. "I haven't much of an example to follow."

"Yes, you do, because you will *not* be like *your* father."

"I suppose." He hesitated. "Do you want children, Em?"

"Eventually, yes, but I'm rather enjoying our time with just the two of us. Mama had such difficulties. I hope I won't be the same."

"I think you will make a wonderful mother, Em."

"Not like mine?"

"No. *Not* like yours," he said, wrapping his arms around her and kissing her.

A little while later, she said, "At the risk of upsetting you, Annis told me in her letter that Bidenden has been packed off to India by his father."

"Hm," he grunted. "He's lucky he didn't get sent to Australia."

"Would that have been worse? They're both hot countries, aren't they?"

"Yes, but India is part of the British Empire, and Australia is a penal colony. I would imagine the facilities are pretty rough."

She nodded and snuggled into his embrace. "Did I tell you today that I love you?" she asked.

"Yes, twice, no three times. Four if you count that one." He smiled.

"Well, you have told me at least"—she counted off on her fingers—"six times!" she said, grinning at him.

"As it should be," he said. "I love you, Emily Frances." He

scooped her up and rose.

"Deo, where are we going?"

"Bedroom. We have time before dinner."

"Oh, Deo." She flung her arms round his neck.

British Antiquities, the journal Deo places his "Wife Wanted" ad in is fictitious, but the *Quarterly Journal* is real, as is the Society of Antiquaries and its President, Lord Aberdeen. The format of the ad follows the pattern of ads for employees from the period.

Deo and Emily's *comes* is a fabrication based on a character in Geoffrey of Monmouth's *History of the Kings of Britain*. At the time that Deo and Emily were doing their investigations, the texts referencing Arthur were still held to have some validity as historical documents, though that understanding was beginning to shift.

All the texts and editions that they consulted would have been available to them in translation except for Wace and Layamon which (as far as I have been able to ascertain) did not have modern English translations until 1836 and 1847 respectively. So Deo would have had to read these in their original languages of French and Middle English.

The description of Iuegyn's tomb is based loosely on Anglo-Celtic burials of the period, in particular the Taplow Burial, and the entrance to the tomb and its construction on Stoney Littleton.

Examples of Celtic crosses of the type described have not been found in the area of England where our story takes place, only in Scotland, Wales, Cornwall, and Ireland, and none have been found as used in this context as a marker for a barrow-type burial. It is a plain cross, not the Chi Rho style covered in elaborate knot work of the later periods. However, the reference to the conflict between King Oswy and Wilfred, the Bishop of York, over the Celtic versus Roman version of Christianity is true. And Wilfred, who sounds like a bombastic ecclesiastic who must have annoyed Oswy to no end, won the argument at the Synod of Whitby in 664.

At the time of this story—the summer of 1819—archaeology as a science was in its infancy. Most archaeologists were nothing more than treasure hunters digging up sites for the treasures they could unearth and taking scant trouble to record any of the historical data that could be gleaned from the site. Deo's methods are as close to authentic for the period as I could make them for a serious scholar who values history over money and fame, although by modern standards they would still be considered rough and crude. The cutthroat nature of scholarly argument and reputation was as nasty then as it is now. And forgeries were not uncommon.

Wives often acted as their husband's amanuensis or secretary and got no credit for their part in the work, where a male secretary would. Deo's insistence on ensuring Emily gets credit and his treatment of her as a colleague worthy of equal respect is, to say the least, unusual for the period.

Acknowledgements

I want to thank my beta reader, Kesha Young, for encouraging comments and pointing out that I needed to explain how to pronounce co-*mees*, and Kathy Golden's editorial expertise for invaluable input to improving the manuscript.

I would also like to thank the team at Dragonblade: Kathryn for taking a chance on me and my series; my lovely editor Courtney Brown who is a delight to work with—you are amazing; and the rest of the team who have made this book shine.

Wren St. Claire has wanted to write since she was twelve and discovered her mother's Georgette Heyer collection. Wren St. Claire lives in Brisbane with one confused Mini Schnauzer and six mad, Bengal cats. She writes steamy historical romance, where the heroes spoil the heroines and readers get to tag along for the ride, enjoying a roller coaster of emotions. Wren has a master's degree in Egyptology and used to lead tours to Egypt up until the revolution during the Arab Spring in 2011.